WICKED GAMES

TYLER COMPTON

Tyler Compton
Los Angeles, CA 90046
www.tylercomptonbooks.com

Publisher's Note: This is a work of fiction. Names, characters, places, and incidents are a product of the author's imagination. Locales and public names are sometimes used for atmospheric purposes. Any resemblance to actual people, living or dead, or to businesses, companies, events, institutions, or locales is completely coincidental.

Book Layout ©2013 BookDesignTemplates.com

Ordering Information:
Quantity sales. Special discounts are available on quantity purchases by corporations, associations, and others. For details, contact the "Special Sales Department" at the address above.

ISBN 978-0-9893845-4-4 (paperback)
ISBN 978-0-9893845-5-1 (ebook)

For Kendra & Jamie

Who each made college memorable in their own ways

ACKNOWLEDGEMENTS

I'd like to thank the many people who have helped make this book possible. Same as before, if I have left anyone out it is truly unintentional. To Dr. George for the quick editing job this time around. To Lori, Davey, Derek & Rita Safady who each read and gave constructive notes. This book exists in large part to all of your help.

Major thanks to Tyler Dille for his awesome job on my website design. I keep getting great kudos about it all the time and it's entirely his doing. A first impression goes a far way, especially in this business, and he helps me look as good as possible. Thanks.

To my family—my parents, brothers & their wives—for their constant support and encouragement, both through this book and the first one. To my grandfather for buying the many copies and pushing them on to other readers I thank you. It means the world to me.

Though this book was written far before *The Poisonous Ten* (you can read more about that in the afterword), it's editing and redevelopment phase occurred a lot during the much figuring out process and release of my first book. Many people have been there either emailing me interesting news articles, harassing me to continue writing, or just giving me positive encouragement. To the many people who follow my progress and daily postings/gripes/etc. on Twitter, Goodreads and Facebook, as well as leaving your feedback about the last book, I thank you. Many of you may be strangers to me but your words to me do keep me going and mean a lot.

And while this book is dedicated to Kendra & Jamie, I would also like to thank everyone at CSUS during my time there. You are *all*, in part, responsible for this book existing.

Of course the game is rigged.
Don't let that stop you—if you don't play, you can't win.

— Robert Heinlein (1907 - 1988)

PROLOGUE

Susan Marsh's last thoughts before she succumbed to death in the back of the speeding ambulance was of the unborn child she had yet to meet. The thought of who would want her husband and her dead, or why, never once having crossed her mind.

Glenn and Susan Marsh always wanted children but knew that they never could. Biologically at least. It had been almost two years to the day since they first filed the paperwork with the agency when Susan received the phone call informing them that they had been approved. They were finally getting a baby. They were going to be a family.

The baby was coming from somewhere overseas. Susan couldn't remember where exactly, as she had been too ecstatic to pay attention to what the adoption agent had been telling her. Luckily, they would get all that information again when they stopped by the agency and signed the last few important documents to finalize the arrangement.

Susan was an attractive if not somewhat large woman, standing at five foot ten, with a full-figured, curviness to her that only added to her merriment. Often smiling, with a rosy complexion to her cheeks, Susan had the sort of happiness that was easily spread to those around her.

With a beaming smile plastered on her face, Susan eagerly waited for her husband to walk through their front door after another fulfilling day at work in downtown Seattle. Glenn Marsh was five years her senior, with the same amber-colored eyes and hair as his wife. Glenn worked in the central business district at Cray Inc. on what she had heard him refer to as "supercomputers" though she couldn't say much more about his job. Besides, once he started talking about processing cores and petaflops, she usually zoned out, thinking up new baby names or what color to make the nursery. Thankfully, as much as her husband loved his job, he preferred to keep the computer talk at work and the baby talk at home.

Glenn walked through the front door, shook off his umbrella before leaning it next to the door and taking off his equally wet black Calvin Klein raincoat that Susan had bought for him for his thirty-fifth birthday. He barely registered something different about his wife—a sort of glow that he would have mistaken for pregnancy had his wife been able to do so—when she jumped into his arms and told him the good news. Glenn Marsh was just as ecstatic.

Glenn was an only child; his parents deciding to have only one so as to give the appearance of being a family though neither ever had any true desire for the one they were regrettably left to raise. The only upside for Glenn was that the senior Marshes were a wealthy family which led to a well-educated upbringing and more possibilities than he was even aware of, though he had always been grateful for the opportunities life presented him. Susan, on the other hand, at least had an older brother to grow up with although now both adults usually only saw each other on the occasional holiday, mostly staying in touch through distant phone calls and annual Christmas cards. A few years before her brother had finally married, to a woman ten years his junior no less, though Susan saw no issue with the difference in ages due to the happiness the woman brought to her brother. In addition, there had been a lavish wedding, which drew Susan and her brother together as an added bonus that particular year.

Despite their personal disadvantages growing up, both Glenn and Susan had always wanted a family.

They decided to celebrate by going out to a charming French restaurant in the historic Pike Place Market. They started the evening with a bottle of Vosne-Romanée Pinot Noir and the two enjoyed their meal, spending more time lost in their thoughts than focused on their food.

The two finished up at half past eleven, after the restaurant had already closed, their server reluctant to usher the generous tippers out onto the streets. They completely ignored the world around them as they made their way to the car, laughter echoing throughout the otherwise barren night. It had rained most of the day but clouds were nowhere to be seen as the stars above shone down on them, proof that this day was to be nothing less than perfect.

The Marshes reached their car and Glenn leaned in toward his wife and kissed her, pressing her up against the side door. Susan laughed and hugged her husband, not noticing the man in the dark grey sweatshirt with the hood pulled over his head, keeping most of his face hidden in the shadows, save for a strong, unshaven chin. Without saying a single word, the stranger quickly took out a gun, fired five shots in rapid succession, and disappeared into the night without even checking the damage he had done.

Three of the bullets hit Glenn.

The first one in the stomach while the second went through his chest, shattering two ribs, one of which punctured the right lung. The third and final bullet ripped through his throat, sending a spray of blood across his wife's face.

Susan screamed, more as a reaction from the deafening sound and the image of her husband's blood flying at her than on account of the two bullets that had hit her. Of the two bullets, one hit her in the chest, missing her ribs, slicing cleanly through her left lung, causing a hitch in her breath without suffocating her. The second bullet grazed her thigh and for a second she laughed, thanking God she had been so lucky to simply be hit in the leg. People were shot in the arms and legs every day and lived. It happened in the movies all the time.

Both of the Marshes fell against their vehicle and slumped to the ground. Glenn held his throat, his life bleeding out through his fingers, drenching his white, Ralph Lauren sweater, which soaked up the blood like a sponge. Unaware of the hypnotic effect the blood in her husband's sweater had on her, tears flowed from her face as Susan tried to stop the blood leaking from his neck.

Glenn felt he was suffocating. His blood flowed through his wife's shaking hands, distracting her from realizing that the bullet wound to her leg had sliced through her femoral artery, causing as much damage to her as his wounds had to him. With each gasp she took, with each pumping of her heart, Susan Marsh's life drained out of her body through her leg.

Susan remained wrapped up next to her dead husband while the wailing of the ambulance sirens got closer. The ruby lights began to reflect off her eyes, creating the illusion of her husband's entire body covered in blood. The EMTs asked her blurring questions that she failed to focus on as her eyes fluttered.

As Susan Marsh succumbed to death in the back of the ambulance, what little coherent consciousness she had left remained focused on her forthcoming baby. Never for one second did she stop to realize that just possibly, she and her husband weren't the unfortunate results of a random attack, but that they may have been sought out and hunted down for an even greater purpose that neither one could have ever guessed or dreamed of.

PART 1
STARTING POSITIONS

ONE

Yellow police caution tape, along with two university campus security vehicles, was used to block off the back entrance to Asmodeus Hall, making sure no one from any of the local news coverage teams could gain access to the crime scene within. An LAPD helicopter circled the campus grounds, flashing its beams haphazardly below, while two uniformed men stood guard at the front of the Psychology building. The wind was unusually strong, even for this late in April, blowing the surrounding trees around campus back and forth, the well-known Santa Anas in full force.

A dark grey Acura TL pulled up to a nearby faculty parking lot and parked next to two more campus security vehicles and three LAPD black-and-whites. The driver's door popped ajar for a second before a leg pushed through and opened the door as Detective Dave Parks exited the vehicle. Parks was dressed in a recently purchased grey Michael Kors suit that didn't look pulled from the hamper, yet was probably the same one he had worn the day before, something he did often when working on several cases around the clock. Parks grabbed his notebook and locked his car up before starting across the grassy knoll toward all the commotion. The place was like a zoo—or

9

a concert: helicopters deafening the University from up above while onlookers gossiped among themselves down below. Parks could swear there was jazz playing somewhere in the background, most likely from the event of the evening. It was twenty minutes to ten and Parks had been on his way home when he had been called to the crime scene. The Pacific Southwest University campus grounds were mere miles from his condo near Brentwood, and the watch commander knew he was more than willing to take on a new case, especially when it might be the last one he and his people took as a team.

As he made his way across the lawn, Parks scanned the crowd of onlookers. Each person standing watch was either an alumnus or working the party that was currently taking place across campus at the Student Union, every attendee dressed expensively in his or her tuxedos or evening gowns and high heels. Thousands of dollars' worth of jewelry stood on parade, as expertly designed dresses, recently coiffed hair and delicately nipped and tucked faces stood on parade. It was as if being at the scene of a crime was a sporting event—the event which one wanted to be seen at this season. The smell of sweet perfume and rancid alcohol filled the air—no doubt the mixture of the two reducing people's sensibilities. Parks took in the faces of each person standing outside the yellow tape, subconsciously rubbing his five o'clock shadow, his hand going along his square jawline up over his head and through his close-cropped mane of grey-infused copper hair.

Was the killer still there? Watching? Waiting to see what they uncovered? Waiting to see if he or she had gotten away with it?

"Looks like someone forgot to invite us to the party," Parks commented to himself.

"Luckily, we've got the dead to invite us to events we'd otherwise never attend." Parks turned to find Assistant Chief Jane Hardwick, his boss and friend for nearly a decade. What was she doing there? Hardwick often stopped by scenes to see her people in action, to see how they worked with one another, but she rarely worked this late at night. And to have beaten him to the scene of the crime? That was almost unheard of. Unless—

"You plan on joining this party sometime this evening?" Hardwick interrupted.

Hardwick signed Parks in on the ledger held by the guard next to the entrance of Asmodeus Hall, which was the university's Social Sciences and Interdisciplinary Studies building, which also housed the entire Psychology department, as well as the crime scene.

Parks smiled to himself. Jane Hardwick was a force to reckon with. Short-fused, yet fair and just, she still commanded attention and respect and always got it. She had intense yet angular features, softened only by her mane of caramel-colored hair and coal-gray eyes that penetrated through one's bullshit. The fact that she stood six feet tall and exuded a tough Chicago demeanor only helped add to why Parks liked the woman. Not just because she was a woman who had fought tooth and nail her entire career just to prove herself—and had done so time and time again—but because she was considered "one of the boys" and highly skilled at the job she performed. Hell, at almost sixty, the woman was still better than half the men that worked for her, and Parks had no problem saying so.

"I thought Wilkes was next in the lineup," Hardwick said as she led him into the building and down the hallway to a pair of waiting elevators.

"Yeah, well, Wilkes is at a homicide up in the Hills." He had been looking forward to going home, relaxing, maybe taking in a quick run and settling down with one of his puzzles. Maybe even just catching up on his sleep, which, after four fifteen-hour days, he was in need of. "I got this, Boss. Really. Which floor?" Hardwick wasn't quite ready to give in, even though both knew she would. "Unless of course there's a reason you don't want me and my team to take on another case this close to the end of the month?"

Parks had been with the department as a detective for over a decade now. He'd had many partners, both competent and not. They came and they went. If you were lucky, the good ones stuck around for a while. The department had played around, forming three, four and five persons mini-squads a few years before, but was currently looking at ways to save money and, more importantly, save face. Having more two-man teams out on the street solving crimes was one of the ways to do that. It wasn't a reality most on the squad would have thought could happen any time soon, until last September, when Detective Wilkes' team had all but been killed, or forced into retirement—thanks to the Palisades Poisoner case—and the cogs had been put into motion. Now, eight months later, Parks's team was the last to be dismantled. Hardwick stared at Parks and he felt momentarily guilty for having put her on the spot. He was just tired of waiting to see what would happen to his team. He also knew her well enough to know she would inform him as to what was what as soon as she could.

"Really, Jane? You want Wilkes on this? I mean, I don't know what's waiting for me, but we are on one of the state's leading universities. Home to many past and potential future governors and senators. Two former Veeps graduated from here. And if those aren't your cup of tea—numerous celebrities." Parks threw on a large smile, knowing he was getting to her. No matter what the situation here was, she did not want Mark Wilkes anywhere near it. Tact was not one of Wilkes' stronger suits. Hardwick knew Parks, on the other hand, could sell an Eskimo dirty ice and come out looking like a prince. "You know, like the Kardashians and whatnot."

"Don't make me regret this."

"Or one of the Hiltons or some other reality TV star," Parks chuckled.

"Four," Hardwick barked, wanting the topic of reality TV stars to end.

"I'm sure there's some housewife from 'lanta or Joy'sey who wants to send their child here. Or Snooki."

"I don't know what the hell a snooki is, but so help me God, Parks, if you don't press the button for four right now..."

Parks pressed the button with a smirk and the doors closed. "So what do we have waiting for us up on four?"

"Double homicide. A student. And a professor." Hardwick paused as she let the facts settle in with Parks. "Professor Fredrick Knott."

Parks let out a deep breath at the idea of dealing with an esteemed professor found in his office afterhours with one of his students when he paused, the name of the professor pinging recognition somewhere in the back alleyways of his mind. He knew that name. But how? Or from where? He rarely paid attention to the acolytes of the local universities.

The doors chimed open. The hallway was busy, seeing more action now than during its normal hours of operation.

"Anyone else been in the room?"

"Tanaka's with the bodies now." Hardwick answered. The medical examiner was one of the few exceptions that wouldn't cause Parks to blow a fuse. He liked her. Her spunk and quips showed she knew how to play with the boys and didn't take life too seriously while taking her job to the extreme. "And the security guard who discovered the bodies."

Parks accepted a pair of blue rubber gloves and booties from a security officer guarding the professor's office while he turned to the guard who called in the crime.

"You found the bodies?"

"Yes, sir," the nervous guard answered. The man was tall, reaching six and a half feet, and barely weighed a hundred and fifty pounds, soaking wet, looking the polar opposite of Parks who was closer to two-hundred pounds of muscle. The guard's campus security uniform was tattered and worn, having been washed numerous times without a proper ironing. He had a pronounced nose and a receding hairline that he tried his best to hide by keeping his hair as closely shaven to the scalp as possible.

"Touch anything?" Parks continued.

"Just flipped on the light switch, sir. Took maybe two steps into the room. That's it, sir."

"Anything else?"

"No, sir," the guard reassured, wiping his forehead with the back of his hand.

"Didn't touch the bodies? Check to make sure they were dead?"

"No need to, sir. You'll see what I mean when you go inside."

"I don't want to get a clear set of latents and find out they're yours."

"No, sir."

"So what brought you here?"

"I was doing my rounds when I noticed the front door to the building was ajar. I came in to check it out and could tell there were people inside. I checked it floor by floor until I discovered the lights in Professor Knott's office were on. The door was open, so I checked inside and found the bodies. Called for assistance right away."

"What time was this?"

"Nine o' nine exactly, sir."

"Okay. Thanks, officer." Parks turned to Hardwick. "Where's my team?"

"They've all been notified and are on their way," Hardwick reassured him.

"Once Fairmont shows up, if I'm busy in the room, have him start out taking photos of the lookieloos. Oh, and have Moore go over the security guard's statement once more."

Hardwick tilted her head in a way that signaled that she had heard his demand. "Remember, Parks. No mistakes on this one."

Parks nodded and stepped into the room, immediately hit with the smell of blood. A scent that could not have begun to prepare him for what he was about to observe with his other four senses.

TWO

Parks took out his notebook and a ball-point pen and began scribbling notes. He surveyed everything around him; the walls—

—mostly adorned with bookcases filled with textbooks, though the space behind the professor's desk was saved for the numerous plaques and awards he had been bestowed with throughout his career—

—the floor below—

—a hard, cheap, carpeted floor covered with several exotic rugs, everything in the office evenly spaced out, the desks and chairs all in perfect harmony—

—and the ceiling above—

—empty, minus the spray of blood that had come during the attack.

Parks cautiously made his way to the professor's desk, noting the path he took, stopping at the body.

"My God," he whispered to himself.

On his back, lying on his desk was Fredrick Knott. He was nude, save for his pants, tangled around his ankles, leaving the rest of his body exposed to show off the numerous stab wounds that covered his stomach, chest and throat. There was even a stab wound through

17

his right cheek, having broken several teeth before slicing through the tongue and down the throat.

The entire top of the desk was covered in blood, having even poured over the sides to the carpet below as if an artist had been playing with an entire can of red paint, the professor's desk his messy canvas. Written in women's lipstick across one corner of the professor's desk, between streaks of the drying blood, was a single word: *JUDAS.*

Parks stared at the word, immediately overwhelmed and exhausted by messages left at crime scenes by killers. The last time he had seen something like this was with the second victim of the Palisades Poisoner, and he was not eager to relive a case like that. In fact, this was eerily similar to that same crime scene. He leaned in closer to the body and noticed a thin white powdery substance blown across the top of the desk. Knowing he could have to have the substance tested before he could get an official verdict, he was still willing to bet his paycheck it was cocaine.

Parks turned around and focused on the woman sitting in the cushioned sofa facing Knott's desk. The young woman—a girl, really—was also nude, with stab wounds adorning her torso, throat and face. Her neck had been gouged so many times that her head was practically decapitated, barely attached on as it hung back against the top of the chair, her eyes eternally staring up at the stark ceiling.

Parks had been so focused on the body that he hadn't noticed Amy Tanaka behind the couch, studying the wounds on the woman's throat. At just a little over five feet, it was often easy to miss the medical examiner, though her loud, opinionated observations usually made it hard to ignore her for long.

"Tanaka." Parks cleared his throat.

"So young. Such a shame," the Japanese woman said as she stood up, staring down at the victim.

"Any one. Any time. Any place. No one's exempt when it comes to murder."

"Don't remind me." Tanaka said. "You look tired. You sleeping okay?"

"Just fine." Parks saw the doubt on the woman's face. "It's just work. Little more than usual, lately. Trying to play catch up."

Someone whistled from behind Parks and he turned to see Jake Fairmont standing at the entrance to the office, his camera in hand. With his curly, blonde hair tied back, he had probably been asleep, dreaming of waking early the next morning and hitting the waves.

"Finished outside?"

Fairmont nodded without saying a word.

"Then start with the scene and work your way to the bodies," Parks said, turning back to the dead girl before him. "Thank you."

When Fairmont wasn't photographing Los Angeles' finest homicides he was usually found at the beaches of Malibu, out on his surfboard, or playing beach volleyball. That was when he wasn't spending time with his fellow detective, Rachel Moore, who just so happened to arrive with him. Detective Moore was a 23-year veteran of the department who specialized in collecting prints and fibers. As the oldest member of the team, she had come to be a sort of motherly-type figure for the rest of the team. When they lacked sleep, or were living off junk food, or needed to release some steam, Rachel Moore made sure each person was taken care of and functioning in tip-top shape. The budding relationship between detectives Moore and Fairmont had, as best as Parks could figure it out, begun around the time of the Palisades Poisoner case when Rachel was hospitalized after an explosion put her in danger. Their romance was becoming an unfortunate "situation" that was still mostly unknown around the department. Now, with the team about to be disbanded, it would soon be someone else's issue to deal with.

Fairmont walked over to the body of Professor Knott, stared down, took a breath and then began taking pictures, working from the head, moving around the body in a clockwise circle, making notes in his own pad when needed. Rachel stood off to the side, also taking notes and waiting for Fairmont and Tanaka to finish before getting closer to the bodies.

Everyone worked silently for a few minutes when someone cleared their throat near the door to the professor's office. Parks turned to find the youngest, and newest, member of his team, Milo Tippin, standing next to Hardwick, awaiting his instructions. Milo had been a computer prodigy who had forsaken a career with the FBI's esteemed Cyber Crimes division for a more in the field, hands-on approach that he so desired. The LAPD had delivered on that promise in full force, especially when on his first case he helped identify the Palisades Poisoner. Ever since that, he had been split between assisting Parks and his team and following Hardwick around as her go-to guy on the computer. While the entire department was still updating their files, as well as the technology they used to carry out their duties, Tippin did his best to help move that progress along at a more rapid pace. So far, money was his biggest obstacle. Simply, that the department had very little of it.

"Start working on a preliminary background check," Parks said. "Thanks."

Milo took out his iPad and began searching on it while he stood off in the corner.

"So what do we know?" Parks asked, turning his attention back to the rest of the group while he let the ME continue with her job.

"He's Fredrick Knott. Age forty-seven. Teaches psychology here on campus," Hardwick rattled off without a pause. "This is his office."

"And the girl?" Parks looked at the woman as Fairmont continued taking pictures.

"Student. Kelli Davis. Twenty-three. She took several of Knott's classes last year. Currently TAs for him."

"Not any more, she don't," Fairmont muttered.

"That all?" Parks tried to get in closer to the bodies but stopped at the sight of all the blood on the floor, which already had numerous prints drying in the coagulated liquid.

"She had an affair with him for a semester about a year ago. He broke it off when his wife threatened to divorce him," Hardwick continued.

"So, he's miserable enough to cheat on his wife, but not miserable enough to divorce her?"

"Maybe he's just a dog," Tanaka commented. "I'm sorry...a man."

"Apparently, when you have as much money as the wife does then you're never really that miserable," Tippin quipped as he played around on his portable computer.

"So he's a user and a dog," Tanaka replied. "He's got 'man' written all over him."

"Just not the kind of man you're used to seeing, huh, Amy?" Fairmont smirked.

"Doesn't have money of his own?" Parks asked trying to keep the room as professional as possible. He could still see Hardwick standing on the outer edge of his peripheral vision, making him tense as she watched over his team's every move. He was fine with his team's personal comments at a crime scene—hell, it was needed. How else were they supposed to stay sane with the stuff they saw day in and day out? It was just usually Hardwick wasn't around to hear their commentary.

"Oh, he does," Hardwick confirmed. "He's got tenure. He's had several books on the bestseller lists. Psycho-sexual, analytical crap. You know? Like why you jerk off to your sister and whether it's wrong to get frisky with the family pet when you're a kid." Parks looked up at Hardwick. Despite the fact that she was a woman, it usually took a hell of a lot to make her blush, and something as simple as sex talk usually never did the job. "That kind of crap. You get me. Anyway, they're big hits. Raking in the dough for him. He's got another book deal too. Something he's been working on. Don't know what about though. He does the professor stuff part-time and the shrink thing the other half. Also did State's testimony work for a few high-profile cases that have been in the news over the past few years."

"Any chance this might have something to do with one of those cases?"

"The cases are being pulled. They'll be on your desk when you get back to the station."

Parks remained quiet. That was quick work, even for her. This case was being expedited at a rapid rate.

"So he's got money. But not enough to compare to the wife?" Parks continued to observe the room, making a mental note of what was where, if it belonged there or not and, if he could figure it out, why.

"Nope. She comes from old money," Hardwick explained. "Newspaper money. Puts his money to shame."

Parks rolled his eyes. "Surprised there's any money left in newspapers. Thought the internet was closing them all down."

"Not yet."

"So she's a socialite."

"She's more than that," Tanaka replied, opening her case and digging through it.

"Oh?" Parks was interested to see what else she could contribute.

"She's an actress," Tanaka said. "Or at least she used to be. Soaps mostly. Did a prime time show with Mary Delancy for half a season but it flopped. I think both of them kinda retired after that. Just bit parts here and there, but she hasn't done anything in over a decade now."

"Well, well…" Parks smiled.

"What? I read my gossip rags."

"So I see."

"Thought I was too good for that, didn't you?"

"Thought never crossed my mind. Promise. She any good?"

Tanaka shrugged as if to say, not really, but who was she to judge.

"She ever get naked?" Fairmont asked with a grin.

"See," Tanaka said. "Dogs. All of 'em."

"What's with the word on the desk?" Parks asked getting his team back on track.

"Judas," Moore answered, since she had examined the desk and all the effects on it around Knott's body.

"The word could mean a million things and refer to either him or her," Fairmont said, wrapping up his finds.

"There's a—" Parks's mind went blank and he snapped a few times, trying to recall the words he was searching for. He closed his eyes and tried to focus, not catching the looks passed between Moore and Fairmont. Their boss needed sleep and it was starting to show. He should have never been called onto another investigation. They knew something was up. "A white powdery substance I noticed on the top of the desk."

"Cocaine," Moore confirmed, holding up a bag with several small vials filled with the drug. "We found this in a secret compartment in the bottom of the professor's desk. Also got a few poppers. Pills. Viagra. And some marijuana as well."

"That all you find?" Tanaka asked from next to the body.

"Was there something else?" Moore asked.

"What have you got?" Parks asked Tanaka.

"Look." Tanaka summoned Parks with her glove-covered fingers and pointed to Knott's forearm where several needle marks were visible.

Parks grimaced. "Those recent?"

"Hard to tell with all this blood everywhere, but they don't appear to be," Tanaka admitted. "I'll get on it once I get the bodies back to the lab."

"Hmmm," Parks huffed. "So, how'd they die?"

"Blood loss due to damage done by multiple stab wounds," Tanaka answered. "Whoever stabbed him didn't just jab him and remove the weapon. They plunged it in deep. The blade is between seven and eight inches in length. Each time he was stabbed most of the blade disappeared into the body. Or so it appears. They never had a chance once the first stab was made."

"They look pretty messed up. How many wounds are we talking about?"

"At least twenty-seven on the girl. Double that for the professor. Whoever did this didn't just want to kill them; they wanted to make sure they were dead. I mean truly dead. Fingers on his left hand are crushed and there are several defensive wounds on both hands. He tried to fight off his attacker. There's also a laceration to the side of his skull."

"What by?"

"Probably this," Moore answered, holding up a plastic bag containing a glass paperweight in the shape of a globe.

"Good. Get it examined and fingerprinted," Parks said when he noticed Hardwick exchanging words in the corner of the room with a man who looked young enough to be a student despite his more formal mannerisms and the semi-expensive suit he wore. Parks had noticed the young man step into the room several minutes before but had kept quiet about it when he saw Hardwick acknowledge his presence and didn't do anything about him. He was in his thirties, fit and trim, with a shaved head, someone who took pride in both his health and physical appearance. He gave the air of possibly being a military brat or having been raised by someone with an authoritative background.

"Who's that and what's he doing contaminating my crime scene?" Parks asked without looking toward his superior. He didn't like an uncontrolled crime scene, and a stranger who had no official business being at one was an "uncontrolled" element as far as he was concerned.

Hardwick stepped forward. "Dave, this is Matthew Bennett. He's with the university's Police Detective Division assigned to Crimes Against Persons. Bennett, this is Dave Parks, one of my finest detectives."

"One of?" Fairmont quipped from somewhere in the background.

"He in charge?" Parks knew there was no way Hardwick would put someone inexperienced in charge of her murder investigation—if she had any choice in the matter—but he also knew a thing or two about jurisdictions. She might not have a say in who was in charge.

"A homicide scene of this nature is somewhat out of the university police's area of expertise," Bennett admitted. The tone in his voice came off as one more with pride of having been in charge of keeping the university as crime-free as it was as opposed to having shame for not knowing how to handle a crime of this magnitude. "Even with my background I've never encountered a crime of this"—he paused ever so slightly, tilting his head as he chose the proper word—"ferocity. I'm more than grateful for whatever help you can offer."

Parks took his words in, not liking the sound of it no matter what they were. It sounded rehearsed. Prepared. Fake. And filled with double meanings.

"That being said, this did happen on university grounds and it would be their case," Hardwick rebutted. "They have priority. However, being as this is a delicate matter and you are the most experienced detective on the scene we have been asked to assume control of the situation, of which I have been assured there will be no arguments about, so long as we keep them informed of the status of the case."

"None whatsoever," Bennett said holding up his hands in a truce. "I have been trained and do have some experience so any help I can offer, I am at your disposal. My main priority is for the university and since, as your AC said, this is a delicate situation, it's one we would like wrapped up as quickly as possible. I'm here to help. This is your case, Detective. No one here is worried about getting glory or any of that bullshit. Think of me more as your personal liaison while on campus grounds. Your own personal walking Google map."

"Glad to meet you," Parks said, shaking Bennett's hand. "Were these two supposed to be on campus this late?"

"There was an alumni party across the courtyard in the Student Union tonight," Bennett said. "It's been confirmed they were both present. He was attending and she worked it. We assume they disappeared up here for a little rendezvous. Everyone that's been questioned so far had no idea about the two. They're all shocked. And not just about the murders."

"Yeah, well, someone knew about them," Parks said, turning back to the two mutilated bodies. "And they weren't very happy about it."

THREE

It was almost an hour before Parks spoke again. He was staring down at the bodies, his head throbbing, veins pulsating, applying more pressure to both his physical and mental being. Tanaka was immersed deeply in her work, but Moore and Fairmont could see Parks's temper building, creeping close to the edge. Fairmont motioned to Tippin, who was trying to focus on his iPad, and held up three fingers before curling each one, counting down to three...two...one—

"Do we really need the soundtrack in the background?" Parks snipped, breaking the silence. He was referring to the music from the party in the Student Union, which was still playing loud enough to be heard across the quad and through closed windows.

Fairmont held back a stifled laugh.

"What's wrong with the music?" Fairmont asked, knowing he was only going to set his boss off, but not able to control himself. It had been a long day for everyone involved. "I thought you liked jazz? You know in the books and movies all the great detectives love jazz."

"Fairmont, I swear, I'll take out my gun and use it on you tonight. I promise you."

29

"Wha?" Fairmont said holding up his hands in defense. "Would you rather it be a thumpa, thumpa, thumpa, thumpa?"

"No, I don't want a thumpa, thumpa, thumpa," Parks hit back. "Why does it have to be anything? Why can't we have peace and quiet? You can't tell me they're back having the party still?"

"Just think of it as our own little CSI background montage music while we work. Only with live jazz instead of techno/pop."

"You know I have no problem taking my weapon out and using it on you. Only that would keep the rest of us out even later tonight and I don't want to be that person."

Tanaka, Moore and Tippin all glared at Fairmont.

"What?" Fairmont asked innocently. "What did I do?"

"So what happened?"

"From the looks of it, they were going at it on the desk here," Rachel Moore stated, collaborating with Amy Tanaka over their notes on the bodies and the scene. "Knott sat on the desk with the girl facing him. The attacker came up at her from behind. We're guessing that the paperweight—which is actually an award from some psychiatry group—was on this table." She pointed to a small end table next to the sofa opposite Knott's desk. "So the attacker comes up, bashes the back of Kelli Davis's head real quick and dazes her. She drops to her knees. The attacker goes to get Knott, maybe gets him but not as good as he hoped."

"Why not?" Parks asked looking back and forth between the two victims.

"They struggled. Shoe prints in the blood show that. Remember, the girl had her back to the attacker, but Knott was facing him. Knott was not able to stop the blow to the head, but maybe he deflected it a little. The skull was cracked, but not as much as it should have been if a full-grown man had been swinging full force. Maybe

Knott was able to get his arm in there just before the blow. Maybe the girl helped block off the attack or was even used as a shield at one point."

"Or maybe it wasn't a man doing the swinging?" Parks offered.

"Possible." Tanaka nodded. "We've still have tests to run on the exact damage that was done to the bodies. I'll get you the results as soon as I get them."

"Thanks. We get anything conclusive out of the prints in the blood?"

"Yes and no," Moore continued. "The few times the attacker stepped in the blood, Knott's feet covered them up while they struggled. All we have are partials. But they're enough."

"To tell what?"

"That the attacker wore male, size twelve, dress shoes."

"There goes our possible female theory," Parks sighed. "But Knott was wearing dress shoes as well. Everyone here tonight is wearing dress shoes. There's a party going on downstairs."

"Yes, but Knott's a size ten. His attacker was bigger. Shoe-wise at least."

"Any identifying marks on the shoes?"

"Like we said, the prints are all pretty messed up. The two men struggled. Most of the prints are destroyed. However, they look like dress shoes. Nothing special. Funny thing is, even though the attacker stepped in the blood there are no prints leading away from the bodies."

"So he cleaned up before he moved around?" Parks surmised. "Then there should be—"

"We've got campus security checking all trash bins and other rooms in the building," Fairmont said slowing his boss down. "So far we've come up empty. However, if this person was smart enough to clean his shoes before traipsing throughout campus then we're probably not going to find his dirty clean-up rags anywhere nearby. But we're still looking."

"Good. So if the paperweight-award-thingy was just to daze them then what was the attack weapon?"

"This," Moore answered as she set down the evidence bag with the paperweight in it and picked up another plastic bag containing a pair of blood-covered scissors. "Straight handle nine-inch cutting shears. Stainless steel handle and blades."

Parks whistled. "Any prints?"

"Not from what I could tell," Moore admitted. "But I'll get it analyzed and let you know as soon as we get something."

"They belong to the professor?"

"Probably," Moore said. "We'll confirm with his secretary. She might not know, but it looks like they were. I mean it's one thing to walk around with a gun or a knife and plan a murder, but a pair of scissors?"

"So it's a weapon of convenience," Parks said with a sigh.

"Rules out premeditation," Fairmont said.

"Not necessarily," Parks corrected. "Convenience of time and place don't necessarily rule out premeditation. This was a crime of opportunity. This murder scene is filled with rage. Passion. This didn't just happen on the spur of the moment. The murder did. But the buildup? No. This crime was a release of pent-up feelings and aggression. This person was more than angry. This is hatred."

"It's sick is what it is." Fairmont commented.

"And they were at the party," Parks commented. "They left together?"

"Not from what we've been told," Tippin finally spoke up. He and the newly acquired Assistant Detective Bennett had just returned from interviewing as many of the guests at the party as possible. Parks noted the obvious physical differences between the two men who were less than a decade apart in age. Both stood six feet tall, though Bennett was built solid and formidable, whereas Tippin was thin as a pencil, his youthful (even for his ripe age of twenty-three), soft looks usually undermining his authority while on the job. There had been rumors throughout the station of the young man's sexuality thanks to his often-impeccable appearance, soft voice and preference for working with computers as opposed to people. Despite all that had been said about him, he had grown over the last nine months, not letting rumors get him down as he excelled in his position on the force, proving himself a reliable and much needed asset to the team. The fact that he had managed to work his way into a detective position while only in his early twenties only fueled the whispers behind his back. "Knott left first. Out a back door. We think. No one actually saw him leave. This is strange because he gave several speeches, and everyone claims to have seen him every moment of the night. He was a popular man."

"And the girl?"

"She was serving cake and refreshments."

"Dressed like that?" Moore asked, referring to the bagged and tagged blue dress that had been found on the ground at Kelli's feet. "Last I checked the help never dressed in thousand-dollar dresses."

"They were told to dress for the occasion," Bennett offered as an excuse. "There wasn't a standard uniform and the help were allowed to mingle after their duties were finished."

"Still," Parks said, "I'm no expert, but that's an expensive dress. How's a college student afford that?"

"You'd be surprised," Bennett said. "If they want it bad enough, they'll do what they have to do to get it."

"Exactly," Moore agreed. "She was dressed to impress tonight. She wanted to be noticed."

"Or someone wanted her to be noticed," Parks suggested.

"What do you mean?"

"Like I said, how's a college girl going to afford a dress like that? Maybe someone bought it for her and wanted her in it for the occasion. Like maybe Fredrick Knott? Let's see if we can find proof of purchase in the girl's belongings when we check out her dorm room," Parks said as he looked to Fairmont who nodded and made a mental note. He then turned to Tippin. "Check out both Knott's and Davis's financial histories. And check their recent phone calls as well." Tippin nodded. "She worked the dessert table. We know when she left her post?"

"Co-worker puts it at about quarter to nine. Give or take," Tippin said. "Said that Miss Davis asked to borrow a... Uh... A tampon, which the co-worker didn't have, then excused herself to the ladies room to take care of business."

"So she was seen leaving. But no one saw him leave? Someone question the wife?"

"Said she never saw him leave," Bennett said.

"She's lying," Parks said without feeling.

"What makes you say that?"

"She's his wife. If he was fooling around, I guarantee you she knew about it. And if she did then she would have known if he had disappeared from a public function. Ask her again."

"I got it," Bennett said with a smile. He was young and ready to prove himself. Besides, Parks figured the more the campus's own people got into the business of the staff and alumni the better it was for him and his team.

"So, they left together. More or less."

"Yeah, but they weren't supposed to."

"How's that?" Parks asked. "They were having an affair, right?"

"Not according to the few who knew about them," Bennett answered, looking around to see who else was in the room.

"What is it?" Parks asked.

"Now, I don't know anything officially," Bennett said. "Only what I hear around campus. And I hear...enough. Rumors. Truths. And everything in between. According to word-of-mouth around campus, they were having an affair. However, it ended about a year ago and they haven't seen each other since. I mean nothing. As though they purposely avoided each other."

"Well, something changed," Parks said. "They were seeing each other again, if they even ever stopped. We need to find out what and when."

"I'll work on it," Bennett said, scribbling something on his notepad. "Anyway, apparently, when the affair ended she went back to her old boyfriend. That's who she was supposed to meet at the party tonight. But when he arrived, she was already gone and he was pissed."

"How pissed?"

"Oh, he made it clear he knew who she was with and where they were." Bennett smiled slyly. "Then he stormed out of the party. Cursing and yelling. Even threw some glasses against the wall."

"Man knows how to make an exit." Parks knew what the next move was even before he said it. "I love it when they make it easy for us. What's his name?"

"Nicholas Martin."

"We know where he is?"

"Not at the moment," Bennett admitted, sounding somewhat defeated but hopeful. "He lives here on campus but he isn't in his room. We're searching for him."

"He's got classes in the morning," Tippin offered, looking up from his iPad.

"Like he'll be at them!" Bennett said snidely.

"You never know," Parks said. "So we'll stop by in the morning and see if the elusive Nicholas Martin shows up. If so, we'll have a chat with him. Until then, I want a car in front of his dorm and a BOLO out on him."

"I'm on it," Bennett agreed. "I'll have someone posted outside his dorm all night. Do it myself if I have to."

"Good," Parks said. "What time is his first class?"

"Nine o'clock, according to his schedule," said Tippin, playing around on his portable computer some more. "He's got Biology in the morning."

"On a Saturday?"

"They have Saturday classes."

"Then we'll be here at eight," Parks said when he noticed Hardwick nodding ever so slightly toward Bennett. He knew what she meant and what he had to do. He recalled the last time the group had a special liaison and it had not ended well. Of course, he had also begun sleeping with the liaison and eventually accused her only son of being a serial killer. But he didn't fear that would happen with Bennett. "You up for it?"

It was through that one simple question that Dave Parks unofficially asked Matt Bennett if he wanted to tag along and be his partner, thereby giving him his temporary seal of approval.

"Really?" Bennett asked.

"This is your campus and you do know it better than me. If I'm going to be traipsing around on it best to have a guide. Besides, most of my team will be busy tomorrow."

"Then I'm your man," Bennett smiled.

"Rachel?" Parks asked before he removed his eyes from Bennett. "Get me any prints?"

"Are you serious?" Moore asked, staring at her superior and re-thinking her response. "This guy was a teacher. Not to mention a counselor for the psych majors and he also offered therapy session to various students on campus who needed it. You know how many different sets of fingerprints we're going to find in here?"

"I don't care," Hardwick interrupted. "If you need help, I'll find it. This is a priority. Just get it done."

"I'll get Milo and we'll start on it right away." Moore sighed as she turned and smiled at him. "He works faster than anyone else I know, anyway."

"All right, everyone," Parks said liking their progress. "With Hardwick here looming over our shoulders all night you can tell this entire case is a class-A priority. We're dealing with a very public and established state university. There's a lot of money flowing through these buildings and people of high stature who have children here. This is a highly sensitive case. We need results and we need them as quickly as possible. You all know what to do without me telling you to do it. So let's get moving."

FOUR

At half past seven the following morning, the sun that should have been shining down on the valley below was instead hiding behind an early morning marine layer that had come in from the coast and settled over Los Angeles like another, thicker blanket of smog. The added gloom didn't do much to help Parks's mood as he tried to wake up and muster the necessary energy to properly carry out his required duty. They had stayed in Professor Knott's office until three that morning, going over every inch of the room. When Parks got home he popped a few Tylenol PMs to help him fall asleep quicker, only to be immediately filled with adrenaline, the need to sleep being counterproductive. No sooner had he fallen asleep than he heard his alarm going off and immediately hated the world. Three strong cups of coffee and numerous Vivarins later, Parks tried his best to keep his head clear and his mind focused, waiting to pick up Kelli Davis's ill-tempered—and possibly homicidal—boyfriend Nicholas Martin. He was trying to solve the morning's crossword puzzle, having already finished the daily Sudoku within the first five minutes of arriving at the university grounds.

"So what's your story?" Parks asked as he blew into his throwa-

39

way cup of coffee, trying to cool it down so that he could dive into it quicker.

"What story?" Bennett asked from the passenger seat of Parks's car.

"You know," Parks said, shrugging his shoulders and motioning his head forward as if his movements would be enough to keep Bennett talking. "Here. The university. Security. What got you here? Your story."

"There is no story," Bennett said, opening his passenger door to get out. "Let's do this. It's gonna take us ten minutes just to cross campus and get to the dorms."

The two detectives started across the deserted quad area, like the opening scene of a horror movie where the heroine is being stalked by some masked killer on a college campus. As Parks crossed the campus grounds he couldn't help but feel something was wrong—off—with the place, making him feel even more like an intruder.

Established in the late 1800s, Pacific Southwest University stood on approximately four-hundred and fifty acres of land in the western part of Los Angeles. Today there were close to two hundred various buildings spread across the campus to help with the almost fifty-thousand students who called the university home. The campus was informally divided into two sections, the north and the south, with the north containing the original 1800s buildings, making them more old-fashioned in appearance. The northern half of the campus was home to the arts, humanities, law, and business programs while the southern half contained the physical and life sciences, engineering, psychology, mathematical sciences, all health-related fields, including the medical center.

Seven minutes later, the two men arrived at the student dorms. Bennett pulled Nick's room number from the administration office the night before and the two worked their way effortlessly to the second floor, taking the stairs as opposed to the slower than molasses elevator that appeared to be indefinitely stuck on the ground floor.

"Which one?" Parks asked once they reached the second floor and exited the stairwell.

"Two-fourteen." Bennett pointed down the narrow hallway.

Parks worked his way down the somewhat claustrophobic hallway to room 214 and knocked on the door.

"Nick Martin," he called out as he knocked again. "Nicholas Martin, it's the—"

Parks stopped when someone on the opposite side of the door played around with the lock and cautiously opened the door to reveal a handsome and somewhat confused face that didn't belong to the person they had been expecting to find.

"Nicholas Martin?" Parks asked, doubting the information he had been given.

"No," replied the kid in a pair of gym shorts and plain-white undershirt that were too small and tight for his thin yet muscular frame. The student rubbed his eyes, informing the men that they had woken him up earlier than had been planned for a class-free Saturday morning. "Nick isn't here."

"I'm Detective Parks of the LAPD and this is Detective Bennett of the University PD," Parks announced, flashing his badge and checking to make sure Bennett had retrieved his. "We were informed that this is Nicholas Martin's dorm room?"

"Doesn't mean he's here twenty-four seven," the student replied with a bite that temporarily threw Parks off as he stared at the boy who was too handsome for his own good. He was fair skinned, without so much as a blemish or proof of teenage acne on his face, though he did have a light speckling of almost unnoticeable freckles across his straight, slightly small nose. The kid probably realized he had answered the detective's question with a less than respectful formality and quickly added, "He's at class."

"Listen, you little shit. We already know he doesn't have class until eight so why don't you quit giving us the run-around and start being straight with us before we have to haul your ass in for questioning," Bennett shot back hoping to shake the kid up.

Parks looked to his recently acquired partner and wanted to say something but knew better than to do it in front of the student, especially since he appeared unfazed by threat. The student, who might have been in his mid—if not early—twenties, took a hand and ran it through his short-cropped, cocoa-colored hair. He stared at the detectives with his brilliant, emerald and turquoise eyes and smirked with two thin yet even lips, liking Bennett's initiative but not falling for the bait. As it was, Bennett didn't look that much older than the student, although he'd been on this earth at least a decade longer.

"He has weights from five-thirty to seven-thirty," the young man said supplying an answer for the missing roommate. "Guess they don't have that information down at Administration, now do they?" The two detectives looked at each other, not sure what to make of their newfound discovery or the information he had supplied. "Of course he could just be off with some girl. He does that too sometimes. This early in the morning. Some need a good cup of coffee—others a good morning fuck. I don't judge. You want to come in?" The young man stepped aside while staying attached to the door. "Sometimes he comes back before class if he has time. Or if he forgets a book...or something."

"Sure," Parks replied as he stepped into the room with his partner following. He doubted Nick Martin was coming back, but figured they may learn a thing or two about the man they were searching for by being in his dorm room. "Thanks."

"No problem," the student smiled, closing the door. "So why are you guys looking for Nick anyways? He's a good guy, you know?"

"Sure he is," Bennett sneered.

"There was a murder on campus last night," Parks continued.

"Yeah, Professor Knott and some girl." The student brushed off the information as if it was last week's gossip.

"You know Knott?"

"I'm not a psych major."

"What's your major?" Bennett asked.

"I'm sort of in-between majors you could say," the student replied. "Been focusing on international business as of late though. Who knows? Was sociology. English before that. I kinda bounce around."

"Depends on what classes sound like more fun to sit through at the time?" Parks asked.

"Depends on which one has the most to offer to help me through life," the student answered with a smirk. "Who was the girl?"

"What girl?" Bennett asked.

"You said Professor Knott was murdered with a girl."

"No we didn't," Parks said. "We simply said there was a murder. You added that it was Knott and a girl part." The student stared at the two detectives. "Seems like gossip spreads quickly around here," Parks continued. The student shrugged. "But not fast enough to get you a name?"

"I was there last night," the student finally admitted. "At the alumni event. My parents are on the board."

"Go figure. Little trust-fund ass—" Bennett muttered under his breath.

"We heard Nick stopped by," Parks said abruptly, hoping to cover up his partner's comment.

"Momentarily. He—oh, I see. Kelli Davis and Professor Knott. Makes sense. That's why you're after Nick."

Parks glanced briefly at Bennett. Nick Martin's roommate knowing about Nick and Kelli was a step in the right direction.

"So did he?" Parks asked.

"What?" the student asked.

"Stop by the gala?"

"You know he did."

"Heard he made quite a scene."

"He's done worse. But, yeah, he did. Everyone there could testify to that."

"Where did he go once he left?"

"Don't know. I didn't follow him."

"Uh-huh. You mind if I ask you a few questions?" Parks continued.

"What have we been doing? Playing charades?"

Parks ignored the comment. "First off: who are you?"

"Christopher Stone," the student replied with a nod of his head and an air of smugness as if the two detectives should have known the roommate to the "great Nick Martin." Parks had never heard the name before but could feel Bennett suddenly tense up. Bennett hadn't recognized the kid by sight but the name obviously meant something around campus.

"You know Nick to have a short temper?" Parks asked.

"That's not really fair now, is it?"

"What's that?"

"Somewhat incriminating question, isn't it?"

"So he had a short temper," Parks said more as a comment and less as a question.

"I've seen shorter," Christopher said. "But no. Not really. Just when..."

"Just when what?" Parks asked.

"Nick has a temper. Short or not. But he knows how to keep it in check," Christopher explained. "He's been in trouble due to his temper in the past. I think he's learned to control it enough. That's what his sports were for. And he had a scholarship. Didn't want to lose that. He was fine with his temper...except..."

"Except?"

"Except when it came to Kelli."

"She had an effect on him?"

"You could say that. Kelli had an effect on many men. She was like that. She wasn't really a one-man type of a gal. For that matter, Nick wasn't a one-woman type of a guy either. Maybe that's why they fit so well together."

"So they weren't exclusive?"

"I don't know what the rules to their relationship were," Christopher admitted. "Maybe they were. Maybe they weren't. I know he slept around. I'd heard the same about her too. So"—Christopher shrugged—"who knows. But I do know that last year she started sleeping around."

"With Professor Knott?" Parks asked.

"That's just what I'd heard," Christopher nodded. "But so did Nick. And he sure didn't like that. I mean, whether or not you believed the rumors about her and all the other guys, there wasn't any more evidence to support that she was sleeping with Knott. Nick didn't care about the other guys. But for some reason Knott sent him over the edge."

"Did he confront her about Knott?" Bennett asked.

"Eventually."

"When?" Parks asked. "Something happened?"

"They were in here. But I didn't see anything."

Parks started to get Christopher's games even if he didn't understand them yet.

"So you waited in the hallway. What did you hear?"

"He told her to stop seeing him. She laughed at him. Called him a jealous pussy. That type of stuff. Said no man owned her or could tell her what to do or who to see. Et cetera. Stuff like that. They were yelling. Fighting. I'm sure several neighbors heard them as well. Then it got real quiet in there."

"Then what happened?"

"Nick yelled for someone to call for an ambulance."

"An ambulance?"

Christopher nodded and Parks turned to Bennett. "You recall any of this?"

"I've only been here since the fall," Bennett admitted as he shook his head.

"This was last spring. But I'm sure there's a record of it," Christopher added, as if he knew what the detectives were thinking. "She was admitted to Kaiser with a broken nose and jaw. He got her good."

"She pressed charges?" Parks asked.

"Not that I'm aware of," Christopher answered. "She stayed in the hospital for a few days. When she got out, she split."

"What does that mean?"

"Means she wasn't around. Don't know where she went. But she stayed away. Nick was all pissy for a week or so. Then a few months later she was back."

"She came back?" Bennett asked. "To Nick?"

"Yep. Said she called it off with the professor like Nick told her to. Said he was right all along and that she should have listened to him. That she should have never gotten involved with him. Don't know why, but something happened between her and Knott. I don't know what, so don't bother asking. She never said anything. To me personally. But she was shaken up for a bit after she came back. Paranoid-like. On edge. As if something had happened."

"Like she wanted Nick around for protection?" Bennett asked.

"It wasn't anything she said. Just a feeling. Like I said, she was scared."

"And Nick took her back?" Parks felt as though he was catching up with some daytime soap instead of collecting evidence.

"Eh, Nick's sort of a sucker for those blondes. Always has been. Besides, Kelli seemed to have some sort of spell over him. Had him wrapped around her fingers. All ten of them."

"So he took her back without a word about before?" Parks asked.

"She was wrong," Christopher said. "You know a man who doesn't like a woman who comes crawling back admitting she was wrong? Especially a man like Nick? Of course he took her back. Besides, you've seen Kelli. Find me a man on this campus who wouldn't have taken her back."

"Would you?" Parks asked.

"I'm not Nick," Christopher replied.

"So she was out of his league?" Bennett asked.

Christopher gave a tilt of his head and a partial shrug. "Have either of you actually seen Nick?"

Bennett took out a black and white photocopy of Nick's driver's license. Christopher smirked at the picture, though whether it was from the poor quality of the copy or the aged picture of Nick neither detective could tell.

"What? That's not him?"

"Let's just say it doesn't do him justice. Nor does the physical description on the card. That's probably his old info from when he was sixteen and first got the license. Let me see if I can find you guys something more current."

"You didn't answer the question," Parks said when Christopher went to the other side of the room and retrieved his cell.

"What question is that?" Christopher asked as he began to search through something on his phone.

"Was Nick out of Kelli's league?"

"Kelli looks like she belongs on the cover of a Maxim magazine," Christopher said. "Agreed?"

Parks looked to Bennett who nodded. "She could turn a head or two I'm sure."

"So can Nick," Christopher added, handing over his cell. "I mean he might not be the cutest but imagine someone with a six-foot-five body of pure muscle and the cocky attitude to back it up and you've got an image of Nick. The guy's built like an ox. That's his Instagram account."

"Sports?" Parks asked as he quickly flipped through a few photos. "I don't recall seeing any on his transcripts."

Christopher walked over to a basket of fruit on a nearby table and picked up a bright, green apple "Care for one?" Both men shook their heads. "He used to do football. Broke his leg sophomore year. Hasn't been the same ever since."

"Thought you said he had a scholarship?"

"He does."

"For football?"

"Hey, don't ask me," Christopher said as he took a bite of the apple. "I'm not in charge of that type of stuff. You'd have to ask him how he still has it. Sure you guys don't want one?"

"We're fine," Bennett replied handing Christopher back his phone. "Thanks."

"You're right," Parks said. "He is a big guy. Not fair for a one-on-one against Kelli though, wouldn't you say?"

"Would it be fair for *you* against him in a one-on-one?" Christopher answered with another question.

"We could take him," Bennett smiled. "If we have to."

Christopher studied Parks and Bennett, checking them out to see just how fit they were despite their deceiving wardrobe. Parks, having not completely lost his physical build thanks to running seven miles a day and weekly workouts, could probably hold his ground, though nearing forty he was no longer in his prime as he had been at one time. Bennett was younger and though thinner in build, and Christopher was about to write him off as nothing to worry about when he noticed the thickness of the man's neck and figured that he had the body to match.

"Well, maybe both of you together could," Christopher concluded. "But I wouldn't take him on one-on-one. Either one of you might get hurt. Then you'd have to add police brutality along with murder one."

"So you think he did it?" Parks asked. Christopher simply shrugged and remained quiet. "He ever hit her?"

"Not regularly."

"You know that for a fact?" Bennett asked.

"Let's put it this way," Christopher replied in-between another bite. "He's a big guy. He bats her around, it's gonna show. Like the broken jaw and nose. Sure, every now and again, she might have had a slight bruise but she always defended him. And he wasn't the type to think up creative ways to beat a woman without leaving a mark or being caught."

"You sure about that? Some men—" Parks started.

"Look," Christopher interrupted. "They may both be damn near flawless looking but there weren't more than two brain cells between the two of them. I'm talking about academic smarts. Now the two of them had street smarts. Gotta give them that. Scary good street smarts. That's part of why they fit so well with each other. You might not understand what they had between them, but it worked for them. Did he ever hit her? I'm sure of it. But did he beat her? I wouldn't say so."

"And how many times does one have to be hit for it to constitute as beating?"

"Once," Christopher replied flatly. "As long as the attacked doesn't wish to be touched."

The two detectives paused for a moment as they took in what Christopher had told them.

"Are you saying Kelli Davis liked getting hit?" Parks asked somewhat concerned with where this conversation was heading.

"I'm not saying anything on the record," Christopher said. "I'm simply stating a feeling I got when I saw them around each other. It's the way they behaved. I'm not saying she liked getting beat. I'm saying they liked to harass each other. Tease. Like it was a form of fore-play. She liked provoking him. And he liked it when she did that."

"Did Kelli ever hit Nick?"

"She'd slap him every now and again, sure," Christopher said as he threw the remainder of his apple into the trash and grabbed a nearby towel to clean his hands. "Saw it plenty of times. Let me tell you that girl could swing her arm when she needed to. Scratch him every now and again too. I saw marks on his back one time. But then again that could have been in the heat of passion if you catch my drift."

"Did it piss him off?" Bennett asked.

"Like I said, no matter what she did to him, or what he did to her, they didn't like being apart from each other. You would've sworn they were rabbits or something." Christopher paused as he looked at something behind the two detectives. "You two are gonna miss him."

"What?" Parks asked.

"Nick," Christopher replied. "If you're planning on nabbing him before class to avoid a scene then you're going to miss him. Class starts in ten minutes."

Parks checked his watch and realized that they had spent more time interrogating Christopher than he planned.

"Thanks for your time," Parks said as he offered his hand to Christopher. "You've been more than helpful."

"No problem," Christopher replied, leading the men to the door.

Parks stepped out and Bennett followed, offering his hand to Christopher as well.

"Thanks," Bennett stared at Christopher, realizing that the student hadn't released his hand when he finally pulled it free.

"Any time, detectives," Christopher waved from the doorway. "Any time."

*   *   *

"You might want to do me a favor and watch yourself," Parks commented to Bennett as the two made their way out of the dorms and across the campus.

"What's *that* mean?"

"You're not exactly the most politically correct person."

"What's that mean?"

"Look, these guys may be assholes and scumbags and whatever else. But you can't go around talking like that and treating them like anything less than equals to you and me. You have to try and be a little more...smoother. Slick about the way you go about getting your information. You ever heard that saying: you can catch more flies with honey?"

"You have your way of going about things and I have mine. Yours works for you as mine does for me. Nothing against you, but..." Bennett shrugged, trying to find the right words. "I deal with these kids every day. I get them. I know them. Honey may work on flies but on these kids, it won't do anything but get you into a sticky situation. Trust me."

"Speaking of which, you did get one part of the equation correct. Trust fund brats. This entire school is made of money. Old money. Rich money. One call from the wrong student to the right parent and both you and I will be out of a job quicker than you can spit." Parks hoped he got his point across to Bennett but wasn't sure he had. "I've already been chewed out before I even accepted this case. There are a lot of public people associated with this school and they don't like the boat to be rocked. You catch my drift?"

"Look. I work here. I'm sure I get it more than you do. Okay?" Bennett gave Parks a look that said to back off.

"Just try and watch yourself. Okay?" Parks didn't care for Bennett's reply but didn't want to pursue it any further. "Oh, and who was that?"

"Who?"

"Christopher Stone. Kid we just talked to. Who was he?"

"I've never met him before in my life."

"Yeah, but you knew the name. Who is he?"

Bennett stayed quiet for a minute while they continued walking toward the car.

"Just a kid whose family has money," Bennett answered. "He organizes a lot of the on campus gambling and gaming and whatnot. We've never been able to catch him at it but we know he's behind it. High stakes games. Most of the security on campus is in his debt. He is not a stupid kid. That's part of why we've never been able to link him with anything."

Parks felt there was more to the story but decided to keep quiet for now. He had enough to worry about and Nicholas Martin's roommate was not on the top of his list.

FIVE

Parks whistled and Bennett looked to where he had pointed with ever so slight a nod. Walking toward them, standing out from most of the other students was the young man from the pictures Christopher Stone had provided. As he walked through the crowd, the student was scanning everyone around him as if looking out for someone while trying to avoid everyone else. There were bags under his bloodshot eyes, not as if from a single night of sleep deprivation but more like a week of uncomfortable sleep and relentless worries. His clothes appeared as if he had slept in them from the day before, which was a plus for the detectives if he had murdered Professor Knott and Kelli Davis, for the evidence would still be on him.

"Nicholas Martin?" Parks asked as Nick was about to pass by the two detectives.

"Shit," Nick muttered as he stopped at the door without turning around. "What now?"

"Hey. That a yes or a no?" Bennett asked, walking to the other side of Nick, one man taking each side of the student. Nick was wired, hopped up on something. That made him unpredictable and this needed to be done by the book. No mistakes.

"Guess that all depends," Nick replied, turning around and licking his lips like a lion preparing to play with its prey. The student wiped his mouth, but then paused as if the action was a giveaway to some hidden clue and he forced his arm to his side.

"On?" Bennett continued.

"Who the fu—who's lookin' for me," Nick snapped.

"Who is looking for you?" Parks asked.

"Man, quit dickin' me around," Nick huffed. He was agitated and wiped his forehead of sweat when he ran a hand over his head. "I know you two are cops. Whadaya want?"

"What do you think we want?"

"Shit. I heard about what happened to the professor and Kelli. I can put two and two together," Nick answered. "Just thought you guys would have been here sooner is all."

"Why don't we take a walk?" Parks put a hand to Nick's shoulder and started to lead him toward the quad area away from any eavesdropping ears.

"Look," Nick started, brushing Parks's hand off his shoulder, losing his bag that he caught before it hit the ground. "I know why you're here. I'll save you time and cut to the chase. I didn't kill them."

"You were there last night?" Parks asked. "At the gala."

"No shit I was there. You already know that or else you wouldn't be here. Not gonna get me that easy. Musta been over a hundred people who saw me."

"Heard you threw a fit when you found out she wasn't around?" Bennett took a step toward Nick hoping to get in his personal space and give them a slight advantage over the hulking student.

"Man, I don't throw fits," Nick retorted. "Get me?"

"Oh, we get you," Bennett replied. "Heard you like to throw fists instead."

"Man, I don't throw fits," Nick repeated, blinking his eyes several times. "Get me?"

Bennett held his ground as Parks studied the college student. Something was off. He fidgeted like he was tweaking. Parks had seen his fair share of tweakers and users in his day but Nick wasn't giving off the usual signs. He was almost holding himself together. To Parks he was just sleep deprived. His eyes were on the move, in overdrive, waiting to see something, or someone, that he'd rather just avoid. He was scared and it wasn't of the law. Was he meeting someone here? On campus? This morning?

"So where'd you go after you left the party?" Parks stared at Nick to get the young man's reaction. Body language played a big part in following instincts. "Did you know where they went?"

"It ain't brain surgery, man," Nick answered. "Doesn't take too much to figure out where they went."

"Where was that?" Bennett asked. "And try and be quick about it."

"Where'd you find them?" Nick asked rhetorically.

"So you went to Knott's office?" Bennett asked. Parks stared at Bennett, upset that his partner had given away crucial information, and tried to figure out how to move past it. He had to use what he had. Unfortunately, between his lack of sleep and the coffee and pills, his head was a swirling mess.

Nick was about to answer but then shut his mouth. This was getting into iffy territory.

"You know we have a team of forensics going over that entire office. We've lifted dozens—maybe hundreds—of fingerprints from that room," Parks explained. "If you were there, we'll figure it out sooner or later. How do you want to play this, Nick?"

"Shit. Yeah, I was up there," Nick huffed as he shivered. "I knew where they went. His office is the closest place to the party. I took a guess. But I didn't kill them."

"You saw them?" Parks asked.

"Yeah."

"Alive?" Bennett questioned.

Nick glared at him and ignored the question.

"And?" Parks continued.

"And what?"

"What did you see? What happened?"

"You know what they were doing. Everyone does by now. But what did I do? Nothing."

"You watched them?"

"I saw them, yeah."

"I didn't ask if you saw them. Did you watch them?"

"Sorry. Not really my thing."

"So you just walked in, saw them doing their thing, then left?" Parks asked doubtfully.

"More or less," Nick agreed.

"What's more or less?" Parks asked.

"I saw them. She told me to piss off. I left," Nick explained. "That's it. Nothing else. I didn't talk to them. We didn't hold hands 'n write poetry an' shit. I left them alone. And alive."

"She saw you?" Parks asked.

"She told me to piss off," Nick reconfirmed. "That's it. Nothing else happened."

"He saw you?"

"Who? Knott? Naw, man. His back was to me."

That didn't work. Kelli was attacked first, with her back to the door. Nick's description put them in the reverse. Then again, Nick could be lying and switched around the positions he saw them in just to mess with them. But why would he? Parks wasn't giving up. "And he didn't turn around when she told you to leave?"

"Naw. He was really into what he was doing, if you catch my drift. He probably just thought she told him to fuck her or something. You know—"

"Yeah, yeah," Parks said stopping Nick. "We get it.

"I swear to you, man. When I left them, they were alive."

"You see anyone else in the room with them?"

"What do you mean?"

"Was anyone else in the room with them?"

"You mean, like, were they havin' a threesome?"

"Was anyone else in the room besides them and you?"

"Naw, man. Not that I saw."

Parks wasn't sure he believed Nick but could think of no reason for him to lie. Then again that didn't mean he wasn't. Everything about Nick's behavior and body language said the kid was telling the truth. But he was still jumpy. Something was wrong. Maybe he had seen something. Or someone. Someone that scared the kid. Parks needed to get him to calm down.

"What was your relationship with Kelli like?" Parks asked.

Nick paused for a second. "Am I under arrest?"

"We're just trying to get a feel for what's what."

"Bullshit," Nick spat at the two men. "I'm your prime suspect. I know how that shit works."

"Look, Nick," Parks said hoping to get the situation under control before the student made this a public ordeal. "We're simply exploring every possibility at this moment. We're—"

"Fuck that!" Nick shouted.

Suddenly, before either Parks or Bennett could comprehend what was happening, Nick was on the run. Nick turned, planning to get away from the two men as quickly as possible, when Bennett grabbed him by the shoulder, igniting Nick's temper. Nick's backlash wasn't a personal attack on the men so much as a gut reaction to years on various sports fields.

"Get offa me!" Nick shouted with blind fury.

Nick spun around and shoved Bennett back, infuriating the detective who went after the student again. No matter what they may have thought, Nick was a much bigger and stronger man than either of the detectives. While Bennett attacked Nick from one side, Parks came up on the other and got in the way of Nick's swinging book bag that caught the detective square in the face. Parks fell to the ground, the corner of several rather large books hitting him in the eye.

"Son of a bitch," Parks hissed as he grabbed his face while he stayed low to the ground.

Nick began to kick Parks, getting him twice in the stomach and once in the face, when Bennett tackled the student. Nick spun the man up over his back and onto the ground.

Bennett landed on the concrete sidewalk, getting the wind knocked out of him. Parks started to get to his knees, his hand to the side of his head tending to his swelling eye. Nick took in the scene before him and knew it didn't look good. He had just attacked two officers of the law. This only added to his already guilty stance on the whole murder situation. With his adrenaline pumping, and his brain on freeze, Nicholas Martin did what came naturally to him. He ran.

Nick Martin may have been a heavy guy, but most of his mass was pure muscle. His legs, though not the game-winning glory they had once been, were more than enough to keep him ahead of whoever may have decided to chase after him. It took Bennett half a minute before he was up running after the student, with Parks another twenty seconds behind him.

The one thing Nick had going for him, besides his strength and speed, was his knowledge of the campus. The student had already decided where to run to that would be most helpful in losing his pursuers. And while Parks may not have had the school's layout embedded into his brain, Bennett had been on campus long enough to know several of the nooks and crannies one may have chosen to run through or hide in.

Nick made it across the entire quad, having jumped over a park bench, and a hedge, neither obstacle slowing his speed in any way. Both detectives had to run around the bench, and though Bennett made it over the hedge without any hesitation in his stride, Parks had to rethink the obstacle and chose another path altogether.

Nick made it to the closest building, Eureka Hall, which housed the theatre department, and disappeared inside. Eureka housed two stories worth of classrooms on one end of the building and two performance stages at the other. The theatre in the middle of the building was a 400-seat proscenium theatre for large-scale productions. Past the large stage, at the other end of the building, was an octagonal-shaped theatre that could remove an entire wall to change the stage from a theatre-in-the-round format to a three-quarter seating arrangement.

What neither detective knew was that Nick was quite knowledgeable of the building thanks to working backstage on two productions the year before as part of his liberal arts requirements. Nick first entered Eureka Hall at the end that brought him into an outer hall surrounding the smaller, round theatre.

Bennett entered through the same door a few seconds later and started down the same path after the sprinting student. Parks entered through the same door and immediately started in the opposite direction, hoping to corner the student. On the opposite end of the hallway, both detectives almost ran into each other, Nick having given them the slip somewhere. Bennett started back the way he had come when he noticed that the doors along the hallway leading into the theatre were all open, having only been covered by black sheets of cloth so as to keep the hallway light out of the stage area during classes or productions. Bennett ducked his head through the cloth and found the stage and the seats around it empty as he walked out onto the stage. Four all-black boxes sat sporadically across the otherwise barren stage that was without a backdrop or any other type of scenery or props. Parks entered onto the stage as well and the two men looked around.

Both men scanned over the empty audience seats and then to the manager's booth up toward the back of the theatre. They froze and looked up at the sound of someone walking on the catwalks high above the stage.

"Up there." Bennett started for a black-painted wooden ladder on the side of the stage. "Check out the area behind the stage. He's got to come down somewhere."

Bennett made it up to the catwalk and started after Nick. Parks turned and disappeared through the black cloth doors, heading toward the back where he thought Nick would be. Parks got to the backstage area as Nick disappeared up over a ledge, into the neighboring theatre's catwalk area.

Parks backtracked, working his way out the small theatre's surrounding hallway into the main hallway, and found a doorway leading to the larger, neighboring stage. Parks made it onto the main stage and saw Nick running some forty feet above him. Bennett was not more than twenty steps behind the young man when Nick slipped, falling off the catwalk. Nick dangled over the edge while Parks stood beneath him, not sure what he should do.

"Dammit, Nick, knock this off!" Parks shouted from below. "You're going to kill yourself and it's not worth it. Let's talk. It's not that bad."

"Fuck you!" Nick shouted back as he hoisted himself back up onto the catwalk. Nick was just up on his feet when Bennett collided with him and the two fell, almost rolling off the catwalk to the stage below.

"Shit." Parks held his breath, knowing there was nothing he could do from down below if one of the two men were to fall.

"Knock it off," Bennett ordered, trying to keep Nick under control. "Quit resisting. It's only making things worse for you."

Bennett punched Nick in the face. Nick's head slammed against the catwalk, dazing him, though it did nothing to withdraw the fight in him, only infuriating him more.

"Fuck you!" Nick repeated and brought his knee up into Bennett's groin.

Bennett sucked in his breath and dropped to his knees. Nick pushed the detective off him and hobbled down the catwalk again, disappearing up over a ledge and out of Parks's sight.

Nick made it to the end of the catwalk and turned right, taking a small corridor to a dead end and then turned left and took another small, darkly lit hallway at the end where he pushed open a door that found him outside, on the side of the Eureka Hall building. He started down the second story wooden stairs and hit the ground below, hesitating only to register where he was before he ran around the corner when out of nowhere Parks tackled him to the ground, catching him completely off guard and knocking the wind out of him.

"Stay down!" Parks ordered. He pressed his knee into Nick's back while retrieving his handcuffs. "You have the right to remain silent. And I suggest you shut the hell up."

The door above them flew open and Bennett exited the same way Nick had a minute before. He caught sight of Parks finishing reading Nick his rights.

"Yes," Bennett cheered with a smile, huffing his way down the rickety steps.

"Now," Parks began, getting Nick to his feet. "What do you say we go and have a little chat about Kelli Davis and Fredrick Knott?"

"How about you go fuck yourselves and get me my lawyer?" Nick spat blood on the ground at the detectives' feet and turned away with a sneer on his face.

"Will do," Parks replied. "Hope you have a good one."

SIX

After Parks had Nicholas Martin booked he disappeared into the nearest men's restroom and took the bottle of Vicodin from inside his jacket pocket and tapped two pills into his hand which quickly made their way down his throat and out of sight. He caught sight of himself in one of the mirrors and realized he had seen better days. With a cut lip, a swollen black eye and a scuffed-up face, he tried to straighten out his grass-stained suit and discovered that he was also missing several buttons after his tussle with Kelli's boyfriend. He tried to clean himself up as quickly and efficiently as possible. He wanted to change; knew he needed to, but didn't have time. As soon as he exited the restroom, Hardwick was on him to join her with Mrs. Knott who had come in, along with her lawyer, to help answer any questions they may have had about her husband. Parks buttoned his jacket over his torn and soiled shirt and went into Interrogation Room #2.

Elizabeth Knott sat with her lawyer, whom Parks paid no attention to, opposite Parks and Hardwick. Elizabeth Knott's skin was fair, having the look of rarely ever been graced by the sun, covered in a heavy dose of light freckles that were highlighted by her carrot-blonde colored hair. She had large, beaming brown eyes and a sharp nose that complimented her face nicely, even if her ears stuck out a little more than was proportionate to her face. Her posture was impeccable, the result of many years of some sort of reform girls' schooling. Her wrists, fingers and ears were adorned by jewelry that was both expensive yet unassuming, adding to the air of sophistication and old-school money without being obnoxious. There was a slight, flowery smell about her, as if she had barely touched perfume, preferring her natural odor as opposed to an overpowering and distracting scent.

Hardwick introduced Parks as the lead detective on her husband's homicide and Elizabeth Knott gave the required smile and nod of her head.

"Mrs. Knott, this interview will be conducted by Detective Parks with the aid of myself," Hardwick said. "Assistant District Attorney Dennis Beasley will also be viewing these proceedings."

Parks turned, having not noticed the other man in the room behind them.

"Nice to meet you." Elizabeth nodded toward the ADA. "This is my attorney, Adam Wolfe."

Parks jerked his head in the direction of her lawyer, the name of Peter Kozlov's lawyer stabbing his psyche, and he wondered how he had not recognized the man upon first entering the room. Peter Kozlov had been a substitute teacher from Russia who had been targeting children with razor blade-infused candies the year before. Upon Kozlov's arrest, Adam Wolfe had been retained to defend the man. Parks wondered if Elizabeth Knott was aware that her innocence in all things surrounding her husband was now in question due to her current company. Her lawyer, in his expensive three-thousand dollar suit that just screamed to the entire room that he was worth more than anyone else around and that he damn well earned his keep, was slick and gave off an oily, snake-like charm. He was young, in his late thirties, and had put in more time doing late night client dinners and spending less time at the gym as he pushed the seams of his suit, though he didn't come off as overweight, just big.

"Now, we would like to make it clear that we are here to help with the investigation into the murder of Mrs. Knott's husband and not as a suspect," Mr. Wolfe said.

"Mr. Wolfe, at this time we have not finished gathering all the evidence and so do not fully know what happened concerning your husband's murder," Parks explained, trying his best to keep his temper in check. "So I think it's safe to say that at this time most everyone who knew and or was associated with the late professor can be considered a suspect. This meeting is not to attack your client so much as figure out her part in the greater scheme of things. Your client has already admitted she is not guilty of the crime in question and has nothing to hide. If this is true and she wishes to continue with the interview, then it can only help but eliminate her from our list of suspects and move us along in a more rapid pace toward the right direction in finding her husband's killer."

Elizabeth Knott looked to her attorney and nodded.

"That being said, Mrs. Knott," Parks continued, "if we discover that you are in fact guilty of the murder of your husband and Kelli Davis, then this interview and all information gathered from it can and will be used in a court of law when that time comes. Do you understand everything I've said?"

Elizabeth was about to answer when her attorney placed a hand over hers to stop her.

"Yes." Elizabeth looked at her attorney and then back to the detectives. "I understand. I'm not guilty and therefore have nothing to hide. Besides, how would it look if I obstructed the law from finding my husband's killer by stalling you?"

Parks stared at the woman who sat before him in an all-black St. John skirt and matching jacket. She had kept the jacket on though it was unzipped just enough to reveal the black Chantilly laced camisole that Parks figured would not have been enough to keep her warm in this mildly chilled room. She crossed her right leg over the left, inching up the hem of her skirt and revealing more thigh than he was used to seeing from one in mourning.

"When do you think they'll release the body?" Elizabeth asked as she retrieved a pack of cigarettes and pulled one free from the box. She had managed to hold back the tears but her fingers told a different story. "I have a funeral to plan and it's a little difficult without a body."

"You can't smoke in here," Hardwick stated matter-of-factly. "Your husband's murder has been given top priority. We should be finished with the autopsy and all tests by the end of the week. Your husband's body can be released to you Monday morning so long as there are no unforeseeable events."

"Thank you."

"In a rush?" Parks cleared his throat.

"Excuse me?" Elizabeth asked, caught off guard, playing with the cigarette, wanting to light it up but resisting the urge.

"To get the funeral out of the way?"

"Detective, let's not beat around the bush. There is no great love lost with the death of my husband. We may have been married on paper, but we haven't been in love with each other for several years now."

"Still, there was love at one time. Should be hard—"

"Yes. It still is. I won't lie. Doesn't matter how much you try to fall out of love with a person—even if you do, it still hurts. To see death lying on a slab in front of you—whether it's your husband or a perfect stranger—well, death is still death."

"Mrs. Knott, you do realize that with your husband being found murdered with one of his co-eds that you are a suspect?" Parks was careful so as not to upset the woman. He had a calm, soothing voice that often put people at ease, and the last thing he needed right now was to anger the grieving widow. She had money and the lawyers to prove it. The last thing he needed was a lawsuit against him or the department.

Then again, a suspect was a suspect and facts were facts.

"I didn't love my husband, Detective. However, I didn't hate him either. I didn't kill him. Therefore, I have nothing to hide. You can ask any question of me you wish," Elizabeth assured him.

"All right, Mrs. Knott, how long have you and your husband been married?" Parks began.

"Four years," Elizabeth answered. "Five this upcoming November."

"Does your husband have any other family besides yourself?"

"No. We have no children and Rick was an only child. His father's been dead for, let's see, seventeen years now and his mother...for about six."

"Rick?"

"Sorry," Mrs. Knott smiled. "I called my husband Rick. I don't care for Fredrick or Fred or Freddie as a name. I called him Rick. I was the only one. Something that made us...us."

"Okay. So as far as you're aware, you are the leading beneficiary to your husband's estate?"

"I am his wife."

"That doesn't answer my question." Parks waited patiently.

"So far as I am aware, yes, I am."

"Where were you between eight p.m. and midnight last night?"

"I was at the alumni benefit with my husband. You can ask around. I was there all night."

"Sure you didn't slip away at any point?"

"Detective, not to sound too pompous, but I'm an extremely important person at benefits like the one last night. Especially when it's one I helped put together. I don't have time to just 'disappear'. Ask around. You'll see. I am accounted for all evening up until the police arrived and I was notified of my husband's condition."

"Condition. Yes. Your husband's body was found with one of his students—"

"Kelli Davis," Elizabeth answered, not missing a beat.

"Were you aware of your husband's affair?"

"You're assuming we didn't have an open marriage?"

"Did you?"

"No."

"So it was an affair?"

Elizabeth simply shrugged saying it was but that it didn't bother her.

"Could you please verbalize your response for the recorder?"

"My husband's activities were of no concern to me."

Parks stared at the woman for a moment, patiently waiting for her to continue.

"I had heard the rumors," Elizabeth continued nonchalantly, inspecting her recently manicured nails. "Like I told you earlier, though we were married, the love was no longer there. Besides, despite what I may have heard, I could prove nothing. Rick was good.

At least at keeping his affairs private. Kelli's name was the only one I had heard of. If he'd been sleeping with anyone else, I don't know who."

"What came first, Mrs. Knott?" Parks asked. "The affairs or you falling out of love?"

"What a truly interesting question." Elizabeth smiled, re-crossed her legs and thought about how to answer the question. "I did love Rick. When I first met him, I was wildly in love with him. I mean, I had been in love before. But never like this. Thought I would spend the rest of my life with him. Little did I know, it would only last a short while. Sometimes people grow apart. I think we fell out of love a long time ago. Sometimes I think the marriage was more out of convenience. I don't know what came first. The loss of love or the affairs. Perhaps they were mutual. However, I never stopped caring for him; and him me. I can tell you that. We may not have loved each other the way a husband and wife should have, but we still cared for one another. We had our own system and it worked for us. I never wished him any harm. I just wish we had found a way to end it all a long time ago." Elizabeth Knott paused for a second, her eyes beginning to tear up. "Maybe if we had, he wouldn't have been sneaking around. Maybe then, he might not have been where he was last night. Perhaps, just maybe, he'd still be alive today."

"You can't think like that," Hardwick said, handing over a box of tissues.

"Can't help it," Elizabeth Knott shrugged. "He's dead. Can't help but wonder what part I played in the events that led up to his murder. And that poor girl that was with him. So young. She didn't deserve this. Maybe she should have made some wiser choices in life. But I don't think death is ever an acceptable form of punishment for one's own ignorance."

"Why didn't you leave your husband?" Parks continued unmoved.

"You don't have to answer that," Elizabeth's attorney interjected.

Elizabeth sneered at the man with disdain for him having even been there at all.

"He wouldn't leave me," Elizabeth began. "He stood to inherit too much. And I was too tired to go through a divorce. I just wanted companionship really. What's wrong with that?"

"What do you mean 'too tired'?" Parks asked, noticing the tiredness in the woman's eyes. Not just in them but around them, a look that even the makeup piled on could not hide. She was talking about something that none of them saw. Something bigger. Elizabeth stared back before finally continuing.

"I'm sick," Elizabeth sighed, dabbing her eyes with the tissue.

"I'm sorry to hear that," Parks said sympathetically. "Truly."

"Thank you," Elizabeth said. "I've been sick off and on for the past five years. I keep beating it. But this time the doctors say...I've got maybe six months left."

"You look well," Parks observed.

"Yes, well, since I know there's no chance of stopping it I've opted not to undergo chemo this time," Elizabeth explained. "It makes the time shorter but at least I won't be prolonging the inevitable. I don't want to spend the last year of my life miserable. Not sure if it's the smartest thing, but it's the choice I've made. I didn't want to spend the end of my life fighting." Elizabeth let out a huff, fidgeted with her wedding ring. "So that was part of our agreement. We go on as a happily married couple until my passing. Then he would get everything and could do whatever he wanted. His end of the bargain was to stop seeing anyone else. Just give me until my end."

"Otherwise?"

"Otherwise I'd divorce him on grounds of infidelity," Elizabeth said matter-of-factly. "Or at least keep him out of my will."

"You don't have any other family?" Parks asked.

"No," Elizabeth answered. "My parents are both deceased. I had a younger sister. She succumbed to breast cancer several years ago. There's no one left now."

"I understand you're a wealthy woman," Parks stated.

"I suppose I am," Elizabeth agreed. "I don't count it every day."

"Got an estimate? Give or take?"

"Twenty, maybe thirty million," Elizabeth sighed, bored with the subject but understanding its importance in the picture. "Give or take."

"Would it shock you to learn you're worth forty-seven point four million?"

Elizabeth Knott thought about this, having not known the number but not really surprised by it either. "My father was one of the founders of a newspaper up north in the bay. He bought out failing publishing companies and gave them new life so to speak. Left me a nice piece of change when he and mother passed on a while back."

"Nice piece of change."

"Yes. Though you must realize that by the time my parents passed on he wasn't worth much more than fifteen million. He had lost most of it in gambling and bad investments. Newspapers had begun to take a dive."

"And the rest came from?"

"I suppose you think I just sit around all day waiting for my servants to do my bidding?" Elizabeth snapped. "I am a woman, Detective Parks. I have a brain. I'm not handicapped. I have the means to survive." Parks stared at the woman, trying to judge her short outburst. "I work, Detective. You might have seen me on the television from time to time?"

"I'm sorry, I can't say I have. Do you know what your husband's worth?" Parks asked wanting to move on.

"I'm not sure," Elizabeth said. "Rick and I kept separate accounts. I know he had his books. A few million or so, I'd say. Give or take."

"You don't have a joint account?"

"No," repeated Elizabeth. "We kept our money separate from each other. He had his affairs and I mine. I really don't know what he had or how much he was worth. I never asked."

"But he knew how much you were worth?" Parks asked.

"I suppose so," Elizabeth agreed. "He never asked. But it isn't that hard to find out. The papers toss our name around enough so that it becomes public business whether I like it or not. I didn't care. We rarely ever spoke of money. He never asked me for any. We both paid for our own way in life."

"Did you have a prenup?"

"We both did," Elizabeth admitted. "In the event of infidelity neither one of us would leave with anything more than what we came into the marriage with."

"So that's a pretty good reason to not get a divorce," Parks wondered as he leaned back and sighed. "That is if you agreed to leave him everything if he stayed with you until the end."

"I suppose so."

"Even though he was cheating?"

"I told him to stop."

"But he didn't."

"I guess not."

"So he was set to inherit it all from you?"

"He was," Elizabeth agreed when her skin turned a shade paler and she paused for a moment as if recovering from a spell.

"I think we're finished with this for now," Mr. Wolfe said with authority, forcing Elizabeth to her feet.

"I thought you came in here to help? To eliminate your client from our list of official suspects?"

"We came in here of our own volition to help with the investigation into Mr. Knott's murder. My client is devastated by what has happened. I believe this is enough for now. She needs her rest and this line of questioning isn't helping her condition. Unless you wish to proceed with charging my client with something?"

"Just one last question: Who stands to inherit all of your money now that your husband has passed on?"

"I'm not sure, but I think it will go to the school. And various charities. It is what I'm noted for after all, Detective. Even you should have known that from the gossip rags."

"Yes," Parks smiled. "I am aware of that actually."

"I'll probably leave that to the Nortons to handle," Elizabeth said.

"The Nortons?"

"Yes. Bill and Katherine," Elizabeth explained. "Katherine Norton's my best friend. More like a sister. She never had one. You could say we were meant to be in each other's lives. I met Rick through her, actually. I have her to thank for so much that's in my life right now. I was in a dark place when she came into my life. I truly think she saved me. Anyway, she works on many of the same charities as me. She'll make sure my money gets off to the proper places. Charity wise. Besides, most of it will probably end up back in the school and that's what Fredrick would have wanted. Especially because he spent so much time there. Me too, for that matter."

"How do you know this Mrs. Norton won't keep it all for her-self?"

"You don't know what you're talking about, do you, Detective?"

"How so?" Parks asked.

"Do your homework. If there's one person in the world who doesn't need my money, Detective, it's Katherine Norton. Trust me on that one. Good day."

Adam Wolfe led his client out of the office and started down the hallway toward the elevators with Parks and Hardwick following after. The elevator chimed and the doors opened. Mr. Wolfe got onto the elevator, trying his best to get his client to follow him before anything else was asked of her—or worse, she said anything damaging.

"I take it we're all good, Detective?" Elizabeth asked from the safety of the elevator as if Parks couldn't step onto it like a vampire forced outside a home waiting for an invitation.

"We're all good for now, Mrs. Knott," Parks nodded. "Again, I apologize."

Elizabeth threw on a fake smile for the detective, the deep crimson cutting a horizontal slice across her chalk-powdered face. Parks just noticed for the first time the deep royal blue tint to the woman's eyes, surrounded by a complimenting smoky eye shadow. Just one of the many smaller details he had noticed; something he had trained himself to do after a decade of reading the finer points on suspects.

"I'll be home the rest of the day, preparing for the funeral. You are welcome to come by if you need to look through any of Fredrick's things for...clues or whatever. I haven't touched any of his stuff in his office. I'll make sure it stays as is until you stop by."

"A couple of detectives will be by later today."

"Thank you," Elizabeth nodded as the doors began to close.

Parks started to walk away when Mrs. Knott stuck her hand out the elevator, blocking the doors from closing, and called out after him. "Detective?"

"Yes?" Parks replied turning back.

"There is one other thing," Elizabeth admitted. "It's not a big thing, but now that I think of it, I feel it's only fair. There is one other person part of Rick's money should go to. I mean, after all that my husband and the school put that poor girl through."

"Oh?"

"She was the only other name I ever heard associated with my husband's extracurricular activities," Elizabeth said.

"And who would that be?"

"Meredith Langer."

SEVEN

"You ever heard of her?" Parks asked Hardwick.

The two walked together, side by side, from the elevators through the hallways, past the interrogation rooms and back toward the main squad room.

"Can't say that I have," Hardwick admitted. "You?"

Parks shook his head and shrugged.

"Well, you better get someone on it quick. If she stands in line to inherit half that fortune I want to know who she is."

"You really think some girl who slept with Knott several years ago murdered him in hopes that his wife would remember her and put her in his will?"

"I think she stands in line to inherit a small fortune due to Mrs. Knott feeling guilty about the way her husband treated her. I want to know what he did."

"You got it," Parks agreed as Fairmont walked into the room. The younger detective moved slowly, with bags forming under his eyes and a doped-up, exhausted look on his face. Parks had handed over the interrogation of Nicholas Martin to Fairmont when Hardwick asked him to assist with Elizabeth Knott. He usually conducted the interviews himself, but he hadn't been expecting the student to do a whole lot of talking before his lawyer showed up and he had wanted to let Fairmont handle more aspects of the investigations.

"So what did you find out about the boyfriend?" Hardwick asked, arms crossed.

"Pretty much what we expected," Fairmont replied, sounding disappointed. "Nick Martin's a prick with a short temper but that doesn't make him a killer. He's a spoiled brat and, thanks to mommy and daddy, I'm lucky I got anything out of him before they showed up. We managed to get his clothes, which are being checked for biologicals. However, so far there are no obvious signs of an attack. No rips or tears. No blood anywhere on them. If he was wearing them during the murders it's some kind of miracle."

"Maybe those aren't the same clothes," Hardwick suggested.

"They're what he was wearing last night," Fairmont corrected. "We have photos of him from when he was at the party and they're the same. And there's no evidence of them having been washed with bleach or detergents or anything like that. No time recently, anyway."

"And his parents and legal counsel didn't object to you having taken them to test them?"

"He gave them over before they all showed up," Fairmont explained. Then they started throwing a fit. But once I showed them the initial results, and explained how it only helped prove their son's innocence they shut up real quick. They still felt it was an invasion of his privacy, blah, blah, blah, but they couldn't argue when we're helping prove his innocence. They still didn't want him just sitting around waiting to say something incriminating, so they got him out of here. Apparently they have high expectations for him."

"I think he's a waste of time. He didn't do it," Parks commented.

Fairmont wasn't sure what to say. "We could have booked him for drugs—"

"You found drugs on him?" Hardwick asked.

Parks began shaking his head when Fairmont answered, "No. But he's using."

"He's not using," Parks disagreed.

"Did you see him?" Fairmont rebutted. "He's using."

"He needs a hit," Parks corrected. "He's going through withdrawals. Besides, if he didn't have anything on him then we can't book him for possession. And if his parents have half a brain, then I guarantee you, he's on his way to rehab as we speak. He's going to be a pain in the ass to reach again."

"Rehab doesn't equal immunity." Hardwick loved a good fight and had no problem busting down the doors of a rehabilitation center to drag out one of Hollywood's most famous stars if it meant solving a crime.

"No. But like Jake said, his family's got money. They're going to protect him. He'll be hard to reach. And personally, until we know he did it, I don't want to waste the time."

"You're giving up on him?" Hardwick asked.

"No. But the evidence is making him look less likely as our killer. I'll just add him to the list of a hundred or so suspects we've got going so far," Parks reassured. "We're going to make damn well sure he's our guy before we try and haul his ass in here again because we won't get a third try with him. We'll keep digging. If there's something connecting him to the murders then we'll find it. Either way, his clothes are clean. He's going through withdrawals, which is affecting his stability. While that may cloud his judgment between right and wrong, I think it would more likely affect his ability to get away with murder without leaving behind or dragging along any trace of them. Again, for the record, I think it's highly unlikely he did it."

"What else do we have?" Hardwick continued without a response. "Any other suspects? Leads? Anything?"

"This guy was a professor at a high end university," Parks said defensively as Tippin walked onto the floor holding a Dr. Pepper and a bag of Cool Ranch Doritos. "You want to know how many people he's pissed off? We have his wife whom he was sleeping around on. Students he didn't pass. Students he embarrassed, publicly, in class. Some numerous times. Parents of students he didn't pass who don't like to see their hard earned money going down the drain. Other faculty members who felt his teaching abilities were too far out there and not conducive to the teaching environment. Patients. Both former and current, all of whom could be certifiably nuts for all we know. From what we gathered, this guy was the type that everyone loved and hated at the same time. He was your best friend and your worst enemy all within the same week. For every person who loved him there were two who hated him."

"Guess it depended what day of the week it was," Fairmont laughed.

"No kidding," Parks agreed. "And we're not even talking about all the girls he was sleeping with."

"How many?" Hardwick asked.

Parks motioned to Tippin.

"Well, apparently he's been cheating on his wife since before they said 'I do'," Tippin continued. "The reason she probably doesn't know about them is because he was good at hiding it. I mean *really* good. Always home when he said he would be. No anonymous phone callers; or anything like that. Of course, his home number is not listed, and there is no way to get a hold of it. And he had two cell phones."

"Oh?"

"One that was public. The other basically an electronic black book," Tippin said.

"How many names?" Parks asked.

"No names," Tippin corrected. "Just numbers."

"How many?"

"Close to two hundred."

"How does he know which one is which if there are no names attached to them?"

Tippin shrugged.

"You're telling me he had close to two hundred women's identities memorized by their phone numbers?" Parks asked.

"Some people are numbers people," Tippin suggested.

"I want every number in that cell identified," Hardwick ordered.

"Already working on it." Tippin flipped through his notes.

"Good."

"Well..." Tippin paused and smiled. "There was one woman he didn't keep quite so hidden."

"Please let it be—what's her name?" Hardwick pleaded, snapping her fingers at Parks for help with the answer.

"Meredith Langer?" Parks replied.

Tippin stared at the two, somewhat surprised. "Yeah. How'd you know?"

"The wife mentioned her," Hardwick answered.

"Mrs. Knott?"

"No, his other wife," Hardwick snapped. "For Christ's sake. He's got a hundred girlfriends. How many wives you going to give him?

Don't tell me he's got more than one?"

"No. Just the one," Tippin said. "Never been married before her."

"So?" Parks shrugged. "Who is she?"

"About four years ago he slept with one of his students," Tippin said. "This Meredith Langer person."

"We figured that much," Hardwick said getting impatient.

"She got pregnant," Tippin continued. "And she wanted to keep the baby and he wanted her to terminate it."

"Go figure," Hardwick said with a roll of her eyes. Knott was beginning to astound even her.

"She also wanted him to leave his wife for her."

"And he wasn't up for that," Parks surmised. "Not with his wife's money on the line."

"Nope," Tippin agreed. "So then the girl threatened to tell his wife and the school board about his behavior with his students."

"Oh?" Hardwick was getting into the story.

"So he got one up on her and had her expelled for cheating and plagiarism," Tippin continued cautiously, eyeing Parks for a reaction. The story was familiar and he waited for the recognition to click in with the detective. "He also told the school board that she had come to him as a patient seeking therapy, telling him about a boyfriend that had knocked her up and ditched her. That she also had a fixation on him and acted out on her fantasies and expected him to take over the parental duties."

"But this is bullshit, right?"

"According to what I got from the board, he had pretty substantial evidence to back his story up," Tippin said. "He had files and paperwork galore on this girl. I mean Knott is a player and a creep, but it genuinely looks like the girl was obsessed. He had letters, cards, and emails from her; in her handwriting too. And he had a file on her as a patient. Also, Knott agreed to a paternity test and Meredith objected." Tippin paused a second as he let that information sink in with everyone. "And her ex-boyfriend at the time testified against her as well. Said the kid was his and he was willing to take a paternity test to prove it."

"Really?" Hardwick was yet again surprised by Knott.

"Really."

"So the school kicked her out?" Parks asked not needing an answer.

"And the court put a restraining order on her," Tippin added. "Her parents believed the school and wanted nothing to do with her. Hardcore religious types. They shipped her down south to live with an aunt to have the baby. Still lives there."

"Her own parents abandoned her?" Parks asked skeptically.

"Well, I guess it's the mom and a stepdad," Tippin said glancing at his notes. "None of them got along. But, yeah. Shipped her off to be with the biological father's sister or something like that."

"So we think that four years later she snuck back up here to take out the good Professor for what—revenge?" Parks asked doubtfully. "Seems kinda iffy to me." Parks thought for a moment. "But we should probably still check her out. So Knott had a file on her? We're going to need to subpoena his files."

"Already working on a warrant for a special magistrate for Knott's patients' files. That file should be included," Hardwick said.

"There's more to her," Tippin added.

"Oh? What's that?"

"She sent letters," Tippin said as Fairmont began digging through a pile of papers for their copies of the threatening notes. "Like, nasty, I'm gonna kill you letters."

Fairmont handed over a handful of letters, some handwritten, some typed on typewriters, some printed on computers, each threatening in one way or another. Each promising pain and dismemberment of vital body parts beyond imagination. Some even threatened his wife.

"These are brutal," Parks said, handing a few over to Hardwick. "How long ago were these sent? She could still be harboring hatred for Knott if these were sent recently." Parks held onto one of the letters as he focused on it more. Some of the letters were concise and eloquent, almost poetic, whereas the others were child-like, blunt, over the top. "Were these all from Meredith Langer?"

"To answer your first question, we're not sure when these were sent because Knott was the one who received them and he's obviously not around to ask. We'll see if maybe he said anything to his secretary or kept any kind of a record. As for your second one, no, we don't think so. We have CSU going over each of the originals but so far they're thinking that these were from more than one person. Five different people actually. And these were just what we had found so far. We have a feeling there are more. We are checking with other divisions of LAPD to see if maybe he was smart enough to have them recorded in a file with them to keep track of. We'll see. So far nothing."

Parks stood and continued to think, beginning to space out.

"What's up?" Hardwick asked.

"Something doesn't fit," Parks said.

"Such as?"

"According to Knott, and the school board, there was proof that this Meredith was loony. Paternity tests. First hand testimonies. The works. So Knott's in the clear."

"Yes...?"

"If Meredith made everything up and more or less got what she deserved then why does Mrs. Knott feel bad for what her husband and the school did to her and is willing to give her a portion of her husband's small fortune?"

"You smell a cover up?" Hardwick asked. Parks shrugged. "Check her out."

"There is one other thing," Tippin said mildly from his desk.

"What is it?" Parks asked.

"You reacted the first time you heard about Knott. The name Fredrick Knott sounds familiar to you, doesn't it?"

"In a general, vague sort of way," Parks admitted, showing that it wasn't eating him up inside. "I know I've heard of him. I can't recall how. Why? I saw pictures of the man. I've never met him before."

"No, you haven't," Tippin agreed. "But we have heard of him."

"In connection with what?" Parks asked.

Everyone continued to stare at Tippin.

"Meredith Langer isn't the only one to have made accusations against Knott."

"There were others?"

"Yeah."

"But you mean one in particular?"

"Julie Hammond," Tippin finally answered.

"Son of a bitch," Parks cursed.

"Julie Hammond?" Fairmont said still trying to place all of the pieces together. "You mean Lewis Hayward's daughter? What's he have to do with this?"

"Knott was..." Parks trailed off, trying to recall the events that led the man the City of Angels came to know as the Palisades Poisoner (so dubbed by the media despite the fact that he neither came from nor ever poisoned anyone from or in the Palisades area) to begin his spree of murders.

"Yes," Tippin nodded, agreeing with Parks.

"Hayward began his whole escapade of death because he couldn't handle Julie Hammond's alleged suicide."

"I thought Hayward killed her himself when she became hysterical because he kidnapped her or something?" Fairmont asked.

The events of what actually took place were still foggy, as Lewis Hayward had all but refused to talk to anyone about the motives behind his rash, violent poisonings. Only Parks had spoken one-on-one with the man. Since the closing of the case, every avenue Parks had used to try and follow up on had led only to dead ends.

"That's not the point. His daughter died. Before that, she suffered from depression due to events that took place at PSU. Knott was the professor behind the accusations that spread around the campus. He was the psychiatrist who used to help Julie with her depression but instead, allegedly, turned on her and drove her deeper into her depression on behalf of the university who faced several lawsuits." Parks let the information sink in. "I pulled several of the lawsuits last fall after we wrapped the case. I looked into the accusations. Fredrick Knott was not as well loved as we've been led to believe. In fact, he was not a nice man at all. I mean everything surrounding him is 'allegedly this' and 'allegedly that,' nothing proven, but still. Where there's smoke… We're sure this is the man whose murder we have to give a shit about?"

Hardwick ignored Parks's comment. "What are the chances Knott's murder might be connected to Lewis Hayward?"

"You know," Parks began. "I'll be honest with you. I always thought it was weird that Hayward never went after the man who had one-on-one contact with his daughter. We all know he tried to harm the university by using poisons from there. And he went after several people connected to or related to people connected to the allegations and lawsuits. But never after the man who had actually contributed to his daughter's destruction."

"So what do you think?" Hardwick asked as she noticed her secretary waving for her, signaling that she was needed on the phone.

"I think it's probably just a coincidence. But it's too big a coincidence not to look into," Parks sighed. "Everyone work all the other angles. I'll deal with Hayward myself."

"He hasn't talked to anyone since he's been locked away. He even skipped out on a public trial. What makes you think he'll talk to you?"

"I don't think he will," Parks admitted. "But there's only one way to find out."

EIGHT

"Rachel," Parks called out as she and Tanaka walked up to the group and set a stack of files down on his desk. "What have you got for me?"

"The DA's looking at this as a sex crime," Rachel Moore answered.

"Well they were screwing when they got offed," Fairmont commented as if no one else was aware of the fact.

"Found traces of semen at the crime scene," Moore continued.

"What did I just say? They were—"

"We know that, Jake," Parks interrupted. He was somewhat confused and turned to Tanaka. "You showed us that under the infrared light at the crime scene. Stuff was all over the desk, floor, and bodies. What of it?"

"But what we didn't know then, and we found out now, is that there were two different types of semen found at the crime scene," Tanaka explained. "One set on the girl's vaginal area and mouth and another around the anus area."

"Two different? So this happened during?"

"No way to tell for sure," Tanaka admitted. "But from what we

91

can tell, both samples appeared to have found their way onto the victim's body at around the same time."

"So it could have been during or it could have been after?" Parks asked.

"It's a possibility," Tanaka admitted. "Killer could have killed them and then did them both."

"Whoa, wait," Fairmont interrupted. "You saying—"

"It's hard to tell," Tanaka said sternly. "Traces of semen were found all over her body and his. Can't tell if it was put there intentionally or if—"

"They were just one messy group," Fairmont finished. "Kinda sick."

"Kinda not safe is what it is," Moore commented.

"Well considering they're dead I wouldn't think that catching anything is of great concern to any of them," Parks said. "Speaking of which…"

"No, nothing," Tanaka answered. "Might not have been the wisest thing to do but according to test results all three participants are one hundred percent clean of all STDs."

"See," Fairmont smiled. "Who says sex kills?"

"So we are working on a third person in the room after all," Parks said. "You peg Nick Martin for it?"

Fairmont rolled his eyes. "You see him shacking up with another guy much less sharing his woman?"

"True. We get an ID on the paraphernalia found in the Professor's desk?"

"Cocaine," Rachel Moore said referring to her notes. "Six dime bags and an eight ball."

"Cut?"

Moore nodded. "But here's a kicker. It was cut with methamphetamines."

"Say what?"

"You heard me. This guy was looking for some major stimuli. Also, found three-dozen Viagra pills. Fifty milligrams each. Eight ounces of marijuana. Two empty syringes, which had traces of heroin in them, and a dozen containers, which tested positive for alkyl nitrates."

Parks scrunched his face at the information.

"Poppers. Uppers," Moore explained.

Tanaka continued when she saw Rachel going through her pad to look up what she had just described. "They're used to enhance sexual pleasure. Helps relax the muscles of the body particularly around the vagina and anus."

"My God," Parks said, silently cursing Wilkes for passing him this case. "Well that fits with what we found at the crime scene. What was he doing? Prescribing to his patients? His students?"

"Possibly," Moore said. "But not legally. He didn't have the authority to prescribe. So he wasn't getting them through legal channels."

"Great. Illegal prescriptions and drugs. So we get to add drug dealers to our list of potential murderers? We get anything on—"

Hardwick entered the floor and interrupted the group of detectives. "Everybody ready to work under pressure? Because you're about to get some. The governor has a daughter at the school and a son joining the student population next fall. Take the governor, plus the school's stance on this incident already, and that's a lot of heat. They all want this case solved and buried and we're talking, like, yesterday."

"We got that, sir," Fairmont said, realizing what he had just said.

"I mean—"

"Do you?" Hardwick barked. "The school's just beginning to recover from a drop in student admissions thanks to the economy and the board is worried how a murder like this might affect the enrollment numbers next fall. Since the governor has promised rising numbers in the economy this might not look so good."

"We get you," Parks said trying to keep Hardwick calm.

"And you tackling students across the school grounds might not look so good for this department either. You're just lucky it's Saturday and most of the campus was empty or else I'm sure the whole thing would be up on YouTube already. The school isn't the only one with a reputation to protect. All I'm saying is wrap this up, ladies and gents. Quickly." Hardwick turned to leave the floor. "Oh, hey, before I forget, you have a four o'clock meeting with Bill Norton."

"Why am I meeting him?" Parks asked.

"He's the president of the university and one of his professors was murdered on school grounds. Besides an update of some sorts, he's agreed to help with any questions about Professor Knott and his teachings. That is, if you have any. And take that new kid from the campus security with you."

"Bennett? Sure thing. Fine. We'll be there," Parks assured his boss as she walked out of the room. "Look, everyone. Sorry about the pressure. And thanks for the hard work. Oh, speaking of which, Rachel, prints?"

"You do realize I hate you right now, right?" Moore quipped.

"What have you got?" Parks asked.

Rachel nudged Milo.

"There were seventy-four sets of identifiable prints found in Knott's office," Tippin explained. "Mind you those were the ones that we could fully pick up and use to identify someone. There's at least another two hundred partials spread throughout that office."

"How long is it going to take us to start getting IDs on them?" Parks asked.

"Well, this is where you're lucky," Moore said proudly. "Knott works in a rather controlled environment. When you consider that fact, it actually helps us out a lot. And I mean *a lot*. With the knowledge that most of the prints in the room should belong to students, whether they be actual students or patients, they're still students nonetheless. Therefore, most of their identities and fingerprints are on file already."

"You mean all seventy-four sets of prints belong to students with criminal records with prints on file?" Fairmont asked skeptically.

"Missing children," Parks shot back.

"Huh?" Fairmont asked genuinely lost.

"Starting back in the eighties all children in public elementary schools were required to be fingerprinted and kept on file in case they were abducted or went missing," Parks explained. "Most everyone at the university should be on file due to that fact. So how many have you been able to identify so far and how much longer is it going to take you?"

Parks prepared himself for a verbal lashing.

"We made this a priority," Moore explained. "Just like Hardwick said to. Pulled everyone off everything else."

"And?"

Rachel tossed a file down next to Parks on his desk.

"You're telling me you got all seventy-four prints identified?" Parks asked in amazement while he stared at the file.

"Hardly," Moore smirked. "We've got about fifteen of them done so far. That's them. The computer program's working on it nonstop and will keep spitting out the results as we get them."

"That's a start," Parks said genuinely pleased with their work so far. "Now comes the fun part. Cross referencing names with Knott's students, patients and whoever else had a reason for being in his office."

"Jake and I are on it," Tippin smiled slyly at Fairmont. Paperwork was never anyone's idea of a good time, so Milo had to be getting Jake back for something going on between the two of them. Parks didn't want to know what.

"Good man." Parks looked to Fairmont and nodded off toward Milo, leaving the men to their work as he retrieved his cell and phoned Bennett.

"What's up?" Bennett answered.

"Apparently I have a meeting with the president of the university at four today. And you're coming with me."

"I'm at your disposal."

"So...what's your boss like, exactly?"

"In simplest terms? He's a bit of a bastard."

NINE

"Fredrick Knott was what you might call a bit of a bastard," Bill Norton said with a Cheshire cat-like grin on his face as if he prided himself on the fact that he had hired a bastard as part of his staff. "Then again you could say I'm a bit of one as well. And I'm sure more than a fair share of my colleagues has said just that."

Bill Norton was exactly as Dave Parks pictured a man of his stature would be: professor-like with a handsome yet slightly rugged look to his face. If he hadn't known better, and had met the two men randomly, Parks would have sworn Bill Norton and Fredrick Knott were related—cousins, maybe, possibly even brothers. Both men were regal and composed in their appearance, with pronounced noses and strong chins, though Norton had a full head of silver-blonde hair and a paler complexion as opposed to Knott's darker looks and hair. Bill Norton wore an expensive two-thousand dollar suit, tailored for his large being. His hands were neat and manicured, adorned with a class ring of some sort on his right pinky and his wedding band on the appropriate finger. His hair was trim, not a single strand out of place, the onset of grey growing ever stronger around the ears, though he probably dyed his hair to somewhat keep up a youthful appearance.

There was a set of Montblanc pens and other various, just as expensive, decorations spread out perfectly across the desk. Not a single item was out of line, each placed according to their function and amount of use. Across the walls of the room hung several degrees and other awards that the man had been fortunate enough to collect throughout his twenty-year career as an education professional.

"You don't appear to be bothered by that."

"No such thing as bad publicity, right?"

"Including murder?" Parks said, trying to read the man.

"There is such a thing as going too far," Norton breathed loudly. "What happened to Fredrick Knott is truly a tragedy and I feel deeply, both professionally and personally, for the loss of a great man."

"What about the legal issues concerning him and several students over the past few years?" Parks pushed. "Besides Kelli Davis, there was also Meredith Langer?"

"Miss Langer was proven to be...unstable. That was an unfortunate event. Fortunately, truth was on our side and we proved victorious."

Victorious? Parks took the man's choice of words in.

"And Julie Hammond?"

"By now we all know Miss Hammond's father and what he has done to this city. There's no shock considering her upbringing that she would come to cause trouble here as well. I would like to blame her, but really, with a madman who poisons people as a father it's so easy to see her as a victim as well. But again, we succeeded over her accusations."

"What was your relationship with Knott like?" Parks asked keeping the conversation going.

"He was one of my best professors."

"So you two saw eye to eye?"

"Hardly," Norton laughed. "You don't get to be a great educator without making a few waves. You have to make people think; not just your students but everyone around you as well. He was challenging. I can promise you that. Nevertheless, Knott, being the man he was, he helped make me a better man. Both professionally and personally. Just as he helped to make and hold this university at a higher level of standards. I think I do a better job here at this university now thanks to Knott's contributions."

"So he was challenging?" Parks asked. Bennett and he had agreed that he would do all the talking. In case this conversation happened to step on a few feet, it was probably better for Bennett's career if he was not the cause.

Bill Norton laughed. "Yes. Very. Nevertheless, I love a good challenge. I welcome it. You ever do the crossword puzzle, Detective?"

Parks didn't reply. He did the crossword puzzle every morning. Along with the Sudoku and the thousand-piece puzzles that were spread all over his condo. He loved puzzles. Couldn't help himself. Had to solve every one he ever started. One of the few tics he had picked up during childhood, most likely spawning from the unanswered questions concerning his father's suicide and his mother's abandonment.

"I do the crossword puzzle every morning. It helps wake me up. Gets my brain working. Thinking. The blood flowing."

"I like the Sudoku," Parks replied.

Norton smiled with the shake of his head.

"So how did the students feel about Professor Knott?" Parks asked.

"They loved him. Some of them. The ones who did, worshiped

him. Considered him one of the best we have ever had here. Then again, there were those that despised him just as much."

"You know, one might say false idol worship leads to sacrifice."

"You're not suggesting—"

"A young mind just waiting to be molded is quite impressionable. Anything's possible. What's your take on the situation?"

"Are you asking me to speculate—"

"I'm asking for your viewpoint into a world I'm not as equipped to fully comprehend," Parks continued, cutting off the man. He hoped false praise would cloud the man's judgment and get him to talk. "I'm not expecting you to name me the killer. I can do my job. I'm asking if there's anything you think I should know about. Threats? Did Knott complain about anything out of the ordinary over the last few weeks? Months? What about Kelli Davis?"

"Nothing Fredrick Knott did was ordinary. But unfortunately nothing out of the ordinary comes to mind."

Bill Norton threw on his fake smile once again and sat patiently, waiting for Parks to make his next move, just as in a game of chess. Norton knew something; Parks had decided that much. But the man wasn't going to incriminate himself or anyone around him for mere speculation.

"I see you're in the middle of a game," Parks finally said commenting on a chess game that was off to the side of the room, never taking his eyes off Norton.

"Observant," Norton said with a smile, pleased at the observations that Parks had made upon entering the office. "Good to know that the LAPD has their best on the case. Yes. Actually, that was a game I was playing with Fredrick."

"So you spoke to him on a regular basis?"

"His wife and mine are good friends," Norton said nonchalantly.

"You could say Fredrick and I have learned to become friends by association."

"Not a friendship you cared for?"

"On the contrary," Norton said brushing off the accusation. "Fredrick was a highly intelligent man. We could have a conversation for hours on the psychology of man. What makes him tick? Why he would choose to carry out certain actions? Speaking with him was always an enlightening event."

"Event? So you loved him. The students loved him. His wife loved him. Everyone loved him," Parks finally said wanting to move along the conversation. "And yet he's dead."

Bill Norton stared at Parks, then looked to Bennett, and finally back to the lead detective.

"Sorry, gentlemen. You know, maybe Knott wasn't the intended target but rather an unfortunate victim. You are looking into Kelli Davis as the potential target, correct? I mean, considering all of the other girls who have attacked him before it would stand to reason that she could be just as troubled as the others."

"We are considering all potential possibilities," Parks said without getting into the details. "We still have to go over Knott's files—"

"I had heard that you had come under possession of some of Knott's files already. Without a warrant from what I hear. I would expect those files returned by the end of the day or I will have to take the appropriate legal actions. Knott's files are now the university's private property. Access to them will, of course, be restricted."

"Those files are his own private—"

"His practice was being conducted on university grounds and so therefore automatically become property of the university. Those are the rules, gentlemen. You know about a doctor's confidentiality.

Can't have you just going around snooping through patients' confidential files."

"I'm conducting a murder investigation here—"

"I'm aware of that, Detective. And I wish you luck in your endeavors."

"We will be back with a warrant."

"Good luck with that," Norton smiled. "You know the governor has a daughter here. I am sure he wouldn't want her privacy to be invaded. I've assured him and other members of our alumni that just such a thing won't happen. Not while I'm around."

"So you've something to hide?" Parks asked aloud. He knew it was a mistake that he'd hear about but he didn't care. He still needed to rattle this man.

"I assure you I have nothing to hide," Norton said. "I'm simply looking out for the safety and well-being of those who come to rely on me for protection."

"Where was Fredrick Knott and Kelli Davis's protection last night? I think there's a serious possibility of the safety of this school being reviewed in the light of recent events. I wonder what your policies on safety on the campus grounds really are."

Bill Norton turned to Bennett, who began to squirm in his chair, caught in the middle and not sure what to say. Parks may have been attacking Norton, but campus security was Bennett's job and both men knew the blame would be passed to him.

"Now you listen here," Norton snapped, his temper beginning to flare.

"Maybe campus safety shouldn't be left up to the university to determine. Perhaps the city, since the campus grounds are within them, should decide how best to protect the students and faculty on site. I wonder what that would do to your standing with the board to lose control of something like that?"

The smile left Bill Norton's face when there was a knock at the office door and his assistant entered the room.

"What is it, Evelyn?" Norton asked.

"I have a message for Detective Parks," the assistant replied.

"Yes?" Parks said turning to the woman.

"It's the security department from here at the university," the woman explained.

"Yes?" Norton asked.

"What is it?" Parks asked.

"They said you should go over to the dorms immediately."

"The dorms? Why? What's up?'

"They said that a Nicholas Martin has been found dead in his room."

TEN

"Son of a bitch." Parks hissed from the common room bathrooms at the end of the hall on the second floor of the co-ed dorms.

Nicholas Martin lay in one of the tiled corners of the shower area, completely nude, with both of his underarms slit from the wrist up to the elbow, with blood everywhere. Written in smeared, near illegible writing on the cruddy white, tiled wall above his head was a single word:

Sorry

"Shit," Bennett spat, jerking his head out of the room, not from the sight before him but from the stench that had begun to build thanks to the room being sealed off. "It reeks in here."

"Then stay out," Parks snipped, trying to maneuver around without stepping in any of the blood. "Has anybody been in this room?"

"No, sir," one of the dorm security guards replied immediately.

"Didn't want to touch nothing. It's just the way we found it."

"Didn't check the body?" Bennett asked.

"That look like he's still alive?" the security guard quipped.

Nick Martin's head lay back against the wall, his mouth agape and his eyes wide open, glossed over, damned for all eternity to stare up at the ceiling of the dorm room. For a split second, the scene reminded Parks of the way he had found Kelli Davis's body and he wondered what twisted karma it was that the lovers had both been found in nearly the same position.

"M.E. coming through," Amy Tanaka called from behind Parks.

"Who called it in? The vic's roommate?" Parks asked, backing out to make space for Tanaka to get in and do her work.

"Naw. Roommate's been out of town for about three weeks now," the guard answered. "One of the other students on the floor called it in. Came in here to shower and saw the body. Ran back to her room and called security."

"Which one?" Parks asked as he walked back into the hallway and then into Nick's room to look around.

He glanced around to see if he noticed anything off from earlier that day. The room was just as disheveled as he remembered; though nothing too out of the ordinary considering two college boys were the room's occupants. Several posters of women adorned the walls, along with a twelve-month, sports wall-calendar containing various notes scribbled across it. A few potted plants sat sporadically throughout the room, catching Parks's attention as he felt they didn't belong with the rest of the decor. There was a TV with a sofa in front of it and off to the side an Ikea table with two barstools on either side of it. In the center of the table were the dozen or so empty alcoholic beverage bottles and cans that the detectives had remembered from earlier that day. Their room was quite spacious and,

Parks noted for the first time, somewhat nicer than most dorm rooms that he could recall.

"Who said the roommate's been gone?"

Parks walked back out into the hallway where the security guard pointed to the room two doors down on the opposite side from Nick's. "Name's Kim Larson."

"All right," Parks said as he saw the hallway fill with onlookers, each standing around and gossiping. "Get these people out of here."

"But that doesn't make sense," Bennett whispered to Parks.

Parks glared at him to keep him quiet as he knocked on the door to 217 while the security guards emptied the hallway for some privacy.

"What?" snapped a young woman, eyeing the two men suspiciously. The woman brushed several dreads out of her face, giving off the air of someone who did not like disturbances.

"Detectives Parks and Bennett," Parks answered, retrieving his identification. "Kim Larson?"

The woman stared at the men with her large dark eyes that showed only a sliver of brown along the rims. The woman had a protective aura about her and Parks concluded that she was not who they wanted, but was blocking them from the one they did.

"Maybe? What you want?"

"LAPD. We're looking for Kim Larson."

"Well, maybe—"

"It's okay," came a soft, timid voice from behind the woman as the door opened wider and a red-headed girl of no more than nineteen stepped out. Her clothes were simple, modestly priced from Target or Old Navy or some other local shop, not the designer name brands that most of the students wore. Her eyes were red and her nose was runny, most likely since the discovery of the body. Parks felt bad for her. This couldn't have been what she had expected when she moved here for an education from some small Midwest town.

"You okay? Need a doctor or anything?" Parks asked.

"N-no. I'm okay."

"You know him? Nicholas Martin?"

"Just casually."

"You see him today?"

"This afternoon. Arrived with his parents and some other guy. Said they were taking him away because of Kelli's murder n'all."

"He left with his parents?"

"No. They left without him. He said he had to take care of some things and that he'd meet them later."

"That seems like an awful lot to know for just being casual friends with him?"

Kim paused for a moment and thought about this. Her hesitation seamed to spread throughout her whole body as she froze, her brain catching up with the information supplied and was now relaying. "Oh? Well, he asked me to check in and water his plants for him. Being his neighbor n'all. Mostly because he didn't know when Ryan would be back. Though I'm not sure why they had plants. I think they were Kelli's touch."

"Yeah, I noticed that," Parks said. "Who's this Ryan person?"

"Ryan Lockhart," Kim answered. "That's Nick's roommate."

"Ryan Lockhart?"

"Yeah," she nodded.

Parks looked to Bennett and then back to Kim.

"And where would I find this Ryan Lockhart?"

"Not sure," Kim shrugged. "His family's from Laguna. He goes back and visits often. He does modeling and acting and stuff like that. He's usually out traveling most of the year. Not sure how he's planning on graduating. He hasn't been around for about three weeks now. He went up north somewhere. Not sure when he's coming back."

"Then who's Christopher Stone?" Parks asked.

"Christopher?"

"Yes. Christopher Stone."

Kim shrugged, not sure how to answer the question. "Christopher's...Christopher."

"You know him?"

"Christopher?" Kim berated the detectives as if they didn't know who Brad Pitt or Julia Roberts was. "Everyone knows Christopher."

"Nick and him are friends?"

"Sure. I guess so. But I'd say he knows Ryan mostly. But I guess if he's around Ryan enough then he knows Nick. By association."

"And Kelli as well?" Bennett added.

"Kelli was over a lot from what I could hear. So probably."

"So Ryan Lockhart lives here?"

"Yes."

"And Christopher knows Ryan but not Nick."

"I guess so. I wouldn't swear to it. I didn't hang out with them all that much. Kelli...well, she didn't really care for me."

"Why was that?" Parks asked.

"See..." Kim glanced back to her roommate who made a face to let her know that she was on her own now. "See me and Nick kinda hooked up one time. Just once. When Kelli and him were on a break. They had just broken up and I was...well..."

"You were available," Parks commented, trying to be tactful.

Kim shrugged in agreement. "It was all an act. He just wanted to sleep with me. Ignored me once Kelli came back around. Whatever. Anyways, he never said anything to her. But I have a feeling she kinda knew. You know?"

"I understand. So reason stands that Christopher wouldn't be here to see Nick."

"I wouldn't think so."

"So why would Christopher be here if Ryan hasn't been around in a few weeks?"

"You saw him here?"

"This morning."

"Oh, I couldn't say why." Kim looked just as confused.

"You sure maybe Ryan hasn't skipped town and perhaps Christopher is crashing here at his place with him?" asked Parks trying to see if he could figure this out. "Maybe Christopher doesn't like his roommate too much? I mean it happens, right? Students swapping dorm rooms. Even if it's not allowed. It happens?"

"That would never happen," Kim replied. "Christopher doesn't even live on campus."

"But he is a student here?"

"Yes. But he doesn't live on campus. Why would he?"

"I don't quite follow you," Parks replied.

Kim took a step back, comprehension coming to her face. "You two don't know who Christopher Stone is, do you?"

Parks shook his head while Bennett remained neutral, neither gesturing nor commenting one way or the other.

"I'm afraid I don't," Parks admitted.

"He's Bill and Katherine Norton's only son."

"You gotta be kidding me," Parks sighed, glaring at his partner. "You're telling me the son of the president of the university is friends with the roommate of the guy who just killed himself and was boy-friend to the girl who was found murdered having an affair with her professor whose wife is best friends with the wife of the president of the university?"

Bennett stared at Parks, completely lost.

"I don't think I have a midterm as confusing as what you just said," Kim replied.

"Are you kidding me?" Parks pulled Bennett in close. "You didn't know? Christopher Stone. The president's son and you didn't know?"

"I knew his name and what it meant around campus but I swear to you I had no idea who he was related to. He has a different last name and he doesn't go around bragging about it. I never put two and two together," Bennett whispered to Parks. "If word gets out that the president's son is involved with this—"

"We don't know that he is," Parks interjected.

"He was in Nick's room after the murder and Nick wasn't any-where around," Bennett replied. "You tell me what that's about? He could be covering for him for all we know."

"Why don't we find him and ask him?" Parks said, turning back to Kim. "So how do Christopher and Ryan know each other?"

"I don't know anything official..."

"Off the record. What have you heard?"

"He's gay."

"Come again?"

"Ryan. He's—no. He's straight. Or so he says. I guess he's gay-for-pay."

"Gay-for-pay?"

"Yeah. See, when people say Ryan's away filming or doing modeling…well, he does porn. And the modeling stuff he does is usually for adult-type magazines. Or magazines that sell sex stuff. Toys n' things. Things like that. I even hear he's got a cam in his dorm room that people can pay to watch him do whatever."

"You've seen this?"

"Well, not all of it. Like, I haven't seen any of his films. But, yeah. It's kinda known throughout campus that he does that stuff so some of the students are all like, 'Oh my God' and stuff about it when they find him online. Like he's our own celebrity. Not that we don't have bigger ones here. Being in LA."

"I see."

"Except Ryan was supposed to quit."

"The porn?"

"Yeah."

"Why's that?"

"School forbids it."

"School forbids it?"

"Yeah," Kim lectured, as if the detectives should have known school policies. "See, Ryan was on the wrestling team or the swim team or something like that. Anyways, they prefer their publicity come from their wins. Not from one of their team players posing naked and having sex with other guys."

"So the school told him to quit or they would expel him?" Parks asked.

"No. Ryan was done for at this school. You'd be surprised how much porn is a big no-no at schools. Any school. Guys or girls. Gay or straight. But *especially* gay. It's kind of a one time you're out of here rule."

"But Ryan's still a student here? Why?"

"Why do you think? Cuz Ryan—"

"Made nice with the university president's one and only son," Parks said, putting all the pieces together.

"Yup," Kim confirmed. "And I don't know what Ryan had to offer Christopher but it must have been pretty nice for Christopher to speak up on his behalf."

"What do you mean?" Bennett asked.

"Well everyone around campus knows Christopher. I mean, he is the president's stepson. Besides that, his mother's like loaded. I mean like unimaginable, make-believe loaded. She's been married a couple of times. Anyways, Christopher has money. Plus his stepfather's clout. Christopher has connections. To everything. And I mean *everything*. You need anything; it's pretty much known that Christopher can get it. No matter how..."

"Illegal?" Parks finished.

"He always describes it as exotic." Kim paused and Parks nodded at her to continue. "Anyways, he's got connections. To everything and everyone. And not just on campus. I mean in this town as well. He knows people. So in order for Ryan to offer him something in exchange for him getting the school board to go soft on him...well, I'm not sure what it was."

"Sex perhaps?" Parks asked.

"What?"

"Sometimes something as simple as sex can be a powerful motivator. You'd be surprised how far sex can take you. Or sell something. Or blackmail someone."

"I suppose. I mean I guess Ryan would know a thing or two about that. Being as that's what he does. But he really does profess he's only gay-for-pay. Besides Christopher has a girlfriend. Girl named Natalie I think. Or something that starts with an N. She's a model or something. Gorgeous. Real pretty. So I don't know. I wouldn't think so."

"I think Ryan getting an education from an esteemed university in exchange for sex more than counts as 'pay,' don't you think?"

"Well, it's not cash..." Kim wasn't sure what Parks was talking about now.

Parks smiled at her remark and shook it off. "You wouldn't have any idea where we might be able to find Christopher right now, do you?"

"Sorry," Kim apologized. "We don't travel in the same circles. It's Saturday, so he'll probably be out somewhere. Though I don't know where. I can ask around if you want."

"Don't worry about it. You've been a great help to us," Parks replied, retrieving a card from within his jacket. "But if you do happen to hear anything or think of anything else, could you please give us a call?"

"Will do," Kim agreed as she retreated into her room.

Parks glanced down the hallway both ways to find it completely empty as he had wanted.

"Well—" was all Bennett got out when Amy Tanaka interrupted him.

"You two ought to come in here and take a look at this mess," the medical examiner ordered as she waved a hand back toward the bathrooms.

"What's up?" Parks asked.

"Something doesn't add up."

"What do we have?" Parks asked, following Tanaka into the bathroom. He tried to maneuver his way as close to Nick Martin's body as he would allow himself to get.

"I want you to take a look at this," Tanaka said, kneeling down next to the body. She grabbed Nick's arms and turned them right side up, exposing the wounds for Parks and Bennett to see. "Look at the incisions along the forearms."

"It's customary to go vertical instead of horizontal when actually meaning to kill oneself as opposed to looking for attention," Parks stated as if reading from a textbook. He wasn't sure what she was asking him to notice that was out of the ordinary for a suicide.

"That's not what I'm referring to. Look. From what you can tell by looking at the body would you say the victim is right handed or left?"

"Right handed," Parks answered as Bennett looked to him questioningly. "He's got a tan line across his left wrist indicating a watch."

"Correct," Tanaka agreed. "Now look at the wounds on his arms. If you were right handed and you went to cut your left arm how would the wound look?"

"I don't—"

"Clean. Precise. To the point so to speak. Because your right hand is your dominant hand and you'd have more control over your actions. This means when you went to go cut your right arm with your left hand—"

"The cuts would be less precise. Less deep and more jagged possibly," Parks suggested.

"I don't get it," Bennett said. "His left arm is cut clean and precise while it looks like he might have started a couple of times on the right. Wouldn't that mean he's right handed like you suspect?"

"That's what I thought at first too," Tanaka said. "Bear with me. Now hold out your arms and show me the motion of how you'd do what happened to Nick?"

"What do you mean what happened to him?" Parks asked. "Are

you saying he didn't kill himself?"

"Just do what I tell you, okay? Sheesh. No wonder you're single," Tanaka ordered, turning from Parks to Bennett. "Remember, when the woman speaks, the man obeys. Got it?"

Parks rolled his eyes, mimed as if a razor was in his right hand, reached for his left wrist, and moved it toward his elbow. Then he did the same with his right arm.

"And you, detective?" Tanaka asked Bennett.

"I'd do it the same way," Bennett said as he quickly went through the motions.

"Agreed," Tanaka said. "Only by studying the wounds on the victim that's not how he did it. Or how it was done to him. His wounds start at his elbow area and work their way up to his wrists."

"Would he do that?" Parks asked.

"It's not unheard of. And it has happened before, I'm sure of it. But I wouldn't suspect so," Tanaka said shaking her head. "Especially with the other evidence here. I'd say someone did this to him. But whoever it was didn't do it from behind. Instead, they sat in front of him and cut the victim's arms for him. I'll to run a toxicology report as soon as I get the body to the lab. I have a feeling he may have been drugged."

"Drugged?"

"I've got a needle puncture on the left arm," Tanaka said pointing to it.

"Maybe he was a user," Parks said. "We found needle marks on Professor Knott's body."

"And the girl's," Tanaka added. "And I'm willing to bet our vic here is a user too. But not in his arms. It's too visible. He'd be caught. This is why I searched and found several puncture wounds near his groin area on the inside of his thighs." Amy pulled back the skin on

one of his legs and pointed to a few needle marks. "Now these puncture wounds are older. His skin's discolored and there are several.
The one on his arm is fresh. It just happened. Not postmortem, but
close. Like I said—I think he was drugged."

"So would you say he died of blood loss or poisoning?"

"Won't know without a tox report," Tanaka shrugged. "Not for
sure. But my opinion—and this is off the record—he died of blood
loss. Whoever did this did it while the vic was still alive because the
incisions on his arms bled out after they were cut. His heart was still
beating. I don't even know if he felt anything or knew what was
being done to him as he was being cut. He may have been unconscious. It will depend on what the tox reports come up with."

"Wait a minute," Parks said stopping her. "So you're saying that
someone drugged him. Then sat in front of him and cut his arms for
him, which made the wounds match the way a right handed person
would have done it to himself."

"Correct."

"But the person who did this wasn't behind Nick. They faced
him," Parks said as Tanaka nodded in agreement. "That means a left-
handed person cut Nick's arms."

"Bingo," Tanaka beamed. "Now. A lot of this could be circum-
stantial. There is a chance that he could have started from the elbow
and worked his way to the wrists. But look at the handwriting."

Both detectives reread the bloody confession written up on the
wall.

"Assuming the blood on the wall comes up positive for a match
with the vic's blood—"

"That's a good guess," Tanaka said.

"And that whoever did this used the vic's fingers to write it."

"Fingerprints were taken and a match is being worked on back in the lab. But you'll notice that the vic's left index finger is covered in blood while all of the rest of his fingers are clean. Why? He wasn't left-handed. Why would he have used his left hand to write a message?" Amy set Nick's hand back down after showing the bloody finger to Parks and Bennett. "Now, I'm not an 'expert' in the field, so I took some pictures and will send them over to Riley, but I think she'll concur with what I found."

"The letters are slanted in the wrong direction for a right-handed person to have written them," Parks said aloud. "Then again...what if that was done intentionally to also throw us off?"

Though the handwriting would be analyzed by an expert, Parks knew already just by looking at the words on the wall. He hadn't been doing this for over ten years to not know what he was looking at. He had seen his fair share of suicide notes, death threats and fan mail. He knew handwriting better than he would have cared for. That got him thinking. Someone desperate to wrap this case up wanted Nicholas Martin to take the fall for Kelli Davis and Fredrick Knott's murders.

Someone left handed.

ELEVEN

Parks breathed deeply as he sat at his desk and rubbed his hands over his face, massaging his temples, trying gently to avoid the migraine he could feel building. This case would be the death of him yet. He just knew it. And technically this was only day one. It hadn't even been twenty-four hours since the murders of Fredrick Knott and Kelli Davis. And all this on less than four hours of sleep. Internally, his body was at a war with itself, the coffee and Vivarin he was taking in to keep himself awake with his body's natural impulses to sleep.

"So…what do we have on the phone numbers?"

"Dead ends," Fairmont answered from his desk as he hung up his phone.

"Dead ends?"

"Mostly. It's exactly what we thought it was. An electronic black book. Though half of the numbers are disconnected, out of the ones that do work, every number was someone that Knott had slept with. And I mean literally slept with and that's it. No relationships. Not a single jealous or pissed off person on that list. I'm willing to bet that not a single girl on that list knew about anyone else on it."

119

"Besides, it's not a crime to sleep with as many different people as you choose," Tippin interjected, walking into the room with two mugs off coffee, handing one off to Parks. From the beginning Milo Tippin was always bringing coffees or had files ready almost before Parks even knew to ask for them. At first it was seen as brown nosing by several of the other members of the department but was soon known to be a simple sign of admiration that Tippin had for anyone in a leadership or seniority position over him. He simply paid attention to the little details. It's what made him him. Those and the many different colored Converse low-tops he was always wearing. "Guy may be a creep, but every girl we've managed to talk to so far was a willing partner. They knew what they were getting themselves into."

"Do we have a list of names for those numbers?" Parks asked.

Fairmont tossed over a printout of each number and its corresponding owner.

"What about alibis?"

"So far everyone we have talked to has given us one. Mostly flimsy but provable. The list is p[probably a dead end. But we'll keep chipping away at it."

Parks sighed. "What about Knott's cases?"

"His what?" Fairmont asked.

"Hardwick said Knott had testified on a few important trials? She was going to get us the case files." Parks looked from each member of his team to the next. "Did someone check into seeing if maybe his death had something to do with one of them?"

"I did," Rachel Moore said as she walked onto the floor.

"What's the point?" Fairmont asked. "I thought I heard that the girl's boyfriend admitted to the murders and then offed himself?"

Hardwick walked through the room and made her way over to

Parks's side.

"He wrote the word 'Sorry' on the bathroom wall where we found his body," Parks said as he looked to Bennett, telling him to keep his mouth shut. Bennett had no jurisdiction off the university campus and so hadn't been to the LAPD station before but Parks had things to go over with him and so brought him along, on the agreement that he keep quiet and only observe. "Which, considering the source, could be an apology for anything from sleeping with someone's wife to cheating on a test. The kid's no angel. And until I get the C.O.D. and final reports on all three bodies we're still treating this as an open case. I want all the t's crossed and i's dotted. You know the pressure the governor is putting on this department. We keep working on this until I say so."

Hardwick leaned in to Parks to have a private conversation with him. "You're looking a little worse for wear. How are you doing with everything else? I don't need you falling apart on me. Not on this one."

"I'm fine," Parks replied with a semi-shrug. "I'm fine. I promise."

"Okay. Oh, and you have a meeting with"—Hardwick paused when she finally noticed Bennett sitting off to the side at Parks's desk—"you-know-who in San Quentin." Hardwick enlarged her eyes and changed the infliction in her voice to let Parks know she was talking about Louis Hayward without naming him around anyone else. She didn't know Matthew Bennett from the man in the moon and, worse off, she didn't trust him. Last thing she needed was a leak that they thought there could be a connection between the university murders and the Palisades Poisoner.

"Really? On the weekend?"

"Let's just say I pulled a few strings. This is strictly off the books.

You hear? They've agreed to a one-on-one with him. Interview's set for tomorrow afternoon. Even though it's a Sunday they'll let you in. You got a flight leaving LAX for San Francisco at noon. Don't be late."

"Will do, Chief," Parks smiled as Hardwick left the room. "So where were we?"

"Knott's legal testimonies," Moore answered, picking up a notepad. "He testified at three trials over the last five years. Two of them were simple testimonies for the state about key witnesses. His testimonies didn't necessarily sway the jury one way or the other. From what I could dig up about them, I don't see there being any hostility toward him."

"And the third?"

"The third's a different story."

"What was the case?"

"Child molestation charges brought against a pediatrician in Long Beach. A Dr. Kendrick. Four different families filed claims. Big to-do. Might have heard of it in the news?"

"Sounds familiar. When did it wrap up?"

"Nine months ago."

"Wasn't it declared a mistrial?" Hardwick asked.

"It was," Moore nodded. "But before that, Professor Knott testified. On behalf of the good doctor, Kendrick. Pissed off all the plaintiffs, I can tell you that."

"But he wasn't the reason why it was declared a mistrial, was he?" Parks asked.

"No," Moore replied. "But he wasn't exactly the kindest person on the stand. Opened up a lot of skeletons in the closets so to speak. He discovered that one family's stepfather molested his own kids and another had an uncle worth looking into. He put a lot of doubt on the guilt of the defendant. And he received threats."

"Threats? As in plural?"

"Yep. Several."

"Serious?" Parks was intrigued.

"Some," Moore handed over a file to him. "They're all logged in there. He reported every one. These"—Moore held up another file—"are other threats he's received over the years. Not having to do with the case. Just random threats."

"He reported all of these?" Parks was genuinely shocked.

"He was nothing if not methodical," Moore smiled. "At least it helps us keep track of his life for the past ten years."

"Have you gone over each and every single one of these?" Parks asked.

"I just finished with the ones associated with the molestation trial. I was planning on tackling the others in the morning."

"Good. Cross reference these with the threats we found in his office. If any of them from his office weren't reported I want to know why. What makes them so special?" Parks took a deep breath and stood up. "It all sounds good to me. Oh, and someone look into a...Ryan Lockhart. He's Nick Martin's roommate. I want to know who he is."

"On it," Tippin answered.

"Oh, and Tippin," Parks pulled Tippin aside and lowered his voice.

"Yeah, boss?"

"See if you can get on Facebook or the Twittersphere or whatever the kids are using these days and see if you can find out where a Christopher Stone is. He's Bill Norton's son, so I need this completely on the hush-hush. You hear me?"

"Where he is?"

"Like now. Tonight. Tomorrow. Anything. Then let me know. Without alerting anyone if possible."

"I'll see what I can find."

"Thanks. All of you go home. Rest. Relax. Recuperate. Tomorrow's going to be another long day. Amy should wrap up all three autopsies tomorrow so we'll see what's what at that time. Until then we still have work to do. But I want to thank you guys for all of your help on this. You're all doing a good job." Parks turned to Bennett. "You feel like grabbing a drink?"

"I could do with some food right about now," Bennett said.

"Good. Let's go."

*   *   *

"You really think Nick Martin's death was a suicide?" Bennett sat opposite Parks in one of the booths at the back of Canter's on Fairfax, halfway between Parker center and the university grounds where Parks had left his vehicle when Bennett drove them downtown. The restaurant was dark, perfect for seclusion and privacy. "You think that Nick's suicide and Knott's murder are related?" Bennett asked. "I mean besides the obvious links."

"Something about this whole case stinks," Parks replied. "Knott's got too many different possibilities as to who could have killed him. I mean this guy literally has dozens of potential people out to get him. We could be following a lead and have it go straight to a dead end and have to start completely over again. There are dozens of possibilities. I can't wrap this whole case up because one of those so-called leads appears to be the answer. I need definitive conclusions. I'm just surprised Knott wasn't killed sooner."

Their server came over and took the two detectives' orders.

"Just coffee, thanks," Parks smiled up at the girl who looked no more than eighteen.

"You should eat something," Bennett scolded as he ordered a BLT with a side of fries.

"I'll take a Denver omelet with a side of bacon and an English muffin," said Parks changing his mind. "That's all. And the coffee. Wait, I need to sleep tonight. Forget the coffee. An orange juice. And water. Thanks."

The waitress smiled at the two men and skipped off.

"Little late for breakfast, isn't it?" Bennett questioned.

"I'll just pick at it," added Parks. "My stomach's too unsettled for me to eat right now."

Parks's stomach was a mess and all of the pills he kept popping over the last twenty-four hours—pills to help him sleep, to keep him awake, to take the pain from Nicholas Martin's attack—weren't doing him any help. Perhaps he should have a few bites to help settle his stomach.

"You don't trust me," Bennett said out of nowhere. "Do you?"

"Why shouldn't I?"

"I didn't say you shouldn't."

"But you know me well enough to know that I don't. Why is that?"

"Because I work for the university. And they have their own agenda."

"And you're saying they don't?" Parks asked, still as a rock.

"What if I told you what it was? Everything that I had been told to do."

"You don't need to."

"Meaning you don't think I'd actually tell you everything," Bennett surmised.

Parks stared at the kid, took him in, assessing what he saw and felt.

"No, you wouldn't," Parks began. "And maybe even you would think you have told me everything. At least everything you think I should need to know. Not realizing that you would be keeping things from me. Even if you felt they didn't matter. You can't help it. Just like I can't help but not trust you one-hundred percent. It's not anyone's fault. It's just life. We work for opposite sides. We both want the same outcome. To a degree. But how we get it, and what we're willing to do to get it and what we do with that information in the end are two completely different things though. You know this. I know this. We're both aware that we're both aware of this. It can't be helped." Parks breathed. "I don't think you're a bad person. Or that you're intentionally trying to sabotage this case. If I did, then you and I wouldn't be having this conversation. You'd be out of everything. I think you truly do want to help. I don't fully know what you want out of this whole experience, but I know that in the end, what I—the LAPD—want and what the university—Norton—want won't matter. Because in the end, what will matter, is what you want. And who will be able to best help you achieve that." Parks took a sip of his water. "Do I trust you? About as far as I can throw you. But...you are still a part of this investigation. And that alone should say enough."

Bennett sat quietly and took this information in.

"You ever read Agatha Christie?" Bennett asked. "Or Raymond Chandler?"

"I spend all day chasing down killers," Parks said nonchalantly, though somewhat surprised that Bennett knew who either author was and that he had read something by them. "You think I want to go home and read about them?" Considering his love for puzzles,

Parks was surprised at his lack of interest in reading crime novels. He did back in high school, but ever since he joined the force he found himself reading less and less. He'd rather head out in the middle of the night, all alone, and patrol the streets that were talked about by Raymond Chandler or Michael Connelly than read about them in a book.

"I first read a Christie novel in high school. I think it's what got me interested in the law. But what I love about their books is the complexity of it all. The twists and turns. You never see the killer coming until the final twist at the end. See, real life is never like that."

"What are you saying? I should read a Christie novel to calm down?"

"No," Bennett chuckled. "I'm saying that's fiction. It's all fiction. That's not real life. It's never that complicated. That complex. Usually the simplest answer is the answer. Husband or wife finds out the other is cheating on them and bam, one of them is dead. Man loses his job and can't support his family any more so he kills himself for the insurance. People get jealous. Greedy. Angry. Love. Hate. Those are simple emotions. Layered? Yes. But still simple nonetheless. At least the outcomes usually are. If a jealous boyfriend witnesses his girlfriend cheating on him and loses it—chances are he went nuts and killed them both in the heat of the moment. Then later on he realizes what he did and has some clarity which results in his guilt-filled suicide? Tell me that's so hard to believe."

"Not at all," Parks agreed. "And ten years ago I would have told you that was the answer. But times change. The climate changes. Society changes. People change. Nothing is that simple any more. Even when it is, could what you suggested be the answer? Sure. But ten years on the job has got my spider-sense tingling and telling me something's off. Not all of the pieces of the puzzle are fitting together quite the way they should. Nick Martin feeling uncontrollable rage and murdering the love of his life with her new lover? I can see that. Nick Martin feeling remorse for doing so and being suicidal? Now I just feel played."

Both men sat silently. Parks stared out the back window toward the mostly empty parking lot while Bennett surveyed the sporadically seated customers throughout the diner.

"Makes you wonder, doesn't it?" Bennett said, barely audible, this time. "Marriage and all that. Fidelity. Consequences. For our actions."

"And how's that?"

"Well it's kind of like Knott's wife said. Maybe if they weren't having trouble he wouldn't have been sneaking around. And if he hadn't been sneaking around—"

"Let me just stop you right there," Parks began, reaching into his jacket pocket for a small plastic container containing his pills. It was a simple travel container for Tylenol that had been emptied and now contained his current prescriptions. "You can believe that butterfly effect bullshit all you want. But I don't do 'what ifs'. They're pointless. They don't solve anything. I can't deal in a world of 'what ifs'. Only what is. And what has happened. There's a million 'what ifs' every day of the week. Every hour of the day. Every second of the minute. But it won't fix anything. I can only fix what's wrong and what's wrong can't be fixed with a 'what if'."

He took out two pills, popping them in his mouth and following them with a swallow of water. Bennett looked away, guiltily.

"I'm not a pessimist," Parks continued. "I genuinely believe in people. Look for the good. Hope for the best. I have to. I think. With what all I see. I have to be."

"How long have you been doing this?"

Parks caught Bennett staring at the container of pills in his hands. He paused for a second before realizing the young man was asking about his career as a detective.

"Longer than most."

"How would you say I'm doing?" Bennett asked genuinely wanting Parks's opinion.

Parks buttoned up as their server brought their food. She asked if there was anything else they needed and when both men shook their heads she continued on to the next table with the same plastic smile.

"Never ask," Parks answered. "To each his own. Everyone has something to offer in every situation and honestly, it doesn't matter what anyone else thinks. Well, except for the boss man. Being a street cop you get better the longer you patrol. Years of experience help you with split second decisions that can save a life. That's why the LAPD has a minimum requirement of being a patrol officer before applying for detective. And that's not just police work, that's with every profession out there. Same as with being a detective. Problem is they'll yank you out of here before you get good enough to know what's what. But a lot of what we use as detectives is the same as what's learned on patrol. Being observant. Most people glance over the small details but a detective needs to seek them out. Hunt them down. Details can make all the difference. Experience makes the difference. Then again, you being younger gives you a different viewpoint on things than me. Just like a woman has a different one than a man. Age. Race. Gender. Ethnicity. Sexuality. Background. Variety. Diversity. It all helps."

Bennett dug into his sandwich while Parks began cutting up his omelet. He then left it alone and nibbled on some bacon. He was used to being alone most of the time and wasn't sure why he felt compelled to talk. He was beginning to feel like one of his suspects, filling the void with senseless gibberish. Hell, he didn't do this much talking when he was in a relationship. Maybe that was one of the problems he and his ex-wife had had.

"I was married once." Parks continued. Bennett wasn't sure what to say, but figured it was best to stay quiet. "Didn't work out. Don't regret it though. Loved her very much. But sometimes...sometimes people just mess up. It happens. But neither one of us are dead. Cheating happens every day. Usually just results in broken hearts. Not stabbed ones."

The two men remained quiet as they continued with their dinners when Parks's phone began to vibrate and light up with the sound of the crickets chirping. Parks stared at his phone, wondering how or why it made that noise, and realized that Tippin, or more likely Tippin at Fairmont's behest, was behind the changes made on his cell.

Parks sighed and reached for his phone on the table. He read the neon-green number that flashed across the screen and pressed a button to activate the phone and address the caller.

"I suggest you fix my phone before it rings again," Parks said by way of greeting.

"I'm sure I don't know what you're talking about," Tippin said from the other end. "But if you messed up one of your settings again, I'll be more than happy to look at it."

"Tippin—"

"I got that information on Christopher Stone," Tippin interrupted. The kid was smart. He was distracting Parks and both of them knew it. Parks couldn't help but smile.

"Shoot."

"You know where Skybar up on Sunset is?"

"When?"

"He's there right now. At least according to some girl's Instagram profile."

"Thank you, Tippin," Parks said as he hung up.

"So we got a location on Christopher Stone?"

"Sounds like it."

"No kidding. Where?"

"Feel like being social?" Parks asked with a smile.

TWELVE

Parks drove north on Fairfax to Sunset and turned left until he came to the Mondrian Hotel. There was no parking anywhere close to the hotel, so he stopped by valet and told the kid taking his keys to keep the car accessible. The young man nodded and verbally agreed as he moved the vehicle. The two men made their way to the front door until a doorman stopped them. The bouncer hesitated for a moment but accepted the men were on official business and not simply trying to crash ahead of the rest of the line. Having been at the Mondrian before, Bennett led the way out to the back patio bar where he figured Christopher Stone would most likely be hanging out.

There was no breeze in the air, keeping it just right for the amount of skin being shown off due to the revealing and lacking outfits worn by the patrons of the place. At half past nine the place was already up and running, not crowded, yet busy. Women stood around in groups, drinking their cosmos and other drinks of choice while somewhat expensively dressed men tried to act up their bravado and put on a secure face in hopes of actually succeeding in gaining access into one of the various women's lives or, more preferably, just their beds for the night.

Yellow and gold accented lounges surrounded a portion of the patio while ivy covered the walls without obstructing the glamorous and breathtaking view of the city below. The lighting was dim enough to not blind the men and women in attendance, yet didn't leave that much to the imagination of the viewer.

Both men stood in the center of the back patio, actually blending in.

"You sure he's here?" Bennett asked.

"Who knows?" Parks shrugged. "That was almost thirty minutes ago. He could have moved on by now."

"Wait a minute," said Bennett as he left Parks's side for the nearby bar.

Parks watched as the bartender ignored Bennett while he flirted with several women trying to get free drinks, though he didn't appear to be making any. The bartender finally glanced over and noticed Bennett holding up his badge and a fifty. The bartender came over and the two men exchanged words until Bennett left the fifty and the bartender pointed somewhere off in the corner behind the men. Bennett made his way back over to Parks.

"He's here. Somewhere with a view."

Parks and Bennett turned and looked toward the back end of the patio. It wasn't until a few guests moved to the side when they noticed Christopher sitting in the corner, with a beautiful woman on each side.

On Christopher's right sat a girl who was in her mid-twenties with shoulder-length, shimmering brown hair and long, slender legs. She had exotic features with a sharp nose, luminous lips and clear-blue eyes. A deep, royal purple dress plunged to her navel despite the hem barely covering her thighs, accentuated her enticing body.

The girl who sat on the other side of Christopher barely looked legal and showed off her youthful age and inexperience as she continued to look at the hectic goings-on around her while preferring the protection Christopher had to offer from the big, bad world. Parks had a feeling the brunette was Christopher's girlfriend, while the blonde was simply arm candy for the night. Christopher's face was buried in the brunette's neck and she whispered something into his ear at the sight of them approaching. He slowly turned, greeted the men with a beaming smile and took another sip of his martini.

"Ladies," Christopher smiled, not taking his eyes off the two men who stood before him. "This is Detectives Dave Parks and Matthew Bennett. Or is it David? And Matt?"

"We need to talk," Parks announced.

"This official police business?" Christopher asked with a knowing smile.

"You need to ask?" Parks answered as he watched Christopher take another sip of his drink. "This is about your roommate."

"Oh? Which one is that? My mother or stepfather?"

The brunette smiled at Christopher's statement while the blonde was simply confused; intimidated by the fact the police were talking to Christopher, as if she was guilty simply by association, though she was guilty of nothing more serious than being too young to drink.

"Nicholas Martin," Parks replied not missing a beat.

"Oh? Gave you that black eye and sore lip you're sporting there, Detective?"

"He's dead."

Christopher stared at the two men, not giving them a single body movement or facial expression they could use to identify how he felt about the knowledge, or if he was even surprised by it. Christopher turned to the brunette and whispered something in her ear. She nodded once and kissed him before she got up and reached down for the blonde to follow.

"Guess this will have to wait until another time." Christopher kissed the blonde and nodded toward the standing woman, instructing her to leave.

The blonde stood up, taking the brunette's hand, their fingers interlocking in an intimate manner as she allowed the other woman to escort her away from the group of men. Christopher finished his martini, picked up the brunette's clear-colored drink and stood up to face the two men. He retrieved the blue cheese filled olives from his own martini glass and walked toward the end of the balcony, away from everyone else.

"How did it happen?" Christopher asked, staring out at the city below.

The sun had fully disappeared, but the remains of its light shimmered behind the buildings on the horizon while the city below came to life. Cars were backed up, even on the side streets throughout Hollywood, as the sounds of honking could be heard echoing throughout the hills, despite how much the music in the bar tried to drown them out.

"It appears he killed himself," Parks answered.

"But you don't buy it," Christopher surmised.

"Do you?"

"Does suicide sound like something Nicholas Martin would do?"

"Hardly."

"Yeah, I don't think so either," Christopher said shaking his head and turning to face the men. "That doesn't sound like the Nick I knew."

"Knew him well?" Parks asked, noticing Christopher held his martini glass in his left hand while he finished the last olive from the other.

"What?" Christopher flinched when he noticed what Parks had been looking at. "Was the person who killed Nick a lefty?"

"Who said he was killed?" Bennett asked quickly. "And what makes you say that?"

"Because right handed people are all too common for you to pay any special attention to my hands," Christopher said holding up his hands as he passed the glass from one hand to the next. "I, alas, am quite *versatile*. Sorry. Besides, I didn't see Nick before I left his place this morning after your visit. And I was at home with my mother and stepfather all afternoon."

"Your stepfather was at school today," Parks commented. "We met with him earlier."

"Not this morning, he wasn't," Christopher said. "He went in after lunch. About two o'clock I would say. Maybe a little earlier than that. But around that time."

"But you can write with your left hand?" Bennett asked, though he was sure he already knew the answer.

"I can do many things with my left hand," Christopher grinned.

"But you were there this morning?" Parks interrupted.

"At his dorm room? I was," Christopher agreed.

"What were you doing there?"

"Sleeping. Until you woke me up."

"Alone?"

"Did you see anyone else?"

"Why were you there?"

"Sometimes I crash in Ryan's bed if I've been on campus at a par-

ty and I'm too drunk to get home. You know. Responsible 'n all."
Christopher finished off his drink and set the empty glass down on
the end of the banister.

"No personal driver?" Bennett threw on a fake smile to add to
the bite of his question. "Or Uber?"

"Sometimes. Then again, sometimes I just like to get away. You
know?"

"Ryan doesn't mind you crashing?" Bennett asked before adding,
"When he's not around?"

"Ryan and I have an understanding. Sometimes I just need to get
away. So I crash with him. Sometimes he needs to get away and so
he crashes with me. It happens."

"How did you two meet?" Parks asked. "I mean out of everyone
on campus you could have befriended..."

"Actually, we've known each other for about six years now,"
Christopher began to explain. "We met back in high school. When
my mother first moved us here. We've been friends since then. You
know, youthful exploration and all that. He taught me things and in
return I helped open doors for him."

"You mean the porn?"

"I see you've been talking to Kim. But yes. I guess that. He used
to accompany me to parties and you never know who you'll meet up
in the hills. His family doesn't have money, and though I helped him
when and how I could, he's a prideful boy and wanted to make it on
his own. He's a good looking guy. Certain people with money are
more than willing to part with it for a good looking guy. Or girl. Just
all depends what you're willing to do for it."

"And what was he willing to do for it?"

"Other than the porn? I wouldn't know. You'd have to ask him."

"I'm going to go under the assumption that you care for him,"

Parks said, throwing out the observation. "Though you probably don't have a say in what he does or doesn't do?"

"It's true we were lovers at one time," Christopher agrees. "But that was years ago. I do care for him. But I can't live his life for him. I can suggest and offer, yes. But he is his own man, stubborn and head-strong as he is. He has to make his own choices and mistakes, and learn from them. Do I approve of everything he's done? No, I do not. Again, I can't control him. I can only be there to support him when he needs it."

"And what help would he have needed recently?"

"Drugs were his vice as of recently," Christopher said. "Cocaine. Meth. Heroin even. Though I never saw proof he was doing it, I know he was. I'd offered to pay for rehab if he ever wanted to go, being as he was always near broke, but so far he has yet to take me up on it."

"We found numerous drugs, including all you just mentioned, in Knott's office," Parks said, making sure to tread carefully. "Any connection between the two?"

Christopher shrugged. "Ryan was a patient of Knott's. Or something like that. I'm not sure if he was actually a patient or if they just had a more professional relationship concerning the drugs. But they did meet several times a week, for the past year. I'd even warned him against it, but he didn't listen."

"Was Knott a user?"

"Recreationally. However, lately I came to believe it was becoming more of an addiction with him. He liked to mix up his own little concoctions and see what the outcomes would be."

"He gave his patents homemade mix-n-matches just to see what the outcomes would be?"

"Something like that."

"That's a pretty big accusation."

"I didn't realize I was making one," Christopher said. "I was just telling you what the word around campus was. Not that this was common knowledge. Otherwise, how would he get new patients? And keep his job."

"But you have ears everywhere," Bennett commented.

"That I do."

"So where is Ryan? Word around campus has he's been missing for three weeks."

"I don't know," Christopher shrugged. "I had kept hoping he'd pop up back at campus. Or in one of the rehab facilities. But so far he hasn't. I'm not sure where he went off to. Not to his family, I know that much. I've overheard something about him going up north, but I don't know what that means, or where, or for what reason. Maybe you guys should try pinging his cell. I'm sure no matter where he is he still has that on him."

"Would Ryan have had a reason to want Knott or Kelli dead?"

"Ryan's said he's only been in love once and he was willing to screw anything on two legs. So I highly doubt that he'd have had any romantic feelings toward Kelli, if that's what you're asking. But he and Knott could have been conducting their little drug deals so that is a possibility for some type of a motive. Or maybe they owed the wrong people money or pissed off the wrong patient. Or maybe their deaths have nothing to do with drugs. Who knows?"

The three men stared at one another as if in a showdown.

"Do you think Nick killed Knott and Kelli?"

"I didn't ask him."

"But you saw him after the murders, correct?"

"Did I?"

"There was blood on the floor of the dorm room when we were there this morning," Parks commented. "What do you want to bet if we check it and find that it matches with either Knott's or Kelli's?"

"Doubtful," Christopher shrugged. "After his little scene at the Student Union last night I was concerned. So I went to his room to check on him. I found him in the shower. Shaking and babbling. His clothes were in a pile next to the shower. I may have noticed blood on them."

"And?"

"And when he got out I gave him a nightcap with a couple of Tylenol PMs and put him to bed. I stayed around to keep an eye on him. Make sure nothing else happened. When I woke up in the morning, you guys were knocking on the door and he wasn't around. Neither were any of his clothes. I don't know what he did with them or where he went. Or when he left. I never heard a thing."

"And with his temper and blood on his clothes you don't think he could have killed them?"

"Nick doesn't have the brain power or control to carry out a murder and be smart enough not to get caught. If he had killed them, you would have proof of it already and he would have been in jail. I think it's more likely he got pissed and went to a nearby, off-campus bar. Drank and got in a fight with some random stranger. Check it out. I'm sure there's a report of it somewhere. He didn't kill them, and you guys know that. Or should."

Christopher finished his drink and placed the glass on the edge of the balcony before starting through the crowd of people toward the front entrance to the hotel. He stopped once to hug and kiss some up-and-coming actor and his conquest for the evening. He also waved and smiled a few other goodbyes at some other random people in the crowd. A minute later Christopher ended up in front of the hotel, out on Sunset Boulevard, where he waited for his car; the two detectives right on his heels.

"And where were you last night? Before you went to Nick's dorm room."

"I was at the alumni association all night with my parents. Posing for pictures and smiling like a jackass. Mother thought I could make some good connections. Besides, I had to put on a good face for daddy dearest. The party broke up when we heard the police sirens. That's when we all headed over to Asmodeus Hall. Some guy took pictures of the crowd. Check with him. You'll see. Once I realized what had happened I walked across campus to Nick's room. You know the rest." An emerald green 2014 convertible Lamborghini Gallardo Spyder pulled up with the brunette behind the wheel. "You're wasting your time with me, detectives. I didn't kill anybody."

"You don't have an alibi for last night," Bennett pointed out.

"I have an airtight alibi that you can neither prove nor disprove," Christopher replied. "You already know where I was this morning and I told you where I was last night. And I told you about Nick. Or did I? That's the problem with my alibi. No proof. I mean you can check with Ni—oh, right. You can't. He's dead. Doesn't mean it's not true. Just means you'll have to take my word for it now, won't you?"

Parks was pissed. They were backed into a corner he didn't know how to get out of.

"Look," Christopher said as he walked to the passenger door of the car. "I feel bad for you guys, I really do. I know you work hard. So I'm going to help you a bit here. Number one. Knott was broke. I assume you've checked his bank records? But he was still living the high life. So where did that money come from? Follow the money."

"You're saying he owed someone a large sum of money and they killed him for it?" Bennett asked.

Christopher laughed. "Boy, you guys sure do like to jump to conclusions. And fast. Quit talking and just listen. I didn't say that. Follow the money. I doubt the person who gave him money killed him. But the reason he got the money he was living off might have been the reason he was killed."

"Why don't you quit playing—?"

"Number two," Christopher interrupted. "Everyone knows Knott slept around. Try interviewing some of the women he slept with. You might find some interesting things about our little professor."

"We're interested in the truth, Mr. Stone, not gossip," Parks shot back.

"Besides," Bennett said. "We're already interviewing some of Knott's former lovers."

"Please," Christopher laughed and got into the convertible. "Meredith Langer did no more kill Knott than a fly on the wall. Besides, I said women he had affairs with. See you around boys."

The brunette pulled out onto Sunset Boulevard and flipped a bitch as she turned from heading east to going west toward the coast.

"I didn't say we were interviewing Meredith Langer," Bennett said to his partner.

"I know," Parks replied solemnly.

"He slipped."

Parks remained quiet, neither denying the accusation nor agreeing with it.

PART 2
3 to 6 Players
Ages 8 to Adult

THIRTEEN

"You don't look so good," Bennett noted as he drove south down the I-5 toward San Diego early the next morning. "You sleep well?"

"Probably stayed up later than I planned." Parks wasn't in the mood to talk. He hadn't gotten a good night's worth of sleep; troubled dreams plaguing him, causing him to spend most of the night tossing and turning until he eventually woke up at four-thirty in the morning and continued playing with his puzzles while drinking endless cups of coffee. He was rested more so than the day before, but what was that to really compare to? Between the case and the fate of his team, he was a train wreck of nerves and he simply wanted the week to be over. "I'll grab some more coffee the next time we stop. I'll be fine."

"Coffee sounds good," Bennett agreed.

The two men drove the rest of the way in silence. Parks took the 36 exit from the I-5 southbound and drove into Del Mar, pulling up all the way onto the beach. They drove through a part of town with housing that had been repeatedly abused until it had become the run-down semi-standing structures they were now. The houses

147

were mostly beaten down with boarded windows and walls covered in graffiti. Most of the yards were dirt and weeds, with the occasional potted plant that had died several seasons before. Toys were left scattered and sun-cracked out in front yards, with matching plastic chairs and cheap card tables.

Parks parked in front of the address he had scribbled down on his pad and stared at the two-bedroom house surrounded by a chain-link fence with a barking pit-bull tied up in the corner. The house wasn't as sketchy as some of the others they had driven past, the windows weren't boarded up or broken, but were guarded by iron bars.

"This is it?" Bennett asked skeptically as he looked over his partner's shoulders at the house.

"It's what the computer gave." Parks got out of the car and took in his surroundings. He couldn't see the ocean but he could hear the occasional gull crying in the clouds somewhere up above. He was used to the smog in LA, but for some reason the air felt dirtier down here in this part of town. It felt as if everything around them had an entire film of filth layered over it.

"Let's get this over with," Bennett sighed and followed his partner through the deserted yard, past the vicious attack dog, up to the porch.

Parks knocked on the door and the two men waited. The dog continued to bark and snarl at the detectives but wasn't getting free any time this century thanks to the chain around its neck. Or so the two men hoped. Two children rode their bikes down the street, laughing as one yelled out obscenities at the other, and disappeared off into the horizon. Parks turned back to the door and pounded on it again.

"Who is it?" shouted a hoarse voice from the other side of the door.

"Meredith Langer? LAPD. Can you please open up?" Parks called out.

The door jerked open to reveal a somewhat overweight woman, with shoulder length dirty-blonde hair, that was even greasier and dirtier than the name could ever reflect. Her eyes were sunken and bloodshot, as if from years of drinking and not enough sleep. The wrinkles around her eyes and mouth had aged the woman a good ten years past her thirty-five years on the planet. She wore raspberry-colored, faded sweatpants and a t-shirt with a strawberry print all over the front. It was one size too big, even for her rather large size. In the woman's arms was her three-year-old daughter who was malnourished and had a matching complexion to her mother.

Both men stared hard at the woman who once carried on an illicit affair with the late Fredrick Knott and figured that she had lost some of her luster since the birth of Knott's alleged, illegitimate child and her subsequent banishment from the university and the rest of the world.

"Meredith Langer?" Parks asked flashing his badge.

"Yeah?" the woman replied, eying one man and then the other. "Who're you?" The smell of alcohol reeked off her breath with every word she spoke. Parks wondered how the woman was even able to stand.

"I'm Detective Parks of the LAPD and this is Detective Bennett," Parks answered.

"L.A.? Little lost, aren't you?"

"If you have a few minutes we'd like to ask you some questions about your relationship with Fredrick Knott."

"Shit," Meredith laughed as she turned and disappeared down the hallway.

Parks opened the rickety screen door and stepped onto the custard-colored fringe carpet. The front entrance opened into a narrow hallway with a doorway on either side. The left door led into a tight bathroom while the right side led into what Parks assumed was a bedroom though he couldn't be sure as the door was closed. Bennett reluctantly closed the door behind them and followed his partner down the hall into the only other room in the house. The lower halves of the walls were paneled faux-wood, while the upper half was wallpapered with pictures of birds and other native wildlife. With all of the windows and doors sealed shut, the house reeked of cigarettes and booze as if Meredith enjoyed soaking in her own pollution. In the back room, Meredith settled down on a couch in front of a television with rabbit ears and an occasionally fuzzy screen. Every now and again, a daytime soap opera flashed across the screen, forcing the volume to blare to life until the images disappeared back into static.

Meredith looked up at the two men who stood timidly near the entrance to the room and uttered a constricted laugh. "Shit. Relationship? You can read about our relationship in the fuckin' Times. Nothing I can tell you that you don't already know or couldn't find out."

"So you had an affair with him?" Parks asked.

"Had an affair? We were screwin', if that's what you mean," Meredith snapped, grabbing a pack of cigarettes off the nearby end table and fished for one from inside.

Bennett looked down at Meredith's daughter who sucked her thumb and stared at the fuzzy television. He felt an overwhelming urge to grab the child and leave the house.

"That's Bethany." Meredith nodded at her daughter and lit the cigarette. "She's his too. Wouldn't claim her though. Said I was a whore. Screwin' everything in sight. Lying bastard. Now I live here with my aunt. In this shit hole. He fucked up my life, the prick. He should be paying me alimony every month. Instead I'm workin' three jobs and barely scraping by."

"I'm assuming by your lack of surprise from our visit that you've heard the news?"

"I heard." Meredith took a puff of her cigarette and blew the smoke in the detectives' direction. "Been all over the damn news all weekend."

"What was your reaction when you heard that Mr. Knott had been murdered?" Parks wasn't sure whether to pity the woman or be repulsed.

"You see that," Meredith nodded to a single glass that sat on the end table next to her cigarettes. The glass was three-quarters filled with a dark liquid that Parks assumed was some form of whiskey. "That's four fingers of my friend Jack. I have one of those—just one— every day. Every day. But on the day I heard about Knott being offed I skipped my drink. I wanted to stay sober the whole day just so I could remember it. Cause for celebration, you know?"

"And where were you the night before?" Parks asked wanting to get the questioning moving and done with. Meredith's words were beginning to slur.

Meredith cackled and took a swallow of her Jack.

"You gotta be shittin' me! I was working my second job. That's what I was doing. And you can call up my manager if you don't believe me. Think I murdered that bastard? Sure I wanted him dead. But I didn't kill him. Not worth my time or effort. Not like I'm gonna benefit from him being dead. He's been dead to me for years now.

She"—Meredith nodded toward her daughter—"is the only thing that matters to me now. And as much as I might have wanted him dead, I wouldn't jeopardize my daughter's safety in any way just for that prick."

"Is there anything else you can tell us about Knott?" Parks wasn't sure what else to ask. He already knew it was unlikely Meredith had murdered Knott. It's not like it was ever that easy. But he still felt as if there was a reason he had been led to her. There had to be something he was supposed to learn from her. Why else would Elizabeth Knott feel so guilty about not leaving Meredith any money?

"Just what the hell did you expect to find out from me?" Meredith asked. "I was one of his students. I had an affair with the prick five years ago. I wasn't the only one. That bastard slept with more pussy than any man I know. Then I got knocked up and he kicked my ass out. I haven't seen or spoken to him since. Never been back either. I don't know nothing else."

Meredith swallowed the rest of her drink and stood up to escort the men out of her house.

"It was reported that Knott had you expelled—"

"I know what he told them. Fuck him. It was all lies. I've never done nothing wrong toward that man. I wasn't 'obsessed' like he said. I wasn't living a fairy tale. I just wanted what was rightfully mine. I had his kid. I deserved something for that. The kid's his. I didn't need any test to tell me that. I don't care what he said. It wasn't some ex of mine. And I didn't send him those letters he said were from me either. Don't know where they came from. But they weren't from me. Lies. All lies from that man's mouth. I wasn't even a patient of his."

"Beg your pardon?"

"You heard me. Said he found out all this psycho-babble bullshit from our sessions and whatnot. I wasn't ever a patient of his. We never had any sessions. He wasn't my doctor. I was his student. That's it. Other than that, all we ever did was fuck."

"But according to the report, he had files—"

"Weren't mine. He made all that shit up. I don't doubt someone sent him those scary-ass love letters. Don't doubt it was a patient. Just wasn't me. Switched names or something. If the stupid school board would have taken two seconds to check things out, they would have seen that. I was never a patient of his. I'd say to check his scheduling book but he probably doctored that too. I'm telling you. I was never a patient of his. Though my boyfriend was."

"Excuse me?" Parks asked, his interest growing.

"Oh, yeah. Connor Hargrove. There's a fucking asshole's name if ever I heard one. He was one of Knott's as well. Was seeing him for over a year. Little lapdog. Did whatever Knott told him to do. Or suggested he should do."

"But he was your boyfriend? Or ex?"

"We had gone out on three dates. And even that I would have sworn it was only cuz Knott told him to for the reason of discrediting me. But he was never my boyfriend. We'd only had sex once. Wasn't that good either if you ask me." Parks took this information in. "Funny thing is," Meredith continued, "if you check, Connor was planning on dropping out of school before all that happened."

"He was? Why?"

"Couldn't afford the tuition. Which is funny, cuz I could have sworn he was a rich prick's son. But after this whole debacle suddenly he's got no financial worries. Wonder what you make of that."

"We'll have our people look into that."

"You should. Cuz I sure as hell didn't kill 'em. Wish I had."

Parks had interviewed his fair share of suspects and criminals over the years and had concluded that Meredith was telling the truth or had come to believe her own lies to the point that for her they were reality.

"You went to PSU," Parks muttered, mulling some thoughts through his mind.

"Yeah? So?"

Parks sat there, trying to find the most tactful way to approach this subject.

"I beg your pardon, and I don't mean to be rude or disrespectful, but you attended a state university. I know it's been a few years, hard times and whatnot but..." Parks didn't know what he was saying, or why. It was probably best to drop it.

"But you wanna know why I seem so white trash and un-edju'macated?" She was mispronouncing her words on purpose, poking fun at the detectives. "Shit, yeah, I get you. Truth is, my family is trash. I was the first one to ever get close to college let alone in one. I had a scholarship. Did my mother proud with it. Not that I should give a rat's ass what that bitch thinks. Or cares about. But I had one, just the same. Further proof."

"Of?"

"That I wouldn't do the shit they said I did. I wouldn't have done nothing to screw up that free ride. But that was part of the problem. When I didn't play along with Knott's games...well, he saw fit to just rid the school of me." Meredith's eyes glazed over as she thought back to her glory days. "Three years of working double and triple shifts, having people shit all over you, your family. Extended family. Coworkers. Clients. Whatnot. People shitting all over you every day for any amount of time and it's real easy to think low of yourself. Real easy to get lost."

"We're sorry to have bothered, you ma'am," Parks said as he turned to start down the hallway with Bennett in the lead. "We're sorry we took up your time. Have a good day."

"That's it?"

"Well, we'll check with your places of employment as a formality but if all checks out, as I feel it will, then you won't hear from us again." Parks wanted to mention the inheritance that the woman stood to gain but figured it was something best left for the attorneys. You never knew. Just because Elizabeth Knott felt the woman was owed something, didn't mean she'd actually see a penny of it. No sense in getting the woman's hopes up.

Bennett stepped out onto the wooden porch and the pit-bull immediately began to snap and snarl at the two men.

"Fucking—" Bennett cursed under his breath at the psychotic pet. "Hate dogs. Well, that was pointless."

The two detectives stood just outside of the chain link fence surrounding Meredith Langer's property, neither one satisfied with the information—or lack thereof—that they had gathered from their visit. From the first mention of her name, Parks hadn't thought the woman was capable of or behind Knott's murder but still felt they needed to check her out. Meredith, not trusting either man, followed the two outside and began to water her dirt yard while she kept an eye on them. Both men noticed the woman and the poor job at eavesdropping on their conversation she did but thought nothing of moving to the privacy inside their vehicle.

Parks leaned against the car and thought about what Christopher had told them the night before. Why he had still let them go interview Meredith when he surely could have told them what little they had learned and saved everyone the time? It was as if they were following the breadcrumbs to—

"He wasn't talking about students," Parks realized.

"Who? What?"

"Christopher. He wasn't talking about the students Knott slept with, he was talking about faculty. Knott was sleeping with other faculty members."

"Not likely," Meredith retorted from on her porch, startling the two men.

"How's that?" Parks wondered.

"Well, I can't speak for what's going on around there now," Meredith said. "But back when I was there—ain't no way a faculty member would have touched Knott. Not possible."

"Why's that?"

"Everyone knew. No one talked about it—but everyone knew," Meredith said as if that explained it all. "*She* wouldn't allow it."

"Elizabeth Knott?" Parks asked.

"No. The other woman," Meredith corrected. "Before he was married."

"There was someone else before he married Elizabeth?"

Meredith held back a laugh as she remembered something. "She was the woman he was gonna marry before he met Elizabeth. The woman he did marry was Elizabeth Something-or-other. But there had been the other woman before her. Elizabeth started out the woman on the side. Even after he married her, she was still the other woman. Didn't matter that she had a ring on her finger."

"You remember a name?" Parks asked. "For this first lady?"

"No," Meredith answered. "But don't matter. I know who she is. She and his wife were best friends."

Parks was somewhat surprised. "Knott was seeing Katherine Norton?"

"That's it," Meredith said. "They were seeing each other for a while. Then he said no to her and moved on to Elizabeth. Katherine moved on as well. She's the school president's wife you know?"

"Yeah," Parks said. "So Knott and Katherine were seeing each other, then broke up to marry other people, but continued to see each other on the side?"

"Something like that," Meredith confirmed. "Supposedly there was some bad blood between Knott and Katherine when they both married other people. Some say that they didn't really love their spouses. That it was just a cover and that they continued to see each other anyways."

"But why?" Bennett asked. "If Knott and Katherine were already seeing each other, why did they stop and marry other people they didn't love? What, it—it doesn't make sense."

"We're missing something," Parks agreed and turned to Meredith. "So Katherine more or less put the word out for faculty members to leave Knott alone? To not touch him?"

Even Parks wasn't sure about this theory.

"Didn't have to," Meredith said. "She was the wife of the president of the university. No one wanted to touch him. Nor should they have. She was obsessed with him, or something like that. Everyone knew if that shit blew up then it would be a shit storm to end all shit storms. Everyone associated with him would be out of a job. No one wanted anything to do with him socially, let alone sexually. They say that's why he kept seeing her even after he broke things off. Knew if he pissed her off, he'd be out of a job. Being as she was the president's wife 'n all."

"Wait," Parks said. "Why did Knott and Katherine end things?"

"Not sure. All I know is that it got too serious and Knott didn't want nothing more to do with Katherine. Like I said, something happened. Not sure what. But something."

"So she was getting back at him," Parks surmised, thinking about the situation. "She was ruining him. She had to know word would get back about the affair."

"But when was this?" Bennett asked. "Five or so years ago? Back when they all got married? You mean Katherine Norton was still carrying on an affair with Knott in hopes that her husband would find out and fire him? For five years? That's a long time to carry on an affair that means nothing just to hope that your husband will get back at the man who turned you down. I mean why didn't she just tell her husband and have him fired?"

"What if Bill Norton did find out about the affair? Maybe firing one of his leading professors with tenure wasn't an option."

"You mean it's a good motive for murder?" Bennett asked.

"It's worth checking up on," Parks said.

"That's what Christopher wanted us to find out," Bennett said. "He knew his mother and Knott were having an affair. He just didn't want to be caught squealing on mommy dearest. That's another thing...Katherine Norton and Elizabeth Knott were best friends, right?"

"Yeah?"

"And best friends—especially best girlfriends—tell each other everything right?"

"You don't think they went down to the salon and gossiped about how Katherine was sleeping with Elizabeth's husband, do you? Unless you think they swapped husbands?"

"These days, anything's possible. But no. What I'm thinking is, if you were sick—I mean terminally ill—isn't that something you'd tell your best friend? Even if you kept it from everyone else? I mean for support?"

"I would say so," Parks shrugged. "For support. But so what?"

"How long would you say she was sick?"

"Not sure. She said she's had it several years on and off."

"You said you couldn't figure out why things ended between Katherine and Knott... What if she knew? What if Katherine knew that her best friend was terminally ill?"

"And what? Convinced the man she loved and wanted to be with to leave her and marry her best friend so he could be there to inherit the woman's fortune when she died several years later? I think that's a big if. I mean who's to say that Elizabeth was going to pass away. That the cancer she had was even terminal? No one knew that. She could keep fighting it. It wasn't until recently she had even decided to give up."

"Even if she didn't die, a divorce alone would have granted him half of her estate," Bennett suggested. "Might seem a bit farfetched but fifteen million is a good motive for a fake marriage, wouldn't you say?"

"But they both had prenups. Besides, he's dead now so he's not getting her fifteen million to go share with Katherine," corrected Parks.

"No, he's not," Bennett agreed. "It's all going straight to Katherine now. Elizabeth said so. And Katherine doesn't have to share a penny of it with anyone else."

"That's still a bit farfetched. I mean what—Katherine killed her lover and his student—?"

"That he cheated on her with?" Bennett interrupted. "I mean if they were still together it is a motive. Why share it when the man's not being faithful? Now it's all hers."

"None of this makes sense," Parks said. "I don't buy it. It's far out there. All this cheating upon cheating. None of it is right."

"Murder isn't supposed to be right. That's why it's called murder."

"But like you said before, murder's usually simple. Revenge. Blind passion. Greed. Anger. Personal advancement. Homicidal mania. All of this—"

"And who says it's not?" Bennett asked. "We're only supposed to solve the murder. The motive's simply a means to help us find out who did it. Really it doesn't matter why. Only who. And the whos all lead to one place."

"The Nortons," Parks said, figuring it out.

"Yep. Either way it leads to him or her. Both have a good motive for murder."

"Let's get back to the station and see if Rachel has IDs on any more of those prints yet. We'll pull their address while we're there and maybe pay them a visit later today," Parks suggested.

Meredith waved them down before they pulled away from the curb.

"What is it?" Parks asked.

"Just remembered why Knott broke up with Katherine," Meredith said from the safety of her porch. "What that something that happened was. He found something out about her."

"And what was that?"

"It's how she acquired the millions she now possesses."

"Where from?"

"From the first three bastards who said 'I do' to the woman and are now all buried six feet under."

FOURTEEN

"So, three husbands?" Bennett said from across the abandoned desk he currently sat at while rummaging through some files. Neither detective had said a single word the entire drive back into town, each man thinking over the information they had acquired. "Technically she's on number four now."

"That's not a crime," Parks muttered.

"What do you think though?"

"Unless she actually murdered Knott her numerous husbands have nothing to do with our case." Parks saw the disappointment on Bennett's face. "But I'm sure it's something that could be looked into."

"Do you think we have a strong enough case for her to be a suspect?"

"She does like money. But that's not a crime."

"No. But how she comes by it can be." Bennett continued. "She's got millions."

"You think she's going to get this elaborate for just a few measly more?"

"Probably not. Do you?"

"Money is money. And greed is greed. You'd be surprised how once some people get a taste for it they'll do anything to get more. Even if they don't need it. It's like feeding a hunger that can't be satisfied."

"Like an addiction."

Parks nodded.

"So how much money does it take for it not to matter how much you have any more?"

Parks shrugged.

"Try close to seventy-four million," Milo Tippin answered. Before they left Meredith's, Parks called and asked him to do some quiet digging so as to not raise any flags. Last thing he needed was word to get out they were investigating the wife of the university's president.

"Say that again?" Bennett shot out flabbergasted.

"Katherine Norton is worth seventy-three point six million dollars according to what I could dig up," Tippin said.

"All from ex-husbands?" Parks asked.

"Well, that's what's funny," Fairmont continued. "Husband number one, whom she married right out of high school, left her with less than three million. It wasn't until husband number two that she got close to forty-five million. Then about another twenty from the third. The rest is interests and profit and loss stuff."

"Tell me we can bust her. Tell me we can bust her," Bennett chanted in a whisper.

"It's not a crime how she acquired her money," Parks repeated. "Unless it was. In either case, it's not our crime to worry about. We already have one murder to solve."

"Unless they're related," Bennett shrugged.

"A black widow with three dead husbands versus an unrelated

lover with a few measly million? That's highly coincidental if you ask me. And I'm going to need a hell of a lot more than suspicion before I go attacking a woman worth almost a hundred million dollars."

Bennett pouted like a heartbroken child who had just been told he was not going to Disneyland that year for the family vacation.

"Anything else?" Parks asked.

"We also have Knott's patient files," Fairmont offered, leaning back in his chair, his feet up on his desk. "The possibility of his murderer being a disgruntled patient is possible. We haven't done anything with them yet though."

"You haven't?"

"And when was I supposed to get to that?" Fairmont asked. "Before I checked every phone number on his little black book? Or identified all the fingerprints from the office? Or after I did background checks on him, his wife and the Nortons?"

"Hold on. Hold on. You're right," Parks agreed with a chuckle. "Sorry. You have the court files now?"

"Gave those to Rachel." Fairmont looked away, slightly embarrassed.

"Oh, yeah, so overworked. Overworked delegating."

"Hey, now. She asked for them." Fairmont shrugged. "She's working on the prints in Knott's office with Milo."

"Then what the heck *are* you working on?"

Just then Rachel Moore walked up to the gentlemen's club as if having been summoned.

"Gentlemen," Rachel smiled with contempt.

"Why if it isn't the lovely Miss Moore," Fairmont smiled back.

"Bite me, Jake. As if trying to identify all of these fingerprints wasn't hard enough, having to work with the school isn't exactly a piece of pie. No offense," Moore said looking to Bennett who brushed the comment off with no offense.

"Not coming along well?" Parks asked.

"Actually—and you better remember this when Milo and I ask for a raise—we have matched all seventy-four sets of prints with an identification and connection to Knott," she beamed proudly.

"No kidding?"

"Well, remember, we have a fairly controlled environment to work with, so that helped."

"Please tell me you excused all but one set of prints that belong to a homicidal, sex-maniac who recently escaped from prison?" Parks's sarcasm helped to lighten the mood in the office; something greatly needed and he was glad for his ability to do just that.

"Sorry. All were students and or patients of the late Professor Knott. Along with various other university professors. Secretaries and whatnot."

"Dammit," Parks cursed.

"All but two that is," Moore beamed.

"Please say it's the homicidal, sex-maniac."

"First one is a..." Moore looked to Milo who had sat down at a nearby table.

"Christopher Stone," answered Tippin without referring to notes as if his single job was to remember the two sets of prints.

"Close enough," Bennett chuckled under his breath.

"Christopher Stone?" Parks wondered. "We talked with him already. He's tricky. Already considering questioning him some more. And you're saying he has no connection to Knott?"

"According to his school records, he's never had Knott as a professor or advisor," Tippin confirmed. "And according to Knott's online records and calendar, he didn't see Christopher Stone as a patient."

"So he's not a student of Knott's nor is he a patient of his. The little snake," Parks was pleased. "Nice work."

"Could he possibly be our third person?" Bennett asked.

"Who?"

"The third person who was with Knott and Kelli Davis the night they were murdered?"

"Possible. Seems like he swings…in every direction possible," Parks admitted. "Either way, I'd like to question him again. Let's find him. Who do the other set of prints belong to?"

Rachel looked at both detectives, not wanting to answer, hoping that the revelation of Christopher Stone would make her second option void. "Milo?"

Tippin turned from Rachel to Parks. "Katherine Norton."

"Shit," Bennett cursed.

"And she had no reason to be in that office?" Parks asked.

"Other than she had an affair with Knott," Bennett corrected.

"Used to. And that's hearsay for the moment. We have no proof," Parks corrected. "But she was best friends with Knott's wife. And that is a connection. Could make her legit for being in the office."

"We don't think so," Moore rebutted.

"Why's that?"

"Elizabeth Knott. The professor's wife?"

"Yeah? What about her?"

"Her prints were not found anywhere inside of Knott's office," Tippin explained.

"Excuse me?" Parks asked not believing what he had been told. "You're saying that the professor's wife was never in that office?"

"Didn't say that. Just said we couldn't find any proof that she had been."

"And her best friend's prints are there?"

"Well she is the president of the school's wife," Bennett added.

"But does she have any official capacity at the school?" Parks looked to Rachel.

"I don't recall her having an official job at the university but I can go back over it again. Get a more detailed report on her history."

"Can we get it on her various husbands too?" Bennett asked.

"You want to tackle the Nortons' finances and history or Fredrick's court cases?" Moore consulted Fairmont, giving him a choice, when Parks knew she could have just taken one and left him with the other.

"I think career-wise it's smarter to stay as far away from the Nortons as possible," Fairmont replied. "They can be hazardous to your health."

"You got it," Moore smiled.

"Thanks."

"A full history," Moore said as she slapped the back of Milo's head with the files and motioned for him to follow her. "The report will be on your desk as soon as it's finished."

"Thanks," Parks said, standing up.

"Where are you going?" Bennett asked.

"We are going to have a little chat with the Nortons."

FIFTEEN

Parks pulled off Sunset Boulevard and started along several smaller streets heading deeper into the Hollywood hills. He finally found the address he pulled from the DMV for the Nortons, and after figuring out how to work the intercom system at the front gate was finally allowed access. He pulled up the half mile driveway until he circled around a fountain and stopped near the front doors, wondering if this was a lost cause as he failed to see any of the various vehicles the mansion's owners paraded through town.

The Norton property was a seven-bedroom, five and a half bath piece of hillside property that had asked for eighteen million when it was sold two years before. The Hollywood Hills property, which covered seven thousand square feet, not to mention the breathtaking view, was purchased for an even fifteen million—cash. The entire south side of the house had a view of the valley below thanks to the mostly all glass walls that made up the elegant structure.

Each of the five bedrooms had their own connecting bathrooms, which were more like spa-inspired bath suites, with fully plumbed jet tubs and isolated, stand-alone multi-functioning showers. There were three media rooms (in case one was being occupied by one of

167

the other two tenants of the house) fully equipped with surround sound, state of the art electronics and a fully functioning theatre.

The two detectives made their way to the front door and rang the enchanting chime. Parks was about to ring the bell again when the door was answered by an elegantly dressed elderly man.

"Yes?" the butler inquired of the detectives.

"I'm Detective David Parks, LAPD. This is Detective Matt Bennett," Parks explained as the two men withdrew their badges. "We'd like to speak to Miss Katherine Norton if we may?"

Expecting to be given the runaround, Parks was surprised when the doorman stepped back and allowed the two men entrance into the house. The main foyer was three stories high, with a chandelier in the center that cost more than both detectives made all year. A beautiful spiral staircase led up to the second floor and then split off as it continued on in two opposite directions toward the third. The front room to the house was warmly inviting, with a mixed tone of crème, light green and lavender colors, which helped give the house an open feel, accepting all who came through the front doors.

"This way," the doorman motioned, leading the two detectives down a long, narrow hallway toward what they smelled was the kitchen or dining area.

"Why, I do believe that Detectives Parks and Bennett will be joining us for a late lunch." Parks identified the voice as belonging to Christopher Stone but wondered how the student knew they were there with his back turned to them. Sitting at the head of a table that sat fourteen was Bill Norton. The man was dressed in a three-piece suit and complementing tie, which gave Parks the impression that he was simply home for lunch and might be heading off somewhere official on this Sunday afternoon.

Sitting to Bill's right was his wife, Katherine, who somehow connected the recently deceased professor and her husband, in a lopsided love-triangle that may have somehow included her best friend, Elizabeth Knott. Katherine sat statuesque in her high-backed, thousand dollar chair, a sterling silver knife and fork in each hand, mere inches above her plate, not moving as she waited to see what the detectives wanted from them.

Three seats down, on Bill's left, sat his stepson Christopher who turned his head and smiled at the two men as if he had been expecting them and was pleased with himself at what he had set up.

"Would either of you care for some sautéed Atlantic salmon?" Christopher asked.

"Christopher. Don't be rude," Katherine scolded with a raised eyebrow of intolerance as she set her silverware down and dabbed the side of her mouth with her cloth napkin. "You'll have to excuse my son."

"Actually, if you'll excuse us, ma'am," Parks replied with a smile. He wasn't about to be shown up by the trust-fund brat and was prepared to do what was needed to save face, staying on the family's good side. Though Christopher may have been a spoiled, rich kid he was still an only child and Parks had the feeling his mother was quite protective of him. "We're sorry to intrude on you at this time but we need to ask you a few questions concerning the death of Fredrick Knott."

"Fredrick Knott?" Bill Norton chimed in with concern in his voice. "But my wife hardly knew the man. What's this about? You already got my statement. And I thought the girl's boyfriend took the blame. Isn't the case closed?"

The two detectives stared at the couple and considered how to continue their line of questioning. They were already on thin ice with the school board and the governor as it was. Accusing the university president's wife of infidelity probably wouldn't help their cause much to say nothing of their futures in law enforcement. Parks noticed Christopher staring at them, intently wondering what their next step would be.

"Actually, sir, it's your wife's relationship with Knott's wife, Elizabeth, that we're here to talk to her about," Parks interjected, thinking of a way around the topic of cheating, at least in front of the husband. "Tying up a few loose ends is all, sir."

"Elizabeth?" Norton questioned with the tilt of his head.

"Yes, sir," Parks continued. "Mrs. Knott gave us a statement and now we'd like your wife's help in assessing their validity. We were given the impression from Mrs. Knott that your wife would be able to do that."

"But—"

"Of course I can help," Katherine replied, placing a hand on her husband to calm him from objecting to their requests. Parks figured she knew all too well why the two detectives were really there and had decided to help the drowning men before everything blew up in her face. Obviously there was some truth to the rumors of the affair and her husband was not aware of them. Or maybe that was an act as well. "Anything to help the police finish this dreadful business. We want nothing more than to help in any way possible."

"Oh, quite agreed," Bill Norton nodded, turning from his wife back to the detectives. "Anything you gentlemen need. The university is quite thankful for all you've done so far and have great trust that you will wrap this up quickly."

"I thank you, ma'am. Sir, we hope to do just that." Parks noticed Katherine give her son a knowing look as if she suspected he was the reason they had shown up on her doorstep at all.

"Well I'm sure I can find something to keep myself occupied with while you all conduct your business," Christopher smiled and turned to exit the dining room through a side door, pausing momentarily upon crossing paths with the two men.

"How about we take this out on the terrace?" Katherine asked, eyeing the detectives and nodding to her husband. "That way, dear, you can stay and finish your lunch."

"We promise not to take but a few minutes of your time," Parks said.

"Sure you don't want me to accompany you?" Bill Norton asked.

"I'm sure it's just a few simple, routine questions." Katherine leaned over and kissed her husband. "I'll be just fine. Gentlemen, this way."

Katherine led the two detectives through the room and down a hallway out a side door and onto a balcony-patio that overlooked the valley below.

"This is beautiful," Parks said, truly in awe of the view that lay out before him. On one side was the valley below, while on the other lay the beaches in the west.

"So what can I do for you gentlemen?" Katherine asked standing her ground.

Katherine Norton was a beautiful woman of natural gifts, not appearing to have had any cosmetic surgery done to alter her appearance in any way. Despite approaching fifty years of age she appeared almost a decade younger. Her hair was up, out of her face, and was of a beautiful caramel-color, accented with the occasional blonde highlight. She had warm yet piercing ocean-blue eyes that were emerald in the sunlight; a trait Parks noted she had passed onto her son. She wore a form-fitting, knee-length, grey Michael Kors skirt with a white, button-down, collared shirt tucked into her waist that felt as though it should have been on one of the coeds at her husband's university. The woman was not an unhealthy sort of thin but rather had a sturdy and balancing look as if she practiced yoga and other various daily rituals that helped keep her form so tight and attractive.

"We're actually here to talk to you about your relationship with Fredrick Knott. Not his wife," Parks admitted, checking to make sure they were in fact alone. "In particular, what exactly is your relationship with the deceased?"

"I love my husband," Katherine smiled, giving away a few lines around the mouth and eyes that only enhanced her beauty. "But he can be a jealous man when it comes to me. I have a feeling that if he found out that I had conducted a personal relationship with one of his professors before him…well, I just didn't want to be responsible for the man's termination due to something that happened so long ago. Fredrick Knott was a brilliant man and it would have been foolish for the university to lose him. After all, he was in high demand."

"Other schools were interested in Knott?"

"Yes," Katherine replied. "That's how he was able to get tenure so quickly."

"So it's the university you really care about?" Parks wasn't sure if that question sounded as snide as it did in his head and quickly followed it up with his true inquiry. "The relationship with Knott had ended?"

"What gave you the impression that it hadn't? I haven't had personal contact with Fredrick since I met my husband."

"Your fingerprints were found in Knott's office," Parks said cutting to the chase.

"Yes," Katherine was calm, not missing a beat. "I said I had no personal contact with Fredrick any more. Not no contact at all."

"When was the last time you saw Knott?" Parks asked.

"The night he was murdered," Katherine answered. "Bill and I were at the alumni fundraiser. So were Fredrick and Elizabeth. I helped Elizabeth organize the event. That's why my fingerprints were found in his office. I had visited him earlier this past week to confirm some details about a few of the scholarships we handed out that night. You can check with his secretary. I believe it was last Tuesday."

"So you were around the night Knott was murdered?"

"I was at the benefit, if that's what you mean. Was I out murdering him? No. I hardly had time to do so, gentlemen. I helped run the event. Free time was a luxury I didn't have that night. Ask anyone there. I could be accounted for every minute of the evening. Sorry."

"I wouldn't apologize for not murdering a man and having an alibi to prove it," Parks smiled for a second before controlling himself. He wasn't sure why but the woman made him feel comfortable and relaxed. "How would you describe the breakup of your relationship with Knott?"

"It was so long ago..." Katherine shrugged and stared off into space to think about the timeline which Parks had no doubts she had recently memorized to her liking. That was the problem with a one-sided alibi. Just like her son's, there was no way to prove or disprove so many aspects to her story when the only other person to counter-act the events was dead. "I suppose it was more or less mutual. I mean we were both adults and it was just sex. Then he met Elizabeth and I met Bill. Both around the same time. I guess it was just meant to be."

"No hard feelings? Anger? Jealousy?"

"Detective, we've managed to stay friends for the past five years. I think if there were any hard feelings, they were dealt with internally and then quickly forgotten. We're adults. Not the juveniles running rampant at my husband's school or on some prime-time soap."

"How long have you known Fredrick Knott?" Parks asked.

"Let's see...going on six years now," Katherine calculated. "Give or take."

"And how did you two meet?"

"Through the school," Katherine answered. "Seven years ago I moved Christopher and myself from the east coast out here to Los Angeles. We needed a break from the cold. We were checking out school options for Christopher for a few years down the line. While we were at the university, I was approached by Elizabeth to help with various charities and other social events that she had just recently become chair of. We hit it off and became friends. It was through the various contributions and fundraisers we worked that I met Fredrick. Nothing happened at first. Then a few weeks later we began seeing each other. It lasted for about six months."

"Then what happened?" Bennett asked.

"Well, we weren't exclusive," Katherine admitted. "I had heard about Fredrick's social behavior. I wasn't expecting a commitment from him. We were having fun. Grown-up fun. That's all. Then Bill came down from up north and took over as president and that was the beginning of us. And the end of me and Fredrick."

"So you left Knott?" Parks asked.

"I don't think there was exactly a conversation about us ending things. We simply stopped seeing each other."

"I see," Parks said. "Are you aware of Elizabeth's medical condition?"

"I assume you're referring to her cancer? I am."

"How long have you known?"

"Since she first found out. It's come and gone several times. The first time she found out, I helped her through it."

"Was this back when you and Knott were still together?"

"You could say so. It was around the time we stopped seeing each other. I guess that's part of why we stopped. My time became consumed with helping Elizabeth. Helping a friend face her mortality kind of puts a damper on petty things such as emotionless affairs."

"Emotionless?"

"We were both career-oriented adults, Detective. Neither one of us had time for a personal life. It was just sex. Good sex too. Nothing more for either one of us. So yes, I think it's safe to say it was emotionless. Though we didn't hate each other if that's what you're getting at. We just didn't love each other either."

"So you found out about Elizabeth's cancer before she and Knott got together?"

"Yes," Katherine agreed. "The first time she found out about it was before she had even met Fredrick. It didn't come back until two years later—after they were already married."

"And that's the last time?"

"Until now."

"So you and Knott haven't slept together after you had both married different people?" Bennett asked.

A look came over Katherine's face that would have put Medusa to shame. But she just as quickly composed herself. "No. I've never slept with anyone but my husband since I've been married to him. Unfortunately, I can't say the same for Fredrick."

"You were aware of his extra-curricular activities?"

"I had heard the rumors. But they weren't my affairs."

"Was his wife aware?"

Katherine paused for a moment, considering the answer. The sounds of birds could be heard off in the distance, though they were less of a soft, cooing pigeon or gull sound and had a harsher squawk like a parrot's. The wind picked up and began to blow some clouds in front of the sun, even if only for a few seconds.

"She knew," Katherine confirmed.

"How did she feel about this information?" Parks wondered, knowing that feelings didn't confirm anything officially.

"She was bothered at first," Katherine admitted. "But after a while..."

"Yes?"

"She never confirmed anything with me, but I had the feeling she was seeing someone herself."

Parks didn't know whether to be surprised by this information or if he had somehow been expecting it.

"You don't know who?"

"I don't even have proof that she ever did," Katherine said. "This is just my suspicion. After a while she stopped caring what Fredrick did or with whom. From what I could gather, she had someone on the side."

"Are you saying that the Knotts had an open marriage?"

Katherine shrugged. "You'd have to talk to Elizabeth about that one."

Parks knew that he would get no more on the subject from Katherine. They would need to speak to Elizabeth Knott again.

"Is there anything else, gentlemen?" Katherine asked.

"You've provided us with an easily provable alibi," Parks said warmly. "I think that will be all for now. Is it safe to assume that you won't be leaving town any time soon?"

"We have Fredrick's funeral Tuesday morning," Katherine said. "But no. I'm not planning on leaving the city."

"I thought the funeral was on Monday?"

"Monday's even a little quick for us, Detective. It will be Tuesday morning. Nine o'clock. You must have gotten your information wrong."

"Well, thank you for your time," Parks said, offering his hand to Katherine.

"Not at all," Katherine smiled once again. "Like I said: anything to help with the investigation."

Katherine led the two men back into the house and through several rooms, including the kitchen which was now empty, until they came to the main foyer.

"Again, thank you for your time, Mrs. Norton," Parks said.

"Any time," Katherine nodded.

"Actually, Mrs. Norton, there is one other thing," Bennett said, stopping Parks.

"Oh?"

"Is your son still around? We have a few questions for him as well."

"I would assume he's up in his room," Katherine said. "Unless he's left for somewhere."

Katherine instructed the two men on how to find her son's room before she left to continue on with her day. As Bennett stared up the somewhat intimidating staircase, Parks turned back to Katherine whom he noticed glancing back at him on her way into another room.

"What's this about?" Parks asked, following his partner up the stairs. "You realize you just gave away who tipped us off about Katherine?"

"Like she didn't already know!" Bennett said shrugging off his partner's comment. "Besides, his prints are in Knott's office. He knows more than he's letting on. I'd like to know what. How about you?"

The two men checked what they believed was Christopher's room and found it vacant.

"He's not around," Parks said stating the obvious. "Let's go. We'll question him later."

"Oka—wait," Bennett stopped and stared down the hallway. "This way."

Bennett headed further down the hallway into what they discovered was a game room. Inside the room were various forms of entertainment, including an air hockey table, a poker table and a pool table where Christopher played a one-man game. Christopher leaned over the table and knocked a solid into one of the corner pockets. His back was to the detectives but that didn't deter him from addressing the two men even though they had made no announcement or noise to indicate their presence.

"Gentlemen." Christopher stood up and smiled at the two men. "Either of you care to join? I do enjoy the game so much more when there's more than just me to play with."

"We just have a few questions for you," Bennett said nonchalantly. "Official business."

"Pity," Christopher said, focusing back on his game. "What's up?"

"Why did you feel the need to inform us of your mother's association with Knott?"

"I don't know what you're talking about? I simply told you guys that you were on the wrong track. That's all. The truth can only lead down one path. You'll find it eventually."

"You feel it's your job to help us when we're going in the wrong direction?"

"What? You mean like hot and cold? Sure. Why not? Someone has to bring justice to the tragedy that is collegiate life."

"You know what happened that night in Knott's office."

"Doesn't everybody by now?"

"Then why not just tell us what happened? Why all the games?"

"Oh, Detective," Christopher worked his way around the pool table, sliding in between the two men and the table. "I assure you, this isn't a game."

"You know we could get a warrant," Bennett replied.

"And do what with it? Stick it up your ass? You both know that a warrant wouldn't be worth much more than toilet paper at this junction. You can't prove anything. Besides, I didn't kill Knott or Kelli. So you have nothing."

"What business did you have for being in his office?"

"Was I?" Christopher asked innocently enough.

"Your prints are in his office," Bennett continued, ignoring Christopher's smugness. "They shouldn't be. He wasn't your professor, nor was he your counselor. And you didn't see him as a therapist. So, what gives?"

"You're right," Christopher laughed. "Because if the stepson of the university's president was seeing a shrink that would be posted all over Facebook, right?"

"You don't have a file in with the rest of his patients," Parks retorted.

"I should hope not," Christopher shot back. "I mean, besides the fact that my mother used to fu—I mean sleep with him, and that he is—I mean *was*—a close family friend, we at least should be able to throw enough money at him to keep things hush-hush."

"So you were a patient?" Parks asked.

"Not by choice, I can assure you that. But every Wednesday from noon to one," Christopher smiled. "Of course you don't have to take my word for it. You did think to question his secretary, right? After all, she did see me come every week even if there is no record of me seeing him."

"But how do we know it's legit?" Bennett asked. "How do we know you haven't paid her off to say you were there every week?"

"Oh, I like your way of thinking," Christopher beamed, slightly impressed. "True though. Guess you'd have to question her and find out."

"So did you and Knott talk about his relationship with your mother? Is that how you found out about it?"

"Believe it or not, Detectives, as narcissistic as it sounds, we were really there to talk about me," admitted Christopher. "They were my sessions."

"Unless your mother sleeping with Knott was an issue for you."

"Like I care who my mother sleeps with. More of a conflict of interest than an issue. But no—Knott never spoke of my mother. And I never told him I knew about their relationship."

"Anything else you feel you need to inform us of about this time?" Parks asked.

"Nothing comes to mind," Christopher said with a roll of his shoulders and a smug smile. "But if something comes up I know how to get a hold of—oh, there was one other thing."

"What would that be?"

"You're all so concerned with who he slept with as the motivation behind his murder...how do you know he was even the target? But if he was, then why does it have to be about that? You know about the book, right?"

"What book?"

"Knott was shopping around a book."

"I recall it being mentioned," Parks admitted.

"Have you found it? On his computer? In his files? His notes or anything of that sort?"

Parks looked to Bennett who shook his head. Christopher didn't wait for the men to verbally answer. The looks on their faces was enough to know they hadn't.

"I don't know what the book was about, or who's in it. I only know that he was getting a shitload of money for it. Money being the trail I originally told you gentlemen to follow. There was even a bidding war for the publishing rights. Apparently it's controversial. Quite embarrassing for the people involved in it."

"Is it about his patients? That's illegal you know?"

"I don't know what it was about," Christopher repeated again. "He never mentioned it to me. Though I did try to find out a few times. I just know it was damaging to some people who would rather it never saw the light of day. I'm just thinking that if you can't find any evidence of it around in his office or whatnot then maybe...?"

"You think the motivation for his murder was to cover up a potentially damaging manuscript that may or may not exist?"

"Just asking if you found it was all. Like I said, I don't know what was in it or who it was about," Christopher said. "But I'm sure if you found out...it might help. I can't do all the work for you gentlemen."

"We'll look into it," Parks said.

"Anything I can do to help," Christopher replied as the two men started out of the room. "Oh, Detective Parks...how's Jennifer?"

Parks stopped and turned back to Christopher, wondering what game he was playing this time.

"Who's Jennifer?" Bennett asked.

"Your partner's wife," Christopher answered without turning around, hitting the second to last ball into a hole.

"He isn't married," Bennett corrected.

Parks remained quiet and stared at the student.

"Isn't he?" Christopher asked with the tilt of his head, confused and trying to show it. "I'm sorry. My mistake. Must have gotten...I just must be mixed up. I thought you mentioned—Sorry. No matter. You gentlemen have a good day."

SIXTEEN

Parks dropped Bennett back off at the university and then called into his team to have them start rechecking Fredrick Knott's personal files, phone numbers, DMV and bank records all over again. Anything they could do to try and find out about this mysterious unpublished manuscript. He made a mental note that when they went to Elizabeth Knott's house to check for proof of the manuscript and ask about any bank deposit boxes he or she might have. Rachel informed him that Tanaka wanted to see him at the morgue as soon as possible and he said he would stop by on his way to LAX for his flight up north. Hopefully he'd get some sleep on the way to San Francisco, even if it was only a one hour flight. Both the pressure of the case and waiting to hear the future of his team had left him with insomnia. He considered taking a few more Vicodin for the thrashing he received from Nicholas Martin and decided on waiting until he got to the airport to relieve the pain.

Parks arrived at the morgue an hour later to find Amy Tanaka standing in her scrubs with three dead bodies displayed across three separate tables. They were there to discuss Professor Fredrick Knott, Kelli Davis and Nicholas Martin, each one laid out, all having been cut up, dissected and studied.

"Heard you wanted to see me," Parks said, announcing his presence to the technician. "And before you ask, no, I haven't heard anything new." Parks referred to the disbursement of his team. "But I'll let you know as soon as I do."

"I still have to finish typing up my report, but I figured you might want the verbal sum-up a little quicker," Tanaka replied without looking up from the body she was dissecting. "And you better or I'm going to hunt you down."

Parks stood patiently until Amy removed the oversized, plastic glasses from her face.

"How's the case coming along?" she asked, studying one of the many charts that lined her desk, and made a few quick notes. She hoped to put him at ease. Ever since the end of his last relationship with Jackie Isley, whose office was located in the LA county coroner's office as well, he had been slightly off every time he had to visit her, often preferring phone calls. But it was Sunday and so he figured Jackie had the day off. It was also part of the reason why Amy had agreed to work on her day off. That and the mayor's insistence that she get her portion of the case finished with as quickly as possible.

"If it's possible, I think there are even more suspects and three times as many reasons to have wanted Knott dead," Parks commented, exhaling deeply. "Hopefully you have something that can help us whittle that number down."

"Maybe," Tanaka said with a brightness coming to her face. "Maybe you guys are looking at the wrong person as the target."

"What do you mean?" Parks picked up a pair of latex gloves and put them on.

"You're assuming that Knott was the intended victim and that

Kelli Davis simply got in the way."

"We are. Though we haven't ruled out the possibility that Kelli may have been the intended victim. Until we know who did this and why, we're not ruling anything out. Why? What did you find?"

"You're trying to find connections between the victims through their lives," Tanaka began. "But I only have their bodies to help me make a connection. What's your current theory?"

"The logical story is Nicholas Martin caught Kelli Davis with Fredrick Knott and killed them both and then killed himself the next day out of guilt," Parks grimaced.

"But you don't really believe that."

"No. The evidence suggests that Nicholas knew about Kelli's affairs for some time. So why suddenly turn to rage and kill them? I don't buy it. I think there's a connection here. And I don't mean that Kelli was sleeping with both men."

Amy Tanaka nodded silently as she took this in.

"What did you find?" Parks was excited to know what she knew.

"We found trace amounts of cocaine both in Knott's nostril cavities and in his mouth." Tanaka started pointing to the bodies to further explain her discoveries. "We also found some in Kelli's nostril cavities and in her mouth between her gums and her lips."

"They were both high," Parks said. "So what? We figured they were."

Tanaka went to Kelli's body and turned her arms over. "What do you see?"

Parks noticed a network of needle marks on both of Kelli Davis's arms, leaving behind a large yellow-and-purplish hemorrhage under the skin.

"We didn't notice it at first because she was wearing body paint,"

Tanaka explained.

"Body paint?"

"It's like make-up, but thicker. They use it in the movies to cover up tattoos on actors. Plus, most of these wounds are old. Only this one"—She held up Kelli's left arm—"is new. She may have been a user but she had stopped. This is the only recent puncture wound. Rest of these have all scabbed over and begun to heal."

"Heroin?" Parks asked knowing he didn't really need to. Amy nodded. "So she was using. Stopped. Then started up again."

"And don't forget Nick Martin." Tanaka turned to Nick's body to show track-free arms. "Remember our fella here was a sports player. Would have been noticeable if he had track marks on his arms."

Tanaka spread Nick's legs apart and pulled back the skin on the inside of his thighs. There weren't many, but it appeared to Parks that Nicholas Martin was also a frequent user of needles. There were several yellow and purple hemorrhages under the skin on his upper thighs close to his groin area.

"He was using." Tanaka released the student's leg. "And he had an infection at one time. Recently. I did a tox screen on his blood. I bet we'll find traces of antibiotics, but I won't know for another couple of days until I get the reports back."

"What about Knott?" Parks asked.

"I went over his entire body twice and didn't find a single mark," Tanaka said shaking her head. "He wasn't using."

"But both Nick and Kelli were," Parks said, pleased with the discovery. "And they had to get it from somewhere. Assuming they got it from Knott, how do we prove it?" Parks asked no one in particular. "And if so? Where did he get it from?"

SEVENTEEN

As soon as the plane left the airstrip Parks could have sworn they were already landing. He walked off the plane without anything more than his briefcase containing the documents, files and other forms of paperwork he was expected to use to get him in to interview Lewis Hayward. He obtained a car from the rental agency at the airport and began his drive to San Quentin State Prison. Less than an hour later he arrived, showing the proper credentials before being scanned and checked by a metal detector. Parks was shown to a cold, brick-walled room. A no-contact room. He was told to take a seat and wait. He sat on a steel bench that was attached to the ground and stared through the several-inch Plexiglas wall with small holes that they would speak through.

As he waited, Parks gathered his thoughts and prepared for the questions he would ask. He had them typed up on a sheet, prepared by Moore and checked by Hardwick. He wasn't expecting a response to any of them and tried to calculate for several possible scenarios that might unfold as soon as the serial poisoner was brought in. It had been seven months since the man went on a rampage and poisoned nine people and took the lives of another three, including his own daughter, which set off the whole line of killings in the first place. Lewis Hayward had been calculating, exacting, patient, resourceful and determined. That he had been a Los Angeles detective, and before that a member of both the New York and Philadelphia police departments, kept him close to the investigation, though from what research Parks had been able to determine, the man rarely guided the investigation away from discovering who he was. This concerned Parks, as he hadn't been able to determine the reasoning behind this behavior. Added with it, the fact that Hayward chose to forgo a highly public trial and pleaded guilty for a life sentence also bothered Parks. He wasn't sure why. The man was locked up and never getting out of prison for as long as he lived. But there was still something about it all that threw him off.

The sound of metal scraping, handles being turned and doors opening and closing brought Parks back to the task at hand. Lewis Hayward was brought into the room, guided by two correctional officers, one on each side. He sat down, dressed in his state supplied orange jumpsuit with CDOC stenciled across the front and back, hands still handcuffed. The man was different from what Parks had remembered. Having spent six months in the state prison system had already gotten to him—aged him, though not beaten him. He looked his age, though only in his late forties, the lines around his eyes were more pronounced, his hair finally starting to recede. His eyes were just as wild, sharp and attentive, proving that no matter the situation, he was a survivor and refused to be beat. After all, what did he have to feel bad about? As far as he was concerned he had won. He had set out to accomplish what he wanted: retribution for his daughter's death. The fact that Hayward had directly caused his daughter's death completely escaped his mental facilities, which was partially why Parks had trouble buying the "reasoning" behind the murders.

Both men sat for a moment, taking one another in, enjoying the silence.

"Dave," Lewis Hayward finally said, his voice cutting through the air, his voice had hardened with his time inside.

"Lewis." Parks opened the file before him and began shuffling papers around. "Do you know why I'm here today?"

"I'm assuming it's not to give decorating tips," Hayward smirked as he glanced around the drab room. "Even though you must spend the majority of your time in rooms with wallpaper that consists of portraits of the dead, I'm sure even a single bachelor, like you, could give a few helpful and much needed improvements. Even to a place such as this."

"Do you know why I'm here today?" Parks repeated, ignoring the one-on-one small talk.

"How is the team doing?"

"There's been a death at a local university," Parks continued but then stopped.

Hayward smiled and held up his shackled hands to show Parks that he hadn't committed the crime.

"Are Rachel Moore and Jake Fairmont still sneaking around behind the department's back?" Hayward grinned.

"I'm not here to discuss the personal lives of the members of my team."

"That's a yes," Hayward smiled. "Though from what I hear, your team's working on borrowed time right now, aren't they?"

This paused Parks for a moment. The fact that Hayward knew his team was close to disbanding meant he was up to date on his current events. This unsettled him. This wasn't knowledge that came from the papers or the internet news sites. This was departmental information. Even locked up, in prison, Lewis Hayward still had connections.

"So now you know what it is I am aware of. And you, being the intelligent, thought-provoking man I know you to be, already have the wheels in your brain turning. Don't worry about it. Who's feeding me what information and for what reasons isn't of your concern at this moment. You're here about the death of Professor Knott. That's more pressing, is it not? On your 'borrowed time,' so to speak?"

"How did you—what do you know of the murder of Fredrick Knott?" Parks continued. He could keep playing Hayward's games or stay on track. This was going to be a slippery slope as it was.

"You know I didn't kill him," Hayward smiled, lifting his hands once again. "But you're wondering if I might have had him killed, especially since he had direct contact with my daughter back when she attended that prestigious university." Parks shifted in his seat but remained quiet. "But then you start thinking, why wouldn't I have killed the man back when I had the chance? Which, I obviously had. If Knott was so integral to the downfall of my daughter, then why didn't I take it out on him when I had the chance? Wouldn't I want the pleasure of that man's death on my own hands? So then you think, no. No, I didn't have the man killed and you realize the reasons for why I didn't kill him are still my own. And that Knott's death must, in the end, be coincidental." Hayward smiled and took a breath. "But you're a detective. You don't believe in coincidences. So, is it? Or was this planned? To happen just like this. To drive you...just a little bit mad. You know I do believe we all go a little mad sometimes. I think I heard that in a movie once."

"I'm not the light to your darkness," Parks replied quietly.

"You think because I'm locked up in here that I'm limited from the outside world? Of course I'm not. And you know this. So it will make you wonder. You can't help it. And nothing I can say will placate your thoughts of me or my actions or intentions. That's what you really want to know, isn't it? Why? You think the reasons behind my actions are so mundane. But of course you're not a father, so how could you?"

Parks tensed up for a second, not enough for anyone watching the two men to have noticed, but Hayward was not some casual observer. He sensed things. Knew things. Knew which buttons to push. And just how hard. He smiled ever so comfortably.

"I'll tell you three things right now. Three things and then we're finished," Hayward said, resetting himself in his seat, the adrenaline beginning to pump through him. "Number one: everything I've said to you today, so far, and up until the moment you leave has been and will be the truth. I do not lie. Not to you, dear David. I like you too much for that. And I feel the truth will conflict you far more than lies. That brain of yours. It's a puzzle, wrapped in an enigma. You and your afflictions. Notice I said afflictions and not addictions. You don't yet fully realize the extent of your addictive personality. Your drive for a solution to a question. A problem. A mystery. A murder. You don't realize this quite yet, but one day...I feel you just might. No, you think you are defined by your afflictions and therefore limited by them, not knowing that they may be your greatest asset. Your greatest tool for survival. Both in this world you navigate through and the one you were thrust upon as a child. Our parents, whom we do not chose, and the environment in which we are raised in have so much to contribute to the manifestations of who we will become as adults. This manifest rot as I call it. We cannot choose. It is all chosen for us. We simply adapt and learn to survive. You did not choose your parents, dear Parks, they were chosen for you and so you cannot accept guilt for the events that followed your being brought to them in this world we exist in."

"I think we're off track," Parks interrupted. He couldn't tell what was nonsensical ramble and what had true merit. Or what was intended to sound as nonsensical ramble.

"Your parents have more guilt associated with who you are as a man today than you realize. From your addictive personality—of which I'm not even sure you're aware of just how much plays into your psyche—to the puzzles and games you obsess over. The way your brain *works*. Your astute observational powers. To the little ticks and habits you've yet to figure out how to bend to your command. To your eating habits. Everything in life begins with the beginning of life. You included."

"Now if we can—"

"I have never lied to you!" Hayward said with force as he stood up and leaned in against the glass. His face turned red and the veins in his neck were pulsating. The guard in the room stepped for him but stopped as Hayward lowered himself back to his seat.

"I have never lied to you," Hayward said with a whisper. "I respect you too much for that. You were able to stop me. You figured things out. I respect that. You keep me honest. I need to be better. And I will be. For next time. You'll make sure of that. I know it."

Parks sat quietly, taking in everything Hayward said. It, in fact, was not him who had figured out the Palisades Poisoner's true identity and was once again struck by the knowledge that he was receiving accolades he did not feel he had warranted.

"Two: I am but a minor pebble in a larger quarry. A single drop in an ocean of ideas. A simple corner piece in one of your thousand-plus piece puzzles. I was not the beginning nor am I the end. Simply a never ending Ouroboros. Others will continue where I have failed. I am but a humble servant. Protected by Mehen, I will travel to my ends safely. But to what ideals? For what purpose? All in good time."

Parks rolled his eyes, feeling weary of the gibberish exiting Hayward's mouth. Some of the words sounded familiar, as if he had heard or read of them a long time before. Like from his college days when semesters of philosophy and history were shoved down his throat. But he wasn't sure how Hayward would know of them. He wasn't a college educated man. There was no proof he had ever attended any schooling beyond high school. So far as they knew from what investigations into the man's history they had conducted. He was a lifelong man of the law. A detective by trade. Or had that all been lies as well? What did they truly know about Louis Hayward? Everything they had discovered had been via online documents and Hayward had already proven himself more than adapt at online manipulation. Everyone who knew him before his arrival in Los Angeles, his wife and daughter, were now dead. They had confirmed his employment before arriving at the LAPD but that had all been done online and over the phones. Who had he really talked to face to face? What did they really know about this man? Obviously he had more work to do.

"Three. And finally: I did not kill Professor Fredrick Knott. Nor did I have him killed. His death simply is a coincidence. Hard as that will be for you to believe, it is the truth. Because remember, I have not lied to you once today. But I do believe that whoever killed Knott did so for reasons other than why you think he was killed. Misdirection is a powerful tool in the wrong hands. Or is it the right hands? I wonder…"

"What the hell does that mean?" Parks asked completely lost.

"That is all," Hayward smiled and turned his head. "Guard. I'm finished here."

"What the hell does that mean?"

"You'll figure it out," Hayward said genuinely in awe as he walked to the door. "You always do. Oh, one other thing." Hayward stopped the guard as he was almost out of the room. "Have you ever been to Seattle? It truly is beautiful there this time of year. All that rain. I suggest you visit. Though maybe not with a loved one. I hear it can be tragic for couples. It truly is a great city. Much to take in. So much more than you ever would at Meredith Langer's down south. Trust me. Until next time, and there will be a next time, trust me on that. And perhaps sooner than you think. Have a good day, Detective Parks."

And with those words Louis Hayward left the room and a baffled Parks to try and understand everything that had just been said.

EIGHTEEN

His interview being shorter than he expected, Parks made it back to the San Francisco airport and stared up at the departure board as he tried to figure out his next step. His scheduled flight wasn't until eight that evening and he didn't feel like sitting around for three hours doing nothing. That was when he realized he had other business to attend to.

He found a flight to Santa Barbara on a smaller airline and paid for that himself so as not to leave a trail of paperwork for the department to shuffle through. Less than two hours later he was up in the air again, trying desperately to catch a few moments of sleep, before he was being shaken awake by the flight attendant. He then obtained his second rental vehicle for the day and headed to his new destination.

It had been a few years since he had last visited the seaside town and a decade since he had last visited her, but he was fairly confident that he knew where to go. As it was, he had to pull some records to make sure she still lived at the same address. According to their database, she did.

Parks drove down a road with the beach on his side and watched as the night surf pulled in and gave the surfers something to play on. Despite having been born in Los Angeles and raised in Newport Beach, surfing was one of the few forms of local recreational activity that Parks had never fully participated in. He wasn't sure why; it just wasn't something that had ever interested him, even though most of his friends in high school had enjoyed the ocean waves. Though in general he didn't mind the ocean, there was still something about the water that haunted him, always keeping him further inland and away from the coast as if it was the end of the world and the ocean waters were just waiting to consume everything it touched. Parks continued driving until he found the right street and pulled away from the beach, turning down a few more streets until he found the quaint, two-story house.

What was he doing?

This probably wasn't a good idea. But he had to know. Something was up and he needed to know what. Though he barely knew Christopher Stone, he had come to the conclusion that the young man never did anything by accident and he sure as hell didn't get his information wrong. At least not so far as Parks had been able to see. There was a reason Christopher had mentioned his ex-wife, and he had to find out why. Though it wasn't a secret that he had been married at one time, the identity of his ex-wife was harder to discover, unless one was purposely hunting down the information.

Parks sat in the car, recalling past memories—both the good and the bad. The marriage had lasted less than nine months, though they had known each other since the fifth grade. They had loved each other deeply through the eight years they had been together, but the marriage had been one of convenience, which had turned bitter, and eventually spiteful. Though neither was fully to blame for the dissolution of the marriage, both had participated and were equal participants until all they could do was point fingers to leave nothing behind but hatred.

That's not true. It wasn't his fault. He had tried to help. Ever since the attack...he tried to help her through what had happened. But there were some things he just couldn't do. No matter how much she had begged...he tried his best. That was why he became a cop in the first place. To help her. To show her he still loved her.

Parks shook off the thoughts of the past and finally gathered enough courage to approach the front door. He knocked three times and then backed up a step so as not to be right in his ex's face. He knew it was going to be enough of a shock to see him without totally invading all of her personal space. He waited, fidgeting with his tie and straightening out the front of his jacket as if his appearance would make all the difference in his ex-wife's acceptance of him showing up unannounced on her doorstep after all this time.

After all that had been said—and done—between them, it didn't matter how much time had passed. This would be difficult.

He was about to give up when he heard someone fumble with the lock. The door opened and his ex-wife stood, emotionless, simply staring at him. Despite having been with her for eight years, a decade had passed since he had last seen her and he realized that he no longer knew how to read her like he once did.

She was pretty, in a conventional sort of way. Though now in her late-thirties and showing all the right signs without the cosmetic benefits of LA's top surgeons, she still had the looks that had made her attractive to men. Her hair was straighter and longer than she used to keep it, coming just below her shoulders, with just the faintest hint of grey mixing with the natural sunny color. The crow's feet around her eyes were more pronounced than before, but that didn't take away from the brilliant amber-color that still managed to suck him in without any hesitation.

Jennifer Malone bit her lower lip, not sure if she should smile at the sight of him or be furious and so she constricted herself from both emotions until she found out what he wanted.

"Dave." Jennifer's eyes widened but then resumed to their natural size as she continued to wait, also trying to read a man whom she no longer understood.

"Jenn," Parks replied. "Been a while."

"It's Jennifer." Jennifer threw on a fake smile and then changed her mind, the lines around her mouth not able to disappear as quickly as her action. "I'm sorry. Yes. I know. It has been a while."

"How's um..."

"Richard?"

"Yes. Richard."

"Good."

"He around?" Though he had not named Jennifer's current husband, both knew who he was referring to. Nothing like the new husband to make meeting the ex-wife even more difficult.

"He's picking up dinner. He'll be back any minute."

"Yeah...uh..."

"Dave, what are you doing here?"

Parks wasn't sure how to pursue this discussion with a woman he used to share each and every day of his life with. They had loved each other. Still did in their own way. They had a bond that few couples ever got to form. One that would never allow them to truly separate and be hundred per cent out of each other's lives. Even if they didn't see each other every day, they still thought about one another. Sometimes life left scars like that. Not just the physical kind—but the emotional, life-altering kind that were even more painful. Even after all this time, she still could leave him speechless.

"So um...how's your new job?" Jennifer asked, not able to stand the silence any more.

"I'm still with the L.A.P.D. Haven't left."

"Oh?"

"Yes. Why...? Why did you think I had—?"

"Someone called recently asking up on you. Said it was a background check for a new job. Something university security. Not sure. I wasn't sure why you would take that job though. It seemed below you."

"I never took a new job. I was never up for a new job. That's why I'm here actually. Do you remember who called you?"

"No...I, uh..."

"Someone's been digging around in my life. My past. Our past. Someone who should have no knowledge about you does. And I'm not sure how or why. What did you tell them?"

"No knowledge of me? What's wrong? Disappointed I couldn't be buried as deep as you would have liked?"

"That's not what I mean, Jenn, and you know it. It's for your own protection."

Jennifer looked down the hall behind her, as if remembering something she left in the middle of, but ignored it and turned back to Parks.

"I didn't tell them anything. It was just casual. Nothing serious. I told them I haven't seen you in a decade. What could I tell them? I guess I knew something was off with the questions. Maybe that's why I didn't say anything."

"Did he sound young?"

"Who?"

"The person who called asking about me? You said it was a guy. Did he sound young? In his twenties?"

"I don't know. No. No, he was older. He had that gruff sound to his voice. Like, older, I'd say. But I never met him. We just talked on the phone so I can't be sure. It all happened so quickly."

"Did he leave a contact number?"

"No. What's going on, Dave? Who was that? What do they want?"

"I don't know," Parks said shaking his head. "I don't know why they'd be calling you. You sure you didn't tell them anything?"

"What would I have told him, Dave?"

"I don't—"

"Are you in some sort of trouble?"

"What? No. This just has to do with a case I'm working on. I'm rattling some people and they don't like it. I think this is their way of fighting back."

"Rattling? Haven't changed much in ten years, now have you?"

"Just if anyone else calls back, will you let me know about it?" Parks handed over one of his cards. That was the whole reason behind the trip in the first place, besides wanting to see Jennifer face to face after all this time. He didn't have any way of contacting her. Not that he would ask for her number now. He'd leave it in her hands to communicate again if they needed.

Jennifer nodded. "What should I tell him if he calls back?"

"Nothing. Tell him nothing. Or anyone else. Like you said. We haven't seen each other in a decade. What could you tell them?"

Jennifer threw on her fake smile again and tapped his card against the door she was leaning against. She began to look over her shoulder again, letting him know she had a life to get back to. A life that didn't involve him.

"There's just one thing…and I hate to ask. I know I don't need to. But I have to be sure. To make sure something didn't slip."

"Dave, don't…"

"You didn't say anything—about…you know…"

The pain—the hurt—immediately flashed across Jennifer's face, tears welling up in the corners of her eyes, and he regretted the question as the words shamelessly escaped his mouth. He knew better than to ask. Why did he have to do it? Why did he have to rip open that wound just like he always did? Why did he even have to make this trip? He knew better. He was being selfish. This wasn't accomplishing anything but harm.

"What? The attack? Or the baby? Or the body? Or what I asked you to do that you wouldn't do?"

"What you asked me to do; that you knew I couldn't," Parks snapped back with just as much force as she had delivered. "What you did that put your life in danger? That thing?"

She was hurt and she would want nothing more than to hurt him the same way. But she wouldn't be dragged down to his level. She still felt she was in the right. No matter what side of the law he worked on. She would end this before it turned ugly.

Uglier.

"So I guess there's nothing to say about that, now is there?"

And with those words, Jennifer shut the door in Dave Parks's face, locking out both him and the haunting past they would always share together.

NINETEEN

Parks and his team spent all of Monday going through files and calling phone numbers, trying to get a sensible handle on Fredrick Knott. It wasn't the glamorous fast-paced life that was often portrayed in the movies, and even though they worked in Hollywood, this was reality. They went over the statements of each person who was at the alumni gala, trying their best to recreate the last few hours leading up to the deaths of Fredrick Knott and Kelli Davis. Most people only wanted to help, some more than they should have, and therefore most statements were not all that truthful, and several of them only contradicted each other. Too many people had each seen Fredrick Knott or Kelli Davis in too many different places that would have been physically impossible. Unless the two had learned how to teleport from place to place.

The night before, Parks had made it home close to midnight, followed by a night of uneasy sleep thanks to the visit with his wife. Too many dreams of the past. He just knew his case would be the death of him. He needed a solid night of sleep and had yet to get that, even though this case was only going on its third full day. Maybe, depending on how today went, he'd end the day early, send everyone home and take several Tylenol PMs himself and knock out before the sun went down. Maybe. And maybe pigs would actually fly.

"What about Ryan Lockhart? Who's working on him?"

"I got it covered," Fairmont answered. "I've got several calls into employers, co-workers, neighbors. The works. Going to talk with his family in Laguna Beach later on."

"Good."

"Where are you going?" Moore asked as Parks stood up and put on his jacket.

"Need to check something out back at the school. I want to take a look around. Plus, I want to see the crime scene again. Something's off. Not sure what though."

"Need help?"

Parks mulled the offer over. "Naw, don't worry about it. I'll be on the university grounds so I'll need my usual babysitter. Besides, it's probably a waste of time. You help out Jake. I'll be back."

*   *   *

Parks arrived at the school an hour later to find the front entrance covered with students, each shouting and yelling, holding signs, looks of anger on their faces. Before security waved him on to the faculty parking lot, Parks was informed that Bennett was out on patrol but would meet him in a few minutes.

"What the hell is going on?" Parks asked when Bennett finally arrived.

"Student protests," Bennett huffed. "Half the student body is pissed that we're memorializing Knott when they think we should be celebrating his death. The other half is pissed at that half for de-monizing him. And...well, I know my math is off, but I think half of both sides are just out there to be out there and say they were part of history. This school is being torn apart."

Someone whistled at the two men from behind and they turned to see Christopher Stone circling the lot.

"What are you doing here?" Bennett asked without hesitation.

"I do go here, you know? But actually I was dropping some paperwork off for my stepfather that my mother wanted signed. I might ask what you two are doing here. It's almost beginning to feel as though you're stalking me." Christopher smiled, revealing a row of perfectly straightened and bleached teeth.

The best money can buy, thought Parks. He continued to stare at the student and realized that there wasn't much with him that wasn't perfect—physically at least. His skin was flawless, without a single blemish or patch of acne (current or former) to prove that he had at one time been a teenager plagued with the regular assortment of troubles. His ears were the perfect shape for his head, of equal size and standing just right on both sides of his head. The more Parks studied the student, the more he realized it was as if Christopher had been manufactured out of a test tube—the perfect specimen—made for manipulation and misdirection. Enticement. Seduction. He wondered if there was a person Christopher had met that he hadn't been able to control in one way or another.

"You know more than you should," Bennett accused the student.

Christopher stopped smiling but didn't move his eyes from Bennett, making the detective uncomfortable.

"So you think that even though I didn't do it, I know who did and so—what? I'll just lead you to them? Hand them over on a platter? Or walk up to them and yell out at you guys, this is your killer!"

"How can we trust what you say you know?"

"My birth father died when I was only five," Christopher said sounding serious. "Since then I've gone through several stepfathers.

I'm sure you know this by now."

Neither detective said anything, letting him know that they did.

"My mother moves around. I've grown up not staying in the same place much longer than a few years. Besides that, she's got money. A lot of it. That draws in a questionable crowd. Believe it or not, I'm not some spoiled brat who likes to flaunt his money and just throw it around. I think I'm quite grounded. All things considering. But I'm also a survivor. More than you know. I've had to be. Given my...surroundings. I think that's the most basic human instinct. Survival. Self-preservation is a major motivator. My mother is an intelligent woman but she's not the smartest person out there. She lets people in. Sometimes the wrong people. But again, she has to. Can't make an omelet without breaking a few eggs. So to speak. I've had to watch out for myself more than I think she has."

"I see."

"Do you? I don't easily trust people. When your mother has millions most people don't sincerely care for your well-being. They only care to get through you to what they ultimately want. Money. Truth is I could care less about it, probably because I've had it all my whole life. But still, you wouldn't believe the people I've met and the ways they've tried to screw me over just to get a few lousy dollars."

"You think millions of dollars is just a few lousy bucks?" Bennett asked.

"I do believe in giving credit where credit is due. And if there's one thing my mother knows how to do, that's to get money. And keep a hold of it. You think she's going to let a few million out of her hands just because someone thinks they deserve it? Good luck. You'd be lucky to get away with a ten spot if she didn't want you to have it. She's that good. My mother has been making me see shrinks more or less my whole life. She feels that without a permanent father figure and with all the money in the world at my disposal I need to keep grounded and not get ruined. That's the pot calling the kettle black. But Knott wasn't the first shrink I've seen. Won't be the last either. Probably. But after you've been to a dozen or so of them you get to see who the legit ones are and who's full of shit. Knott was good. An asshole, sure—but still good. But I've still learned how they think, and it's not too hard to get information out of them if you ask the right questions."

"So Knott just told you about everything?"

"No. Like I said: I don't trust people I don't know. Usually when someone new is introduced into my life I do research. Not that difficult. Especially when you have the money to spend. I did my research on Knott. That's all. Then I made sure to ask the right questions once the sessions began and I filled in the blanks with what I couldn't find out. You guys are detectives. That's what you're supposed to do. The research. The detective work. I just did some of it for you." Christopher changed gears, letting them know he was finished with the conversation. "You boys aren't going to learn anything from me that I don't want you to know. Until next time, Detectives. Have a good day."

Bennett stared out after Christopher when Parks started a timer on his watch and began across the lawn. The two then made their way to Asmodeus Hall and rode up the slow elevator after they were permitted entrance to the building by the security officer posted at the front doors twenty-four seven. Parks figured that not only the student population but the faculty as well were all on edge after the murders.

"It's been seven minutes," said Bennett as they got off the elevator on Knott's floor and started down the hallway.

"Yep."

"Seven minutes from the Union to Asmodeus Hall and up this slow-ass elevator and down here to his office," Bennett said in greater detail though Parks knew exactly what he was saying. "And we were moving quickly. Of course there's also the stairwells. What if our killer took those?"

"Then we can take off, what? A minute or two? Tops. So five to seven minutes to get over here. Say five for the murders. Then five to seven to get back?" Parks wasn't buying the timeline. "And what about the blood?"

"What about it?"

"There was blood all over that room," Parks explained. "There's no way whoever did this got out of there without getting covered in blood. So they either had to come prepared and dressed for the occasion or, if they came from or were going back to the party, had to change their clothes."

"Assuming the killer came from the gala," Bennett said. "Or that he or she went back to it."

"That's twenty almost...thirty minutes someone would have to be gone from that event, if they—"

"What's wrong?" Bennett asked when he noticed Parks stop. "What is it?"

"Someone's been inside?" Parks pointed to the office door where the yellow caution tape had been severed. "But who would have—?"

Parks stopped talking when he heard a noise from inside Fredrick Knott's office. Both men instinctively drew their guns. Parks nodded to Bennett who reached for the door handle and threw the door open.

"LAPD! Hold it right there!" Parks ordered as he lowered his gun while his partner kept watch over the situation.

The person in the room was crouched at Professor Knott's desk, his back to the detectives. The intruder flinched at Parks's command but did not move.

"Stand up," Parks ordered. "Slowly."

Parks made his way to the desk as the intruder stood up while Bennett flipped on the light switch next to the door. Parks came face to face with a student no more than twenty-one, maybe twenty-two years old, with curly dark hair and a fair complexion that was enhanced by his somewhat rosy cheeks.

"Who are you?" Parks asked, putting his gun away.

The student looked to the ground, hands shaking and eyes bugging, not sure how to pursue his next action.

"Look, kid," Parks sighed. "What are you doing in here? This is a closed crime scene. Now are you going to tell us what we want to know or am I going to have to book you?"

"Bobby Avalos," the student finally said giving in.

"Okay, Bobby," Parks continued. "Mind telling me what you're doing in here?"

Bobby looked to the ground again as his face flushed.

"Hey, Bobby," Parks said. "You know Knott was murdered, right?" Bobby nodded. "And you know there's an ongoing investigation into his murder, right?" The student nodded again. "So, how smart do you think it looks that we found you breaking into his office? You might want to try and start telling us what's going on here or it's not going to look so good for you."

"I was trying to get..." Bobby broke off as he turned from the detectives.

"What? A term paper? Some notes?"

Bobby was quiet.

"A letter perhaps?"

Bobby looked up, concerned.

"What's wrong, Bobby? Wrote a nasty letter to the Professor and think it might incriminate you?"

Bobby nodded.

"Did you kill Professor Knott?" Parks had to ask.

"Hell no," Bobby was about to cry, his eyes tearing up. "I swear it. I had nothing to do with it. I swear. It was just a letter—"

"What about?"

"I knew."

"Knew what?"

"What he was up to."

"Who? Knott?" Bobby nodded and Parks continued. "Were you a student of his?"

"I was. Until he expelled me. But he had no right to do that."

"Expel you? Really? Then why'd he do it?"

"Cuz I knew. Cuz I saw him."

"Saw him what?"

Bobby looked to the ground again, not sure how much he should say.

"Look at me, Bobby," Parks ordered. "This doesn't look good for you. Try explaining it to me. I'm usually a very understanding guy."

"He was blackmailing Cynthia into sleeping with him," Bobby finally admitted.

"And who's Cynthia?" Bobby remained quiet, probably thinking he was being strong. Parks pushed on. "Your girlfriend?"

A nod.

Parks was both surprised and yet not very, to be hearing this. The more he heard, the less he liked Fredrick Knott. "Okay. How'd he accomplish this?"

"She was flunking," Bobby explained. "So he made a deal with her."

"Did he make this deal with other girls?"

"He makes it with all the girls. That he likes," Bobby continued. "I think he flunks them on purpose. They're not supposed to tell anyone. But Cynthia broke down. She couldn't handle it. Said he practically forced himself on her. Here in this office. I told her to go to the dean or security. But she wouldn't. She was scared. Said she'd flunk out if she didn't do what he told her. She was so ashamed. She felt so humiliated. He takes pictures. Videotapes them. Then threatens to show their families if they say anything."

"So you did what exactly?"

"I confronted him," Bobby said. "Told him I knew and if he didn't leave Cynthia alone I was going to go to the authorities and report him."

"Then what happened?"

"The next day I was expelled from the school," Bobby explained, getting agitated as he explained his story. "That asshole said I plagiarized a term paper. But that's bullshit. I never plagiarized a thing in my damn life. I worked hard for what I got. But they expelled me and I lost my scholarship. I lost everything. So did Cynthia. She got expelled too. Said we copied each other's papers and stuff. But that's bullshit. We never did nothing like that. He lied. He's lying to all of them and getting away with it!"

Bobby stopped talking and took a deep breath.

"So you didn't go to the school with this problem?"

"I tried. But they just ignored me. I mean, who's going to believe me over the great Professor Knott? They knew I was telling the truth. They knew. But they didn't care. They just didn't want to deal with it. They'd rather sweep me under the carpet and forget about me."

"Who did you go to?"

"Norton."

"And he didn't believe you?"

"Believe me? He knew. He was part of it. Him and Knott together. Cynthia said they took turns. They liked to share."

Dammit. Parks hated this case more and more.

"What did you do next, Bobby?" Parks asked.

"I sent him a few letters," Bobby admitted.

"Threatening letters?"

Bobby nodded. "Told him he wasn't going to get away with this. I wasn't going to let him. He ruined my life. He ruined Cynthia's life too. He does it to a lot of the students, but they all keep their mouths shut for him. But I wasn't going to. I wasn't going to let him get away with it. But I didn't murder him. I swear to you. I was getting a lawyer. We were going to file a lawsuit. I swear to you I didn't murder him!"

"I believe you," Parks said, shaking his head. It still didn't look good. "Do you have an alibi for the night of Knott's murder?"

"I was at work. All night. You can call them. They'll tell you."

Bennett touched Parks's elbow and led him away from the student.

"If Norton and Knott were blackmailing students into sleeping with them, then we've just opened a whole new can of worms," he whispered. "If this gets out, the press will have a field day with the university. There's going to be a whole open investigation—"

"I don't care about the school," Parks admitted. "My concern isn't the university. It's finding Knott's murderer. Even if he did deserve it."

"They're going to fight you on this," Bennett said.

"Let them," Parks said. "I don't care. I'm only after the truth. But I understand if you need to back down from this investigation. You have a job to do as well. I understand. But so help me God, if you get in my way, I'll have you arrested for obstruction. You hear me?"

Bobby finally let the tears fall and he frantically wiped them away.

"Fuck 'em," Bennett smirked. "They don't pay me enough anyway."

Bennett looked over to Bobby Avalos.

"Hey, kid. We're going to need an official statement from you to put on the records. Think you can come with us and do that?"

TWENTY

The detectives left the university and made their way back to the station with Bobby, who called his girlfriend on the way so that she could meet them there. The two students gave their statements, going over them for several hours, getting down every last detail. Regardless of his involvement in Knott's murder, Bill Norton had some explaining to do. No doubt his lawyers would put a stop to that as quickly as possible. Parks had Moore fill out a warrant for a copy of all of Knott's students and their semester grades which they wouldn't receive for at least twenty-four hours. If ever. If Bobby and Cynthia were telling the truth, there had to be other victims. The more statements they could get before confronting Norton would be all the better for them. Still, it was their word against Norton's. And they had no physical proof. Only disgruntled, expelled students.

While they waited, Parks and Bennett studied re-created crime scene photos and diagrams while talking with Amy Tanaka about the forensics and any evidence they might have overlooked. The toxicology reports showed up positive for heroin in both Kelli Davis and Nicholas Martin's bodies.

They combed through Knott's files, hoping for a homicidal lunatic for a patient, or someone else with something damaging enough to their person that they would kill to keep it a secret. Alas, they turned up nothing new or out of the ordinary enough to raise a red flag. Fredrick Knott appeared to only know controversial people who would want him dead. They should have been searching for someone who *didn't* want the man killed.

After an entire day of turning up no new evidence and feeling as if they hadn't achieved anything, Parks called it quits and told everyone to go home, recharge and prepare for another day of monotonous research. He would be attending Knott's funeral in the morning, followed by a stop at the Knott's residence, but after that he would be in to help assist with further digging and reading.

"I thought you sent everyone home?"

Dave Parks almost fell out of the chair he was leaning back in as he stared up at the white board with all the information his team had uncovered about the Knott/Davis murders. He acknowledged Hardwick with a slight nod as she sat down on the edge of a desk.

"That should have included you. You look like shit. You need sleep."

"We all need sleep. I couldn't rest, though. Too wired. So I decided to stay a while and take a look at all this without the extra noise," Parks answered, looking down to the empty mug of coffee at his side.

"Guess you ran out and started to doze," Hardwick noted.

"They don't want to let you down."

"Who?" Hardwick suddenly realized he was talking about his team. "And you don't care about that?"

"I just know it won't make a difference. Once this case is over...they'll separate us all."

"You know I fought for you. Hell, still am. With every breath I can muster I'm fighting for you. Best thing going for you isn't even me. It's your record. Your team speaks for itself."

"Thanks. Might not make a difference, but it's good to hear just the same."

"What about Bennett? I keep seeing him here."

"You're the one who told me to keep him around. To keep him involved."

"You know he's reporting everything back to Norton."

"Most things. But not everything."

"You really believe that?"

"I believe that Matthew Bennett doesn't want to be in charge of university security for the rest of his life. I believe he's making Norton promise changes in exchange of information. But I feel he's playing both sides. If Norton is guilty, of anything, and ends up becoming more damaging than helpful to his career, he'll want a second hand to play."

"And you think we're it?"

"Hey, a jump to the LAPD from head of PSU security isn't all that unimaginable. It could happen. Especially if he kept on my good side."

"So you do think he knows more than he's telling you?"

"All I know is that we're not telling him all we know. Trust me on that one. Every time he comes onto the floor Fairmont all but shoots daggers at him with his eyes. All three have learned how to not say what needs to be said when Benett's around. I feel like I'm back in high school and we're passing notes or developing secret codes and languages."

"I get what you're saying. But if push comes to shove, who's he going to help? You? Or half a million dollars?"

"Keep your friends close and your enemies closer," Parks said, as if that said everything. "He's around. Until this case is closed, or he does something to intentionally obstruct this case, he stays."

Parks gazed back at the board at a picture of Katherine Norton.

"Please tell me that no one in that family is a primary suspect."

"Potential. But we're trying our best to eliminate them."

"See that you do. I don't need anyone in that family accused of anything. You know how much money they have? They could close this whole damn station down before we did a bit of good proving they did anything."

"Good to know the rich can still buy their way out of almost anything they do."

"They're not rich. They make the rich look poor."

"I know."

"Yeah, well you make sure if you do accuse anyone with the name of Norton you have unalterable video footage of the murder happening and a bloody weapon with fingerprints and a signed confession. Even then I'm not sure their lawyers wouldn't eat us alive."

"I don't think it will come to that."

"Honestly, Parks," Hardwick said. "How serious are you about investigating them?"

"They all have alibis. Conveniently. And so far I buy them. That's not the problem. It's just that something's off about that whole family." Parks thought about how everything was connected. "The DA's still not going to go after Norton for what he and Knott did to the students?"

"Allegedly. You've yet to find the so-called videotapes of his private sessions with his students. The ADA told you to get him some physical evidence that proves he did what he's being accused of and he'd love to go after the son of a bitch. Hell, with what's going on at

Berkeley and the other UC schools no one wants to look soft. But until then, your focus is on the murder investigation. Not Norton's personal affairs."

"I know. I know. Back at the alumni event there were at least three or four people at any given time who could testify to having seen the Nortons from the beginning of the fundraiser until the police arrived. Not once the entire night did any one of them step out. That we know of. Then again, it is only the word of their peers."

"So it's not those three. Then leave them alone. Move on. Who else? You can't tell me you don't have a list of suspects by now?"

"That's the problem. We do. A long-ass list. Students who hated him? That's an almost never ending list. Parents of pissed off students? Twice as long. You know how much tuition costs at PSU?" Hardwick rolled her eyes and shook her head. She didn't want to know. "Former lovers? That list is almost just as long, but they seem unlikely. Former patients. Current—up until his death, at least—patients. Again: possible and possible. This list is never ending. I mean, Knott's seriously lucky no one had taken him out before this."

"Maybe that will help you figure out who."

"What's that?" Parks asked.

"Why now? If he had such a long list of people who might have wanted him dead, what made our killer decide on doing it now? Was it really convenience that got him killed? Or was there more to it?"

Parks sighed as he turned to the photo of the word 'Judas' written on the professor's desk in Kelli's lipstick.

"No wondering what that means," Hardwick commented. "Whole world knows what 'Judas' means."

"Yes. So the killer feels betrayed...but by whom? Knott or Kelli?"

"Not sure. But it was written on Knott's desk. So he would be my initial guess. But then again it was written in her lipstick, so...her?"

"Which brings me back to the accusations. If those do have to do with the murder then it could be any one of his students. We know there's more than just Bobby and Cynthia. If they're telling the truth which, I think at this point, is safe to assume. But if it is about that, then why haven't they gone after Norton if he was also involved? That's what gives me slight hesitation about that angle. Unless Norton is a target. Think he'd accept if we offered protection?"

"And let him know what angle we're working? Without proof. You really want to tip him off?"

Parks smiled and got quiet as he kept putting the pieces together.

"What's up?"

"Something's off. We're overlooking something. Something simple."

"What?"

"I don't know for su—the lipstick container we found at the crime scene."

"What about it? According to the ballistics report it matches. It's the same tube that was used to write the words on his desk. No prints on the container, of course, but it's the same one."

"No, it's...I'm not sure what it is. But something's off."

"What?"

"Can you hand me the ERL?"

"What are you looking for?" Hardwick asked, handing over the evidence recovery log.

Parks flipped through several pages and then went back to the beginning of the report.

"Where's her purse?" Parks asked quickly.

"What? Whose?"

"Her purse. Kelli Davis's purse. Why isn't it listed on the recovery log?"

"Did you log it from the crime scene?"

"No. But I..."

"Wait—that's because it wasn't at the crime scene," Hardwick recalled. "It was found back at the alumni party. Apparently she was planning on going back for it. Death must not have been a part of her plans that night."

"Do we have it?"

"The purse? I think it was turned in to us and tagged and logged. Should be in evidence."

Parks dropped the log sheets and made his way out of the room and headed down the hallway for the evidence lockup.

"What are you looking for?" Hardwick asked a few steps behind.

Parks approached the guard for the evidence room and Hardwick nodded for the man to step aside, allowing them entrance. Hardwick signed a clipboard before following Parks, who made his way over to the boxes containing the Knott/Davis evidence. He dug through the first box and didn't find the purse. He then tried the next box and also got the same results but he did find a plastic bag sealed with the tube of lipstick that was used to write 'Judas' on the desk. Parks handed the baggie over to Hardwick and began looking in the third box where he finally found what he was looking for.

"Dave? What is it?"

"We know there was a third person in the room."

"Well, since the two bodies found in there are dead, I think that's a good assumption. They didn't kill each other that way."

"And we're looking for a guy, right?"

"There were two sets of semen found at the crime scene."

"So we're assuming that that third person took Kelli's lipstick and wrote the word 'Judas' on Knott's desk?"

"That's the assumption we're going with right now?" Hardwick couldn't believe what she was hearing. "There's evidence all over the room to support that theory you know."

"Collecting evidence isn't just about what's there. It's also about what isn't there."

"So what isn't there?"

"What if the third person—our mystery man—who had sex with them wasn't the killer? What if that person joined in for the sex, did his thing, left them there, and someone else entered the room and killed them?"

"How do you figure that?"

"What were the words written on the desk with?"

"Kelli Davis's lipstick."

"Even though she didn't have her purse with her in Knott's office?"

"So what? So she took her lipstick out to touch up and had it on her."

"Did she?" asked Parks as he reached in and pulled out a tube of lipstick from within Kelli's purse. "And if this is Kelli's lipstick, inside her purse, then who does that other tube that was used to write the words belong to?"

"So another woman was there?"

"It's possible. But not concrete. It could mean several things. And either way, I'm not sure if it gets us any further along. Another woman could have been there. This could be hers. She killed them and used her lipstick to write the message."

"Or...?"

"Or it could still be a man. He simply took this from whomever and when he was finished with his business in the room, used it to write his message."

"So what does that mean?"

"What that means is that if our killer's a man, then he had to have gotten the lipstick from somewhere before the murders with the intention of using it for what it was used for. What that means is that if our killer is a man, then these murders were premeditated."

INTERLUDE: BENNETT

Bennett sat parked across from the Norton residence for almost two hours waiting for Christopher to make his move when the student finally reared his head. He followed intently as Christopher pulled onto Sunset Boulevard and followed him to La Cienega Boulevard where he turned south toward Melrose. A few minutes later Christopher pulled up to a valet, who appeared to know the student; his greeting friendly and familiar. Christopher greeted the bouncer with a smile and a handshake full of cash to avoid the growing line and quickly disappeared into the already active night spot.

The place was crowded but not packed, as it was a Monday night and things were just starting for the evening. Bennett studied the numerous patrons and realized he wasn't that out of place with a suit on, looking as if he belonged with the hip, Hollywood crowd. The lights were dim but lit enough to see where one was and who was around them, while multi-colored lights bounced off the walls to the beat of the music. A bar with four well-muscled men in black tank tops sat in the center of the front room, each bartender quickly taking orders but not forgetting to flash a smile or pump a bicep in order to gain an extra dollar or two for a tip. Girls in short skirts and black, sleeveless, buttoned-up collared shirts made their way through the crowds, taking drink orders.

Bennett walked past the bar through a dining area with a dozen bar tables, each filled with men and women, eating and drinking, each dressed in similar dark-themed wardrobe choices. As the detective continued into the next room he noticed crimson curtains outlining each of the doorways and found a separate bar with its own line of drinkers. A different soundtrack pumped throughout the back room, as people stood around, talking and laughing.

He worked his way out of the room and went up a small set of stairs into the neighboring room where he found Christopher lounging in a cabana with Nicole and a boy he had never seen before with his head in Christopher's lap.

Christopher wore a pair of Armani slacks and a grey buttoned-up dress shirt with a herringbone jacket lying off to his side. Nicole sat next to him, half on the edge of the cabana and half out of it, sipping champagne. She looked stunning to Bennett, in a dark berry, strapless, beaded silk dress that complimented both her warm California tan and slender figure just perfectly. The boy, who was barely twenty-one, glared at Bennett when he felt Christopher acknowledge his presence.

"Why don't you join us?" Christopher asked Bennett.

"I don't really think I—"

"Of course you should," Christopher demanded, despite his male companion's obvious objection to the request. He didn't want any other roosters in the hen house.

"You should," Nicole smiled as she stood up and took two steps toward him. "We have plenty to drink. And I'm bored with our current company." Nicole sneered at the young man in Christopher's lap, the boy oblivious as he focused most of his attention on Christopher. "New guests would be stimulating. And you seem like a stimulating person, Detective Bennett."

"I'm off duty. So it's Matt."

"Well, Matt," Nicole said, correcting herself. "What are you drinking? You are drinking with us, aren't you?"

Christopher sat patiently inside his secluded booth, playing with the hair of the boy in his lap, while the detective built up the courage to continue.

"Jack. Rocks. Four limes," he answered, still staring at Christopher.

"One Jack on the rocks, coming up." Nicole walked past Bennett, brushing up against him, making sure he caught a whiff of her perfume.

"Baby, why don't you go get me a martini," Christopher said to the boy lying in his lap.

"But we have bottle service," the boy whined.

"But I want a martini."

"But—"

"You have a choice," Christopher interrupted with a peck on the boy's lips. "Go get me a martini and come back, or piss off."

The young boy, who looked sad—pathetic, almost—sat up and glared at Bennett before turning back to Christopher and kissed him hard; then bounced away.

"What do you think the chances are you'll get that drink?" Bennett leaned up against a lone standing table a few feet away from the cabana.

"If I wanted a drink I could have the server get me one," Christopher replied.

"So he knew you were dismissing him?"

"He only wants a hookup and I haven't given it to him yet, so he's pissed. He'll find me again later if he really wants it."

"Hookup for what?"

"Take your pick."

"Are you carrying?"

"You gonna frisk me?"

"Sure that's a wise thing to admit to an officer of the law?"

"I thought you were off duty?"

"Now now, boys," Nicole scolded, walking up with a drink. "Play nice. Or I'll have to separate you."

"Yes, mother dear," Christopher smirked.

"That was fast," Bennett commented, accepting his drink from Nicole.

"I'm a good tipper," Nicole winked.

"So, Matt," Christopher interrupted. "What are you doing here?"

"You know why I'm here."

"Our good friend Matt here thinks I killed the professor and his lover," Christopher answered as he turned to Nicole as if she didn't know this already.

"Well, if he's already on your trail then I guess you were sloppy," Nicole commented and took a sip of her martini. The red-stained lights from up above bounced off her berry-painted fingernails which matched her dress.

"True," Christopher admitted solemnly. "And you know what I think of sloppy people."

"Maybe you deserve to be caught then."

"Do you think our good friend Matt here has what it takes to catch me?"

"He does look determined. I'm just not sure how good his stamina is. But I wonder if he might just not surprise us."

"I'm hoping he does."

The two stared up at Bennett, taunting and teasing, when Nicole walked from the table next to him and sat down in the cabana opposite Christopher. Nicole patted the seat next to her, summoning Bennett to join.

"Come on, Matt," Nicole cooed. "We don't bite. Unless you want us to."

"She likes you," Christopher said with a genuine smile while Bennett situated himself inside the booth, against the wall opposite Christopher, Nicole nestled between the two men.

"I should care?" Bennett replied.

"Oh, Matty. You should. See, Nicole is my friend. And when my friends are happy, I'm happy. And when I'm happy, the world can be your oyster."

"Then I apologize," Bennett said turning to Nicole. "Truly. I didn't mean to offend you."

"Manners?" Nicole said pleasantly surprised.

"Told you." Christopher smiled, as if he was ever wrong.

"I do like him," Nicole agreed.

"You have too much information you shouldn't." Bennett turned his attention back to Christopher.

"So what?" Christopher took another swallow of his drink. "That's not a crime."

"Unless you have information about a crime that only the person who committed it should know."

"You'd be surprised what money can buy these days."

"And exactly how much money does it cost to read a police report?"

"Why? Looking to make me a deal? Need help with next month's rent?"

"If you can buy anything you want why didn't you just buy off Knott?"

"As opposed to what? Killing him? You're assuming the killer—I mean *I*—wasn't just pissed off and wanted him out of the way. Really now, what reason would I have for wanting him dead?"

"Maybe you told him something in one of your sessions that you shouldn't have and was afraid he would tell the wrong people."

Christopher hesitated, only for a brief moment, but Bennett had caught the look in his eye. Maybe he was onto something after all.

"Oh, please. You assume there's stuff I've done that I'm ashamed of." Christopher laughed. "You don't know me too well." Nicole shook her head agreeing with Christopher but not saying anything. "There's not a whole lot I feel ashamed about. And you assume I give a shit about what other people have to say or think about me?" Bennett remained quiet. "Or perhaps I did it for the thrill of it?"

"If that's what turns you on, then sure."

"Oh, baby. If you think killing is what gets me off"—Christopher placed a hand on the seat in-between Bennett's thighs as he leaned over and set his empty glass on the counter behind Nicole's head—"then you really don't know me at all."

Christopher worked his way back to his side of the cabana, almost brushing his lips up against Bennett's, causing the detective to jerk back.

"It's the thrill of getting away with it," Bennett replied as if he had just figured something important out.

"Oh?"

"Sure. Why not? You can buy damn near anything you want. You crave attention. And what you can't buy, you create. You did it to see if you could get away with it. And if not—if there was a trial—

then you'd see if you could buy them off. And so on."

"Just to see how far I can get away with something. But what if all that doesn't work? What if I was convicted?"

"You wouldn't let that happen. You'd have someone around to take the fall for you. Even at the last minute. Someone who would want the money bad enough. Need it."

"But you'll stop me before that happens?"

"What do you think?"

Bennett stared at Christopher while the rest of the establishment's occupants completely faded from sight and sound as the two men had their own version of a pissing contest. Bennett finished his drink and looked to Nicole and then back to Christopher. His head began to swirl, though he tried to hide it.

"Feeling alright?" Christopher asked.

"My...eyes...need...It's just a dizzy spell. It's getting stuffy in here. I'm good. I'll be right back."

Bennett got up and looked to his right then his left and disappeared down a hallway that led to the restrooms in the back. Bennett splashed water into his face from the sink as a restroom attendant stood by with a few paper towels, ready to assist him, when Christopher walked into the room. Christopher accepted the few paper towels then tossed a twenty in the tip jar and nodded for the attendant to leave them alone.

"What's wrong?" Christopher asked, holding out the paper towels.

"You put something in my drink." Bennett leaned over the sink and took in his reflection in the mirror.

"Are you sure? Maybe you're just not used to all this excitement. It has been a while since your own college years."

"How—you're messing with me."

"Maybe. But this is my game. And you said you wanted to play."

"I want answers."

"And you'll get them. But you have to play along. You do that; then I'll play nicely with you and you might just be surprised at what you learn."

"I can't—"

"I know you want to," Christopher interrupted. "You need help? Sometimes we just need a little help. Follow the white rabbit and before you know it you'll wake up in Wonderland."

Christopher walked to the last stall in the room and disappeared behind the door. Bennett noted the restroom's clean and tidy appearance. A man peed while watching a small, flat screen television sell alcoholic beverages on the wall above the urinals. Bennett took a deep breath, walked back and disappeared into the stall. Christopher closed and locked the door.

"Here," Christopher said holding up one of his fingers with a flat, round pill on the end of it. "Now be a good boy and follow the white rabbit."

"What is it?"

"You know what it is, Alice. Trust me. You like it. I know."

"How—?"

"I already told you. I know everything. Now take it."

"No."

"You'll like these. Besides, this is far better than any of that poor-man's trash you concocted back in college." Bennett flinched, stunned by Christopher's comment. Christopher rolled his eyes. "You need to relax. You're too tense. You'll have a heart attack by the end of the night. Take. It."

"No."

"Take it...and I'll answer a question. Any question truthfully. Now go on."

"Honestly?"

"Cross my heart and hope to die. Now go on."

Bennett stared at the pill, and he could feel the inside of his mouth beginning to salivate. Before he could think too much about his choices he made the pill disappear.

"Now..." Christopher smiled. "What do you want to know?"

*   *   *

"You owe me an answer," Bennett stammered from the back seat of Christopher's navy blue Porche Panamera while Nicole sped down Sunset toward her condo on the beach. Bennett was in and out of consciousness in the back seat next to Christopher who took sips out of a flask.

"And you want me to tell you now?" Christopher asked. "But baby, I'm afraid that in your condition you won't remember what I tell you come tomorrow. Why don't we wait?"

"I can handle it. I can handle all of this a lot better than you think." The Ecstasy tab Christopher had given to him was kicking in. "You're just trying to get out of it. You're backing down on your word."

"Fine. No."

"No?"

"No."

"Honestly?"

"I don't know what else to say. Would you like me to take a lie detector test? No."

"No, what?" Nicole asked from the front seat.

"He asked if I had ever slept with Fredrick Knott or Kelli Davis."

"Ha," Nicole laughed, barely making it through a yellow light turning red. "I could have told you that one. And I'm sure it wouldn't have cost you whatever you had to pay to get that answer out of him."

"That's probably true," Christopher admitted. "But then our good friend Matt here wouldn't be feeling as relaxed and open as he is. Right?"

"Right," Bennett agreed as he began to make a summoning gesture with his hand.

"What?" Christopher asked.

"You got another pill?"

"Oh, I don't think so," Christopher objected. "One is enough for you right now."

"I can handle it," Bennett insisted. "I have another question."

"Oh, ho ho ho," Christopher laughed. "So his true colors come out. I see how it is. You see that, Nicole? Little Matty has become bold and frisky. He wants to play."

"Christopher," Nicole muttered from the front.

"Relax," Christopher consoled. "Half a pill. He can handle that."

"Bullshit," Bennett shouted. "I can handle the whole thing. You don't know."

"Oh no? I do know," Christopher corrected. "But I also know that to the best of my knowledge—and I'd like to think my knowledge is pretty flawless—it's been a few years since you've partied like this."

"What the hell do you know?" Bennett replied.

"Christopher?" Nicole shot back again.

"Keep driving," Christopher ordered as he reached into his pocket and removed a small plastic vial. He dropped a pill into the palm of his hand and put the plastic vial away. "Half a pill. Do as I say. Half a pill and I'll still give you one question. The other half for me."

"Bullshit," Bennett repeated and grabbed Christopher's hand to retrieve the pill. "If that's the case then the whole pill and I get two questions."

Before Christopher could object, Bennett flung the pill into his mouth and quickly swallowed.

"Why do I think you're going to regret that in the morning?" Christopher wondered.

Bennett smiled and made a humming sound.

"No matter. Too late now. What's done is done. So go ahead, Detective, ask away."

"If you didn't kill Knott and Kelli like you say you didn't—"

"And I didn't."

"Then do you know who did?"

Christopher smiled at Bennett. "Yes."

"Who is it?"

"Sorry. I can't tell you that answer."

"Bullshit. You said I got two questions."

"Actually, I said you got one. You took the pill of your own free will. That answer you haven't quite earned yet. But you can still piece this all together and come out on top if you play your cards right."

"What?"

"I'll give you another question. Just to show I can be fair. So think it through. Make sure it's a good one."

Bennett sat quietly for a second and thought about it while Christopher stared at Nicole through the rearview mirror.

"I got it," Bennett yelled.

"Well...?"

"Have I met the person who killed Fredrick Knott and Kelli Davis?"

"What a truly excellent question." Christopher grinned from ear to ear. "Yes. You have."

*   *   *

Bennett jerked awake, practically jumping up out of the bed he had been sleeping in when he spun around, completely confused and lost. He had no idea where he was, the pounding headache dulling his concentration. He sat up and rubbed his temples, trying to adjust his eyes, which wanted to pop out of his head, running and scream-ing for safety from his pulsating brain which tried to break free from his skull.

He heard noises coming from below him. He stood up, realized he was completely naked, grabbed the bed sheet, and wrapped it around his body. He walked to the edge of the balcony and peered over, immediately identifying the sounds below as that of Christo-pher and Nicole talking. He worked his way down the stairs and stopped at the corner before he was seen. He came up blank as he tried to recall as much of the night before to help him get a handle on what was going on.

"What's wrong?" Christopher asked.

Bennett didn't hear Nicole reply.

"Baby," Christopher said tauntingly. "What's wrong? Don't be cross with me. Are you telling me you didn't enjoy last night?"

"Only the parts with you in it," Nicole said. "Why does he have to be involved?"

"I told you about this already," Christopher scolded. "Everything may not go as planned. I need to have my ass covered. I need him to trust me. Okay?"

"Fine," Nicole agreed and then nodded to the table. "Go sit."

Christopher began to cut the omelet up into two pieces when he noticed Bennett peering around the corner of the kitchen. For a second Bennett was like a child caught where he shouldn't have been and he could feel himself blush as Christopher tried to determine how long he had been standing there listening to them.

"Well, good morning, sleepy head." Christopher took a bite of his eggs and smiled. He was wearing a slick Calvin Klein suit that fit him like a glove.

Nicole dropped the scalding pan she had been cooking in into the sink and flipped on the water faucet, causing steam to fill the air.

"I'll finish getting ready," Nicole said, "so that we're not late. Better get him ready too."

Nicole glared down at Christopher, nodding to the flash drive he had left on the table which he quickly made disappear into his jacket pocket.

Bennett sat down, his eyes sunken in and his color a little on the pasty side as he started for the food on Christopher's plate and received a slap on his hand for trying.

"This is mine. Can't be sharing everything with you," Christopher replied. "You need to shower. It's upstairs next to the bedroom. Knott's funeral is in a few hours and if memory serves me correctly you're scheduled to put in an appearance. I'm sure you need to check in first with the master though."

"Shit." Bennett had forgotten what day it was. "What happened last night?"

Christopher smiled when Nicole called out to him from the upstairs. "Babe, I can't find my black dress. The Armani one."

"Coming," Christopher called out. "You too. You need to get ready."

"Have any coffee?"

"Nicole just brewed a pot," Christopher said nodding in the direction of the pot on a counter in the kitchen. "Get a mug and come up. You need to hurry."

"Christopher," Nicole called out again.

"Hurry," Christopher repeated forcefully and disappeared upstairs.

Bennett poured himself a cup of coffee, shaking his head in mockery at Christopher's orders. He then started for the stairs and stopped by the table, looking down at the plate of half-eaten eggs. He was hung over and famished and needed just a bite or two until he could grab something at the drive-through on the way to the funeral. Bennett took a few bites and then headed upstairs for the shower.

*   *   *

"You've got ten minutes to get dressed and out of here," Christopher called out through the closed bathroom door while Bennett tried to wake up in the shower.

Bennett stared at the door Christopher pounded on and ignored it as he went back to his shower and let the warm water hit him in his face and pour down his body, which felt tense and worn out. Every muscle in his body ached as if he had just fished a triathlon. He opened his mouth and let the water in, dissipating his cotton mouth. He spit the water out and then filled up again. He spit the water out again when he felt his head swirl and he closed his eyes tight and opened them up again to see stars across his field of vision. He shook his head and went to open his mouth to take in more water when suddenly he felt his equilibrium take a dive and the next thing he saw was the water faucet a second before he hit it with his face—

Water poured down over his body as his vision came back and he noticed a swirl of red liquid circling the shower floor as it disappeared into the drain. Bennett couldn't feel his body as he lay there on the tile, barely able to hear the pounding on the other side of the door.

"What's going on?"

"I don't know," Nicole replied, sounding as if she was about to cry. "I heard this thud. When I call for him, he doesn't reply."

"Matt?" Christopher called through the closed door. "Matthew? Matt, open up!"

"What's going on? What's happening?"

"I'm on the same side of the door as you," Christopher replied. "Why is it locked?"

"How the hell should I know?"

"You have the key?"

"There isn't one," Nicole answered. "I've never used one on this door before. It only locks on the inside."

Bennett closed his eyes again, his head throbbing when his breathing began to become constricted and his body heaved.

The door to the bathroom flew open and Christopher and Nicole found Bennett lying on the ground of the shower. Blood seeped from a gash along his left shin and swirled down into the drain. There was also a rather large cut across the top of his head and he hit his nose on the way down, quite possibly breaking it.

"Oh my God." Nicole noticed Bennett foaming at the mouth and she shrieked and jumped back.

"Calm down," Christopher ordered. "Shit. Let's get him out of there. Hold his head. Keep him from banging it on the tile. He's gonna crack his skull. Don't force him though. Don't constrict his movements. Just protect him. Now dammit!"

Christopher jumped up and ran out the room while Nicole got Bennett's head into her lap as she tried to keep him there without touching him.

"Here. Watch out." Christopher said reentering the room as he knelt down next to Bennett and opened a box and took out a syringe. "Told you to stay the hell away from my breakfast, didn't I? Had to go and get greedy and take everything. Stupid ass."

"Now isn't the time to lecture," Nicole cried. "Just fix him."

"I am," Christopher snapped. "Hold him still."

Christopher stabbed the syringe into Bennett's shoulder and pumped the liquid until it was emptied completely into the detective's body.

"There…"

Matthew stopped foaming at the mouth when he suddenly jerked his head back, his eyes rolling in their sockets as he began to spasm again. His hands and feet clenched and his chest heaved as if he was suffocating.

"Matthew," Christopher shouted to the man lying on the ground. "Matt, I need you to listen to me. You're going into anaphylactic shock. I need you to calm down. Breathe for me. Calm down. You hear me. Just relax. Relax, dammit!"

"It isn't working," Nicole cried. "Whatever you gave him isn't working."

"Yes it is," Christopher replied. "This is something else. Dammit. It's too late."

"Wha…" Nicole stopped when she saw Christopher reach down and place one hand over Matt's mouth and the other one over his nose and begin to suffocate the life out of the detective on her bathroom floor.

"What the hell are you doing?" Nicole shouted, staring at Christopher.

"The only thing I can do right now," Christopher replied. "Can't do anything else."

"Stop it! You're killing him," Nicole shrieked and jumped to stop Christopher from suffocating Bennett. "You can't just kill him. Stop it!"

"This is all I can do! Get the hell offa me!" Christopher managed to keep a hand over Bennett's nose while he pushed Nicole off him.

Nicole hit the wall and fell to the floor, tears falling from her eyes, streaks of mascara running down her cheeks while Christopher went back to suffocating the life out of Bennett.

"No!" Nicole sat there, crying, devastated, when Bennett stopped shaking and spasming, his body limp on the wet bathroom floor.

Nicole put a hand to her mouth, her eyes bugging out as she stared at her boyfriend and the dead body in his lap. She couldn't stop shaking. She had helped. What she had given him the night before—

She felt her stomach go and she turned to the side and threw up.

"What did...you du-du—" Nicole heaved heavily as she sat upright and stopped when she noticed Bennett's chest going up and down again. "But...? What?"

"Stupid ass," Christopher hissed at Bennett and slapped the side of his face. "You hear me? Wake up. Wake up, you."

Bennett began to moan and toss his head from side to side.

"Wake up. Now you're really going to be late," Christopher scolded.

"Huh? Wha..." Bennett began to come to.

"Wake up," Christopher ordered with another slap.

"What happened?" Bennett asked, looking around at his surroundings.

"Nicole, babe, can you get me the first aid kit from under the sink? We need to bandage up Matt," Christopher turned from his girlfriend down to Bennett. "You went into anaphylactic shock. Banged up your head and cut your shin real bad. But don't worry. We'll fix you up. Let's get you off this cold tile and onto the carpet. You don't have to move far."

Christopher got up and helped Bennett move over onto the carpet where he continued to lie as he collected his thoughts and tried to regain a steady breathing pattern.

"What did you give him?" Nicole asked, walking back into the room with the first aid kit.

"Are you allergic to fish?" Christopher asked again, digging through the kit.

"Shellfish," Bennett replied.

"See?" Christopher made a face at Nicole before turning back to Bennett. "I told you to stay away from my breakfast, didn't I? That was a crab omelet. Guess next time you'll listen to me. You need to learn to trust me, Matt. I only tell you what to do for your own good. Just thought I was being a prick, huh? Good thing I had an EpiPen or you'd be dead right now. Now calm down."

"Why did you have that Epi-thing?" Nicole stared intently at her boyfriend.

"Never you mind. Just a good thing I did. He went into anaphylactic shock. That's all. I had to give him a shot of epinephrine to take care of it." Nicole stared blankly at Christopher. "Adrenaline. I had to give him a shot of adrenaline. That's what the shot was for."

"It didn't look like it was working."

"Oh, it worked. But by then his body had gone into shock. He was having a panic attack. I'm sure everything he put into his system last night didn't help. It probably slowed down his body from identifying the adrenaline shot. So his body went into the panic attack

mode. His system needed to shut down and start over. Like reboot-
ing a computer."

"So you were..."

"The only way to do that is to knock him out. He needed to pass
out. That's why I cut off his air. I wasn't suffocating him. I was trying
to get him to black out."

"I...I'm sorry I..."

"It's over with," Christopher replied shaking off the apology.
"That's all that matters."

Christopher finished bandaging up Bennett's forehead. "You
have a pretty bad gash on your forehead and your shin is cut almost
all the way from your knee to your ankle. You banged it up good on
the water faucet I'm guessing. I'll take care of them but you're going
to have to go see a doctor and get them stitched up. Looks like you
may have broken your nose as well."

"What do—?" Bennett tried to get up until Christopher put a
hand to his chest to keep him down. "You need to stay put for another ten or so minutes. Nicole, you keep getting ready. We'll drop
Matt off at his car. You can have the campus doctor look at you, if
you wish. We still have time before the funeral."

Nicole continued to stare at the two men as Bennett lay naked in
Christopher's arms.

"Well let's get going," Christopher smiled. "It's only eight a.m.
The day's just begun."

*   *   *

Christopher and Nicole dropped Bennett off at his car in the
parking lot at the club, paid the fee to have the car released from the
valet company who was about to have it towed, and sped off for the
funeral. Bennett walked over to his car, got in, put the key in the

ignition and—

Jerked his head awake to the sound of someone tapping on the side window of his car. He looked around, disorientated, having fallen asleep, and found the front of his shirt covered in blood.

"Man, you okay?" the passerby asked, knocking on the window.

Bennett looked into the rearview mirror and noticed that he had a bloody nose that had been dripping down the front of his shirt for who knew how long.

"You need a doctor?" the passerby asked.

"N-no. No. I'm okay." Bennett said as he remembered he was heading to the doctor's office. "No. Thanks. I'll be okay."

Bennett started his car and drove around the concerned man, pulling out onto the main road leading toward Hollywood. As he drove down Sunset Boulevard, Bennett glanced back at the road, caught a glimpse of the clock and realized he had been asleep for over five hours.

TWENTY-ONE

Even though the funeral was a closed-off event, there were still plenty of onlookers lined up at the gates, including students (who were restricted from attending the services since the university would be holding their own services and day of remembrance that upcoming Friday), again made up of those protesting the funeral and those protesting the protestors. Eggs were thrown, slurs were shouted and the police were used to keep everyone in line. There to record and broadcast everything were the numerous news teams, who were also kept at bay. Thirty minutes after the services had begun; the minister finished and asked all to keep Fredrick Knott in their hearts as they went on about their daily activities.

Parks stood off to the side so as not to take the spot of someone closer to the deceased, while he observed the various mourners, which was the real reason he wanted to be there.

He noted that Elizabeth Knott was surrounded by the Nortons: Katherine and Bill on one side, with Christopher on the other. All four stood silently, grieving for a man none of them appeared all that distraught to see pass on, as though they knew what appearances must be kept for the public. Parks was put off as he looked at Katherine Norton and could have sworn she was staring at him through her dark Ray-Ban sunglasses. As the services ended and people began tossing their white roses onto the lowering casket, he continued to take note of people's behaviors.

Of the many things that he had observed, two things struck him as odd. The first was Elizabeth Knott. Though she had been leaning on the people around her for strength and comfort, as was to be expected, what struck him as peculiar was how she held onto the hand of Katherine throughout most of the service, as if the woman was afraid to let go of her friend. As if she would lose Katherine forever if the bond between the two women was broken. There was a familiarity between the two women, a silent love that only strengthen each other's demeanor.

Another thing that struck him as peculiar was how Elizabeth held onto the hand of Christopher in a way that, Parks thought, was for more than emotional support. The way Elizabeth rubbed her thumb along the side of Christopher's hand had the feel of two people who were more than comfortable with each other and even somewhat intimate. And as he observed them leaving the cemetery, Parks recalled Katherine Norton's words about how she thought her best friend had taken a lover on the side before her husband's death.

There was an after-services reception held at the Norton residence, which both Bill and Katherine had agreed to host for their grieving friend. Parks took mental notes of who showed up and what their relationship to the deceased was.

Who knew who?

Who appeared to like who?

And who avoided who?

After close to ninety minutes of people-watching, he decided to call it quits, realizing that he wasn't noticing anything all that out of the ordinary for a group of people mourning the loss of a friend or esteemed colleague.

"Detective." Katherine approached Parks near the front entrance. "Leaving so soon?"

"I think my duties here are finished for the day."

"Tired of people-watching? Note-taking?"

"Something like that," Parks chuckled. "That's a nice shade of lipstick you're wearing. What is it?"

"I believe it's called Dubonnet. It's from MAC. Would you like to see the receipt?"

"No. Sorry. I do have a few other questions I would like to ask you though. I know now isn't an appropriate time."

"Is this about Knott?"

"It is."

"Then no. Now isn't the appropriate time," Katherine agreed, sweeping the room with her eyes and catching sight of her husband who acknowledged her with a nod of his head.

"Powerful husband."

"He is."

"Rich?"

"Haven't you pulled his records by now, Detective?" Parks gave a smile that neither confirmed nor denied her question. "That is what you want to know about, isn't it? My past husbands? Whether or not I killed them?"

"Actually, it's the relationship between them and your son I wish to discuss further."

Katherine appeared interested. "Or rather my point of view on the topic?

"He was only a child during the time spent with most of them.

Your recollection of past events may be more...accurate."

"Later today, then? After the reception's finished. Say around five. Is this a formal interview?"

"It can be. But I suppose it's more to fill my curiosity and cut off any unwanted leads and dangling questions."

"Then why not back here. The place will be cleaned up. The guests will all be gone. It will be cozier that way."

Parks thought about this. He knew he shouldn't. But it really wasn't any worse than meeting a suspect at a restaurant or park. And he did want Katherine relaxed with her guard down.

"All right. Five o'clock then," Parks agreed without realizing the damage he was setting in motion for the case he had been working on so hard for the past three and a half days.

"I'll see you then, Detective."

*   *   *

"What do we have?" Parks asked as he walked onto the task force room floor to find Rachel Moore and Jake Fairmont going through files together.

"I'll give your Fredrick Knott this," Moore started. "He may have been a creep—and he *was*—but he was at least a smart creep. He knew what he was doing."

"What's up?"

"We got the files from the school," Fairmont said.

"Of?"

"Knott's students' records," Moore answered.

"Wow. Didn't think that was actually going to happen," Parks said amazed.

"Yeah, well, I think certain information is flowing slower in certain circles," Fairmont said. "The governor is delaying because of his daughter. But I found a judge who has a kid at the school and his main concern right now is safety. He doesn't care what information has to be revealed. He wants to know his son is safe there."

"So what do we have?" Parks asked.

"The short version?" Moore replied. "Nothing."

"Nothing?"

"We found fifteen girls who all started off the semester with perfect grades," Fairmont explained, reading from a file containing his scribbled notes. "But about six weeks into the semester, several of these girls' grades took a drastic change. And I mean drastic."

"Like, even if they had flunked a mid-term there's no way their grades should have dropped that far that fast kind of a drop," Moore elaborated.

"Knott fixed their grades?" Parks surmised.

"Most likely."

"So out of the fifteen...?"

"Out of the fifteen, nine of the girls had no idea what we were talking about when we mentioned Knott's little blackmail scheme," Moore continued. "Out of the other six who confessed to know what we were talking about, none was willing to go on record about it. Each girl is prominent. Good grades. Influential families. Knott had it rigged to have each one expelled if they ever talked. Plagiarism all down the page. They know he's dead but they don't want their educational and professional careers scarred. They aren't talking. They just want it in the past now."

"Meredith Langer," Parks muttered to himself.

"I'd be willing to bet the same happened to her," Moore said.

"I wonder how many others?"

"So did we." Moore motioned to Jake. "So we started to do some digging."

"And?"

"So far over the past ten plus years of teaching, Fredrick Knott has expelled thirteen students for plagiarism or cheating in his classes."

"You've got to be kidding me."

"I wish I was."

"But...how? How has he been doing this for that long and no one's noticed it?"

"Good question."

"Someone had to know something. Someone higher up?"

"Exactly," Moore agreed. "All paperwork has been submitted officially and signed by our illustrious president of the university. Norton knew what was going on. He just wasn't doing anything about it."

"But why?"

"Why indeed?" Moore shrugged. "Why would Norton go along with this? What was he getting out of it?"

Parks didn't have time to go over it all now. He'd have to dwell on it.

"I want us to go over the crime scene again. Take down what cold, hard facts we actually do have and what we're simply hypothesizing about."

"What do you mean?" Moore asked.

"The sex. How do we know Knott was having it with Kelli Davis?"

"He was naked," Fairmont objected.

"And how do we know he wasn't stripped down after he was killed as a way to embarrass him?" Parks asked.

"Dave, there was semen," Moore added.

"Again, how do we know he wasn't forced to strip down and jerk off? I'm not saying he didn't have sex with Kelli Davis. And that they weren't caught and then killed. That seems the most likely. But I need to know all the facts to back that up."

"Dave," Moore said quietly. "What are you thinking?"

"What Knott—and possibly Norton—were doing to these students? The sex. The blackmail. Why?"

"It's about power," Moore answered. "But what's that have to do with him not having sex before he was killed?"

"But why? He was a powerful man. Narcissistic as hell. We know that. So why was he doing this? What game was he playing? He was a professor. He already had power over these students. Why do this? Why go this extreme?"

"Cuz he was a sick, twisted fuck," Fairmont answered. "Some people just are."

"Agreed," Parks said excitedly. "But why? I still want to know why. What did he get out of it? And why these students? We already know how this started. We're not stupid and we all know enough basic psychology to understand that. Most likely he expelled a student for plagiarizing and that was it. But the next time, or maybe the third, or maybe that first time some girl he caught and was going to expel had decided to stay in school in exchange for whatever he wanted."

"And that excited him," Fairmont said, getting where Parks was going.

"At first, yes. Sex is sex and everyone wants it. But that wasn't enough. Our doc here is a sociopath. So simply being offered sex isn't enough. He didn't enjoy it like he thought he would. Or maybe he did at first, but then the high wore off. Like with a serial killer. The need to do it again begins to grow."

"But when he offers the deal to the next girl he catches and she says no, or whatever, he realizes he gets turned on more when they don't want to do it."

"When they fight back," Moore said, feeling sad for the students. "Like I said, it's about power. Rape always is."

"So then he begins the false accusations," Parks continues. "It escalates. It has to. He has a risk addiction. That's where the drugs come into play. He had to up the ante, so to speak. I think he was messing with his patients' prescriptions, yes. But I think he was doing that to see what outcomes he could get from doing so."

"You mean like making a psychopath more psychopathic and going out and killing someone else?"

"Yes," Parks said. "Or harming themselves. Whatever. Just to do something. He liked that he was disassociated from actually committing these crimes. Whatever they may be. I think if we pull a list of all of his patients, we'll see a high level of violence."

"I'm on it," Tippin said from his desk.

"Then he started in on the drugs himself," Moore said. "Another high. A different high. Because of this so-called risk addiction. Nothing was working for him. So he keeps moving on to the next addiction, the more risky and life-threatening the better. But why do you think he didn't have sex the night he died?"

"I don't know that he didn't," Parks admitted. "But something tells me that he watched. That was the power he had over Kelli Davis and Nicholas Martin."

"But Nick said—"

"I know what Nick said. And I never in a million years would expect him to say anything different. But I think somehow he did. A big, tough guy like Nick? Imagine forcing him to have sex with his girlfriend, in front of you. What kind of power would you have to have in order to make that happen? And I don't mean just boring ol' missionary sex. I mean—"

"The kind you videotape and blackmail," Moore suggested.

"Exactly," Parks agreed. "I think somehow, he got just that to happen while he jerked off from his place at his desk. His place of power. Once it was over Nick was out of there in a flash. Too embarrassed to face either person. If not, he too might have been killed. But whoever did it, caught Knott and Kelli still in compromising positions and did them both."

"And you're sure it's not Nick?"

"Nick had too much shame. Whatever Knott was using to force him into having sex was enough to keep him safe. Or else Nick might have killed him before any of this could have taken place."

"But what? What could Knott possibly have over Nick and Kelli and whoever else he was doing this to that was enough to force them to do what he wanted?"

"What indeed?"

"Yeah?" Fairmont asked. "How do you force different people with different fears to do what you want? Maybe they all committed a crime or something and he knew about it? One of his patents blabbed about it and he decided to use it against them?"

"No," Parks smiled. "I think we're going a little too much into conspiracy theory territory here. I think it's simpler than that. But still complicated. Jake, if a naked picture of you was suddenly emailed to everyone at the station..."

"Please," Fairmont waved Parks's comment away. "I was in a fraternity. You know how many naked pictures there are of me online? God, I'm scared by what I find online sometimes. I go surfing. I shower at the gym. Whatever. It doesn't bother me."

"Exactly. Now if a naked picture of Milo was emailed to every-one..." Everyone turned to Tippin who immediately blushed. "Sorry, kid. But see?"

"We'd never see Little Man here again," Fairmont said as he winked at Tippin to let him know everything was okay.

"Exactly. We're people. We're all different. No two of us are the same. So...the same could be said about Knott's patients."

"But how—?"

"He was their shrink," Moore interrupted. "He knew about their deep, dark secrets. Then he used them against them. Threatened to expose their dirty little pasts to whomever they would want last to know."

"Like in what? An email? A note? I Know What You Did Last Summer-style?" Fairmont asked, almost sarcastically.

"Close," Parks replied.

"A book," Moore said.

"Exactly," Parks said. "One student. One patient. One chapter. Just one. To show said person to prove that he meant what he said. But one chapter led to two. To three. And before you know it—"

"He's got a whole flippin' book," Fairmont said.

"And when his wife finds out about his infidelities, which he can't stop because he's addicted, she decides to cut him off," Moore continued. "So where's he to get a new source of income?"

"He was actually going to go through and publish a book about his patients. The wrong patient must really be scared about what's in that book," Fairmont said in amazement. "So, then our killer is someone in that book."

Parks stared at his team. "Question is: where is that book? And who's in it?"

"That book, if it hasn't been completely erased from the face of this earth could be anywhere," Fairmont said hopelessly.

"True," Parks agreed. "But if there is one person in the world who might have a copy of it; who would that be?"

"Got me," Fairmont shrugged.

"Tippin," Parks said. "Find out who Knott's literary agent is. If he really was shopping this thing around, he or she would be the one person to have a copy of it."

TWENTY-TWO

Parks returned to the Norton residence at exactly five o'clock. Katherine agreed to forgo the presence of her lawyer if Parks agreed not to record the conversation in any way, shape or form. Since it was not a formal interview, and Parks considered his memory to be fairly good, he saw no reason why this would be unacceptable. He was hoping that since he would make Katherine believe that her son was the focus of his line of questioning she wouldn't see his true intentions. Parks wasn't sure that Christopher was his killer, but thought that since he had been a patient of Knott's there was a good chance he had let something slip that he wouldn't want out in the world. Something in Knott's so-called book? Not something about himself, but maybe something about his mother and her past.

"Where's your husband, Mrs. Norton?"

"He's at the university. Still has to work, you know."

"This late?"

"It's only five, Detective. It's still light outside. I don't expect him until well after ten or eleven tonight. He is the president of the school. Late hours comes with the territory. And now that he's minus one of his best professors I assume he has even more work cut out for him. Know of anyone looking for a position as a psychology professor?"

"Can't say that I do. Not exactly my circle of friends you could say."

"Sorry to hear. Anyway, this gives me more time to do as I like." Katherine wore free-flowing linen pants and an equally suggestive, silky top, both of which Parks made a mental note of. "What would you like to know about first, Detective?"

"Please, Mrs. Norton. Call me Dave."

"Only if you agree to call me Katherine." Katherine settled down on the couch and Parks opposite her on a nearby chair.

Parks stared at Katherine; her makeup had been recently reapplied, though she didn't need any in the first place. She had a natural beauty about her, one of those ageless women who didn't need to cake the colors on thick. She had had her hair redone since the first time he questioned her, as it was shorter and more buoyant. Both the makeup and hair were of a different style than how she had it during the funeral. Parks wondered why the change?

"All right, Katherine. Tell me about your first husband. Christopher's father."

"That would be Phillip Stone. Though I've no doubt you've been able to look that much up by now."

"Actually, there's very little information about your first husband."

"Yes," Katherine smiled. "I suppose that's thanks to my parents. I was only seventeen when I married Phillip. He was a few years older. Working hard. But I loved him and I wanted so desperately to get away from my parents. Phillip supplied a way out."

"Were your parents wealthy?"

"Hardly," Katherine laughed. "My father was a janitor at the local high school and my mother was a seamstress. There are many words I could use to describe my parents, but wealthy is not one of them. They cared for me. I guess I can say that. Their idea of affection was strict love. They weren't abusive. But they were stern. Set in their ways. Didn't like outside influences. Highly spiritual. They weren't rich, but I wasn't left lacking as a child. The basic necessities were always covered. Food. Clothing. Roof over our heads."

"Did your first husband have money?"

"Phillip? Not even close. But I didn't care about money back then."

"But you do now?"

Katherine contemplated her answer. "People change. Priorities change. Having a child changes what you consider important. Even if it still isn't important to you, it might be to the well-being of your child. Have any children yourself, Detective?"

Parks cleared his throat. "I told you to call me Dave. You're making this sound more formal than we agreed."

"Oh, yes. That's right. So, Dave, have you?"

Parks was silent for a moment. "No. I never had any children."

"Too bad. I think you would make a great father. Something about you..." Katherine was interrupted by the arrival of a maid who showed up with a tray of wine and an assortment of cheese, crackers and sliced apples. "You wouldn't believe it with all that food around this place earlier, but being so busy playing hostess I forgot to eat. You don't mind, do you?"

"No," Parks replied. "Help yourself."

"Would you mind?" Katherine handed Parks a bottle of '07 Cakebread Cellars Chardonnay. "So, anyway, where were we? Oh, yes. Money. Money is an unfortunate evil that is required for surviv-al. A necessary evil. Like it or not. Society has built us up that way. Can't live without it."

"Not properly at least?" Parks motioned at the elegantly decorat-ed room about them.

"Well, if you have to have it why not have the best? No crime there."

Parks opened the bottle and handed it to Katherine, who poured two glasses.

"Oh, no thanks," Parks protested. "I'm on duty now."

"I thought this was unofficial?"

"It is."

"Then I think you can officially indulge me." Katherine handed the glass to Parks who let it hang midair before he finally took it from his hostess, so as not to appear rude.

"Phillip Stone?"

"Yes. I loved Phillip. I really did. Planned on having a family and spending the rest of my life with him. I was young. He was fifteen years my senior. Phillip knew what he was getting into, even if I didn't. I mostly needed an escape from my parents. I needed a new life. I thought Phillip was the way to get it. Little did I know...life isn't always what it seems on the outside. People have double lives. Lies. Secrets. Phillip had his share of them. By the time I found out...well...things had changed by then."

"How exactly?"

"We had Christopher. He wasn't planned but he was far from an accident. I love my son with all my heart. He's the only honest and truly decent thing I've done with my life. I think Phillip preferred I had a child as a way to keep me distracted."

"Describe your relationship with your son."

"Oh, like any other typical mother/son relationship I suppose."

"Plus or minus a few millions?"

"Plus or minus a few fathers. Look, we don't always see eye to eye, me and Christopher. But we do love each other. We've been there for each other when everyone else in our lives has come and gone. We generally get along. We do fight but then we forgive and move on. We've been through too much to keep grudges. My son is an adult now. He has his life and I have mine. They intersect when appropriate, but otherwise I try to let him do as he pleases and just hope that I did the best with what I had. How is that not the same as any other mother?"

Katherine stopped talking and reached for the tray, retrieving an apple and biting into the sour slice of fruit, the green of its skin contrasting nicely with her ruby-colored lips.

Parks suddenly felt dizzy. Was it the booze? Or a lack of food? Or most likely, the lack of sleep? He shook his head and came back into focus. "Where was this?"

"Florida. I'm from a small town outside Fort Lauderdale and Phillip was from Miami."

"I see. And how did he die?"

"As much as you swear you know someone it's never enough. There's always something you didn't see. I mean is it really possible to truly know every last intimate detail about someone? Even someone you share your life with every day for six years? I feel there's always something that remains hidden in the darkness. With Phillip it was gambling. Phillip was a brilliant man. Literally. He had a mind like no one I've ever known. But he was also easily bored. I think he passed both of those traits on to Christopher, the bad with the good. Phillip was good. With the cards and playing the odds. He loved to 'play the ponies,' as he called it. But he got bored with winning and had to change the game. He got greedy. And after a while his debt racked up. When he died Christopher was five and we were more than a million in debt. It was horrifying. By that time my parents had both passed on and left me nothing. Phillip had been counting on some sort of inheritance. I could tell. That was a hard time for me in my life. I swear I wasn't going to make it. But I had to. I had to for Christopher's sake. I had to for my son."

"I hate to repeat myself Mrs. Norton but—"

"He was found in an alley. Beaten to death. He owed a lot of different people money. Apparently he owed the wrong ones too much."

"Any arrests?"

"Not that I was ever aware of. At the time, all I wanted was to take my son and get away from that world. A detective who worked on the case kept in touch for a while but after no suspects or plausible leads, what was the point of calling anymore? I still expect one day to receive a phone call from him out of nowhere telling me they caught the man who killed Phillip. I wonder if it will matter by then. He's been dead for almost twenty years now. That was a lifetime ago. I was a different person then. I don't think it really matters anymore."

"And how long after the death of Phillip did you meet and marry your second husband?"

"James?"

"Yes. James Keller."

"We met less than a year after I moved away and were married nine months later. Of course there were things in that marriage I should have been paying attention to. Things I didn't see. Things I didn't want to see. And by the time I admitted them it was too late."

"And where did this all take place?"

"My second husband was from Italy. He had houses in Rome, Greece and Japan. After we met, he moved both Christopher and me overseas to live with him. I had nothing left here in the States so it was an easy decision."

"And what did he do?"

"James was a lawyer. Dealt with the legal affairs of an international clothing manufacturer. Lucrative business. He loved to travel. So did I. It was a match made in heaven. That was how we met. He was on vacation—well, he was in Florida for work. One of the partners in the company had committed suicide or it was a murder/suicide with him and his lover or something like that. I don't remember all the details. But once he was finished the rest of his trip was a vacation. I worked at one of the clothing stores his firm represented. He spotted me on one of his tours of the shops."

"International lawyer. That's quite a step up from a gambler?"

"Yes, it was. I'm just glad I found someone who could appreciate me for what I was worth. I was lucky."

"And how did he die?"

"Boating accident."

"And I suppose you're going to say you were nowhere near your husband when he died?"

"Miles and miles away. Wasn't even in the same country. They left port from San Remo while I was visiting friends in Rome."

"You have friends in Rome?"

"I have friends all over the world, Detective Parks. But actually they were acquaintances I had met through James."

"I see. So your husband was all alone on that boat?"

"No. Christopher was with him. Along with a friend of James's and his son," Katherine answered. "They were the last people to see James alive."

"And how old was Christopher at the time of your second husband's death?" Parks made a mental note to try and keep the timeline as neat and organized in his head as possible.

"Christopher was only eight at the time. I believe. No, maybe nine. As for what happened, I'm not sure. There was some sort of explosion. Christopher was picked up in the middle of the Mediterranean by the Coast Guard a day later. Dehydrated. I had almost lost both my husband and son over the course of that weekend. From the little evidence they had it was determined to be a gas leak of some sort."

"So they found the wreckage?"

"Just bits and pieces. But James had had trouble with the boat before and there were records of him continuously repairing stuff on the boat. Apparently it was not a very safe boat to use. I'm just glad my son was alive."

"Very lucky."

"That's Christopher. He's a survivor. You wouldn't believe all he's been through."

"And how was the relationship between Christopher and his stepfather?"

Katherine finished off her glass of Chardonnay.

"Detective, if you're suggesting that my nine-year-old son set up his stepfather's boat to explode and kill him then you are sorely mistaken and this off-the-record interview is over."

"I wasn't suggesting anything of the sort, Mrs. Norton. I was simply asking what the relationship between your son and your second husband was like."

Katherine remained on edge for another minute.

"How about another glass?" Katherine smiled and reached for his glass. Parks was about to say that he hadn't even finished his first glass when he noticed it was empty. He tried to recall the last time he had taken a few Vicodin and wondered what his limit was while Katherine poured two more glasses of wine, filling both glasses almost to the brim.

"Christopher adored James. The two of them got along famously. Better than he did his own father. They always spent time together. Fishing out on James's boat was a pastime the two loved to share together. When Christopher was a boy he loved the ocean. And James loved taking him out on it. What happened was really a tragedy. I'm sure that not only was Christopher traumatized by being abandoned out at sea for a day but also by the loss of his stepfather. James was more of a father to Christopher than his real father. They truly loved each other."

Parks stared at Katherine's lips as she talked about her son. She had perfectly constructed lips that were even and full, without the slightest hint that they might have ever been tampered with. They were luscious and inviting. When the woman talked of her son, she smiled to reveal an even row of pearl-white teeth that she had passed onto her son. Katherine uncrossed her legs and switched positions. While doing this, Parks noticed that she wore a pair of red laced panties.

"Um...uh...what? Oh, what about your second husband...?" Parks's head swirled once again, his equilibrium giving out from under him.

"What about him, Detect—are you all right?"

"Yes. What about...um...oh, his family. Did he have any?"

"He had some. But he never spoke to any of them. They were a disappointment to him and they were ashamed of him. Though for what reason I don't know. I had never met any of them the entire time we were married."

"A disappointment? A private lawyer?"

"That's their viewpoint, not mine. You'd have to ask them about why. Once again my second husband proved you don't really know everything about a man. Even when you think you do."

"And there's official records of all this?" Parks already knew the answer to that. Interpol had been helpful with all of their requests so far, emailing records, with nothing suspicious turning up. Insurance companies as well.

"There are," Katherine nodded. "You'd have to subpoena them, but you'll get no objection from me. It was all an accident after all."

"And what about your third husband?"

"Howard Price. He was an architect. Built beautiful homes. Including our own home on the east coast. I haven't been in it since his death. Shame really. We met at a party thrown by one of James's friends on the anniversary of his death. Set us up. Thought we would get along. Who knew?"

"And how did he die?"

"He fell down two flights of stairs and broke his neck in three places. I'm not sure why or how he fell. I wasn't at home at the time it happened. I was at mass with Christopher."

"That's a solid alibi if ever there was one."

"I told my husband to come with us. That the sermon would help save his soul. I guess he should have listened to me."

"His soul needed saving?"

"Doesn't everyone's?"

"Any family?"

"Howard? Just his parents. And one sister. I knew them all well.

Know them. Still communicate with them every now and again. Mostly by letter a few times a year. They're thoughtful, caring people. Lovely. His parents felt I was like a second daughter, even after their son's death."

"No hard feelings?"

"Why should there be? It wasn't like I killed their son. It was an accident, Detective. These things do happen, you know?"

"I take it there were full police investigations done into the deaths of your husbands?"

"I stood to inherit millions of dollars, Detective. Of course there were. Both by the police and the insurance companies. I believe both sets of records are available for your viewing. Again, you will receive no objection from me. If I can be of any help with those matters, I'm more than happy to do what I can."

Parks stared at the woman before him, wondering how much the alcohol he had partaken of had affected his judgment. She was mesmerizing, consuming in a way that he had never witnessed or been a part of before. He had never met a woman who so captivated and stimulated him with her every move. Her hands were delicate yet assertive. Her body ached for someone to explore it. Sure, she was physically as close to flawless as he had ever seen but it wasn't just the physical beauty that drew him in. There was more. It was her voice. Her scent. It called to him. Everything about Katherine Norton was engineered and designed to draw men in. Captivate them. Hypnotize them to the point that normal reasoning was thrown out the window and became nothing more than nonsense.

"Is there anything else, Detective?"

"Um...no." Parks retained his focus with Katherine now sitting closer to him. He wasn't sure how she did it. Or when. But she had managed to maneuver closer to him without him noticing it. "No...I, um...I guess not. Oh one quick question. Just to put my mind at ease. Your current husband...?"

"Yes?" Katherine smiled gracefully at him and moved her head closer to him, arching her back slightly, revealing her bra underneath her blouse.

"What's he worth? More or less?"

"He's president of the school. Teachers and professors don't make all that much. Comparatively." Parks jerked when he realized that Katherine had placed a hand on his knee and slightly squeezed it. "His net assets are worth less than three million. How does that work for you? I told you, I'm not with him for the money. I love my husband."

The maid came back into the room to clear away the tray of mostly untouched food when Parks quickly got to his feet. Katherine also stood up, both of them standing a few inches away from each other as they waited for the servant to finish her duty.

"That's what I, uh, I thought," Parks stammered, trying to collect his thoughts. His head began to swirl and he tried his best to keep his balance without being obvious. What was wrong with him? The booze shouldn't he affecting him this bad. Maybe he was worse off than he thought. He needed to get some sleep.

"You sure?"

"More or less. I think we pulled his records anyways. I was just checking."

"Despite my checkered past, I'm a good person, Detective Parks. There may have been some unfortunate accidents surrounding my family but there is no intentional malice on my behalf." Katherine took a step closer to Parks and placed her hands on his arms, with a gentle yet commanding force. "I hope this puts your mind at ease and helps you to move on and find Fredrick's real killer. We may have had something in the past, and it was no longer ongoing, but that doesn't mean I wished him any harm. On the contrary. I wish for his killer to be found and brought to justice. I trust I can count on you to do that?"

"Trust me." Parks breathed in and inhaled Katherine's scent. "I, uh, I want nothing more. Than that. I thank you for your time."

Katherine broke off the trance that she had placed over Parks and led him over to the front door.

"I take it if there's anything else I can help you with that you'll reach me?" Katherine asked, opening the door.

Katherine grabbed Parks's arm and leaned in to give him a comforting, friendly kiss goodbye, grazing just the side of his lips as she touched his cheek. Not knowing why, Parks lost all self-control and grabbed Katherine and began to kiss her. The two stood in the doorway, breathing deeply, filling their lungs as their bodies held strongly onto one another. Katherine pulled him away from the doorway and the two made their way across the foyer, hitting the stairs and collapsing against them.

The two continued to kiss as they rolled around on the bottom of the stairwell. Parks reached into Katherine's blouse and slipped his hand smoothly under her bra and squeezed her breast, causing her to moan in pleasure. As she did this, Katherine worked her way through his zipper into his pants.

"No," Parks moaned, and Katherine gripped him harder and made sure he didn't pull away from her just yet.

"Yes," Katherine hissed into his ear before she began to nibble on it. "I want you. Now."

Katherine guided Parks toward her. When he noticed her panties blocking his intended target he reached down and ripped them off, turning her on even more.

"Yes." Katherine held onto him with one of her legs, making sure he didn't escape her despite his desire to do so.

Katherine bit his lip, sending a shock of pain through his body.

"No," he protested. "No. No!"

Parks broke free from Katherine and backed away, appalled with what he had done. He looked in disgust at the woman who lay on the stairs before him, her linen pants pulled down around her feet as she lay there, enticing him to come to her. Her top was pulled to the side, one of her breasts exposed, taunting him, reminding him of where his mouth had just been just a few seconds before.

"I jus...I can't." Parks repositioned himself in his pants and quickly disappeared out the front door.

Breathing deeply, Katherine closed up her top and then reached down and pulled her pants back up. She looked through the crystal plated glass decorations in the door at Parks as he got into his car and drove away.

"Nina?" Katherine called out as she finished reassembling herself and walked back into the kitchen. "Are these the glasses the detective and I just used?"

"Si, Mrs. Norton," the woman replied.

"I noticed a chip on the detective's glass," Katherine explained, picking up the two glasses. "We don't need someone cutting their lip on this. I'll take care of it. Thank you, Nina."

The servant went back to cleaning the dishes as Katherine walked upstairs.

Upon entering her bedroom, Katherine picked up a remote and turned on the fireplace in the center of the room. She then tossed in the two glasses, watching them shatter and eventually, slowly melt away any evidence that something foul may have been applied to the glass of the good Detective Parks, thereby compromising his judgment.

TWENTY-THREE

"How quickly do you see your team wrapping this case up?"

"No idea," Parks replied. He was feeling off ever since his one-on-one with Katherine. "Hopefully we'll have something a little more concrete by the end of this week. Maybe sooner."

"The higher ups would prefer you wrap this case before any permanent decisions are made concerning your team," Hardwick admitted quietly so as to make sure no one else could hear her. "But you've got until Friday morning to turn out results. Nine a.m. Meeting in Chief Reed's office. You understand?"

Parks stayed quiet but the look on his face conveyed that he did.

"Hey, boss," Fairmont said walking onto the floor. "I got something. And I think it's pretty big."

"What is it?"

"It's Elizabeth Knott."

"What about her?"

"She lied. She's not dying. She's not even sick."

"Come again?" Hardwick said.

"What are you talking about?" Parks asked.

"Elizabeth Knott," Fairmont repeated with a grin. "She doesn't have cancer."

"She never did?" Parks asked.

"No, she did. She just doesn't have it any more."

"What? Did you get a signed note from her doctor?"

"More or less."

"What are you talking about?" Hardwick interjected.

"Elizabeth Knott had cancer," Fairmont explained. "But according to her doctor she currently has a clean bill of health. Cleared of all signs of the disease for about nine months now."

"So she might still be sick," Hardwick replied.

"But she's not right now," Fairmont said.

"And she knows it?" Parks said. "She lied to us."

"Yep."

"How do you know this?" Hardwick asked.

"Well, we were checking out leads, backing up everybody's alibis," Fairmont explained. "When I stopped by Fredrick Knott's doctors to get his general history reports, only I got his and his wife's doctors mixed up. I showed up at Elizabeth Knott's doctor's office. Only problem was it was closed."

"So what?"

"I mean closed as in, 'will not be open for business again this lifetime.' I found the good doctor at home. Looked as if he was going on a vacation out of the country. A long-time, permanent vacation. Apparently he came by a large chunk of money. A five million dollar chunk."

"And?"

"The good doctor wasn't doing too much talking. But after I made a few phone calls to the banks, I found out that the money came from an offshore account. Guess who's got some offshore accounts?"

"Elizabeth Knott?"

"And her husband," Fairmont said. "I wasn't able to get anything concrete, so I bluffed. The doc knew what I was doing but agreed to play along. Technically, he didn't do anything illegal. The doc was already planning on retiring next summer and Elizabeth simply told him it was an advanced retirement present. He knows the Knotts are generous and thought nothing of it. She told him it was also to sort of somewhat keep him on as her own personal physician. He agreed to it. Why not? Five million."

"A five million dollar reason to lie?" Hardwick snapped.

"But he didn't. He filed with the IRS and everything," Fairmont said. "She lied. She told us she was still sick. No one ever checked with him. He was never asked for any records or proof."

"And she knew that. So she was shipping him off on an early re-tirement before anyone could get a hold of his records," Parks sur-mised. "So where is the doctor?"

"He's here in interrogation room one," Fairmont said. "I told him to postpone his trip until we get this all settled out. He's agreed to do so. Doesn't want any trouble. Not this close to retirement. He plans on spending the rest of his breathing days a free man. He'll give us anything we want."

"Good work," Parks said with a slight nod.

"So?" Hardwick asked. "Want to talk to the good doctor?"

"Yes." Parks looked to Hardwick. "Maybe we'll wrap this case up sooner than Friday after all."

*   *   *

"Elizabeth Knott, this is the police. Open up!" Parks pounded on the Knotts's front door and waited for an answer. "Elizabeth Knott!"

Parks looked around at the otherwise peaceful Bel Air neighborhood and realized that he was making a scene. Several yardmen were working on a piece of property across the street, and though none of them were staring, he could tell they were paying attention. Parks pounded again and waited. It was a warm day, getting hotter, while it smelled as though rain might be on the horizon. "Elizabeth Knott!"

"Think she found out we were coming for her?" Fairmont asked.

"Car's still in the driveway," Parks commented, glancing back over his shoulder. "Not that she doesn't probably have three more of them somewhere!"

"Lights are on inside too." Fairmont peered around Parks through the front window whose drapes were pulled back.

"Let's see…" Parks checked the front door and found it unlocked. Parks pushed the door open and took a step inside.

"Elizabeth Knott? This is the LAPD Detective Parks and Detective Levinson. Are you home? We have a warrant. Elizabeth Knott?"

"Well…?"

"Check it out." Parks retrieved his weapon with Fairmont following suit. "Be alert. Not sure what we're dealing with here."

Parks went down the hallway while Fairmont worked his way through the room off to the left. The two circled around until they met in the kitchen near the back of the house, both men coming up with nothing.

"Nothing," Fairmont said, confirming what Parks already suspected.

"Upstairs," Parks said pointing up above him.

Both men walked toward the front again and worked their way up the stairs, checking the first room and finding it vacant. They moved onto the next room which was also abandoned followed by an equally empty bathroom.

"I think she gave us the slip," Fairmont whispered as he wiped his mouth, not realizing how on edge he was. "We might want to call into LAX and Burbank to keep an eye out for her."

"I have a feeling you may be—" Parks stopped talking as he pushed open the last door on the floor.

Sprawled out on her back across the foot of her bed lay Elizabeth Knott, her eyes glossed over, rolled back in her head, giving them an eerily white glow compared to the somewhat bluish-grey tint of her complexion. A foaming mess of vomit that she had choked on had piled up and out of her mouth. The vomit expanded down the side of her face, mixing in with her lipstick and eye shadow, giving the clear upchuck a discolored look as it dripped to the floor below. Her left arm rested across her stomach while her right arm hung out over her head, as if reaching for the floor below her, pointing to an empty bottle of pills that lay just out of reach.

"Shit," Dave Parks shouted. "Shit!"

TWENTY-FOUR

"Where the hell is Matt Bennett?" Parks asked to the rest of the team from the center of the task force room. "Anybody? Anybody have a clue?"

Everyone else on the team stood silently without an answer.

"This is what happens when you get a liaison," Parks said through clenched teeth. "Comes so that you can't do a damn thing without them. Milo? Think you can rustle up a number and find out where he is? This is going on for way too long now. Someone find him. I just want to know he's off at some frat party and not dead in his bathtub."

"And what if he is?" Fairmont asked with a smile.

"Then I'll chew him out a new asshole. But find out. We have shit to do with the campus and I don't need any problems. I want to know if there's something wrong with him or if this is just a delay tactic on the university's behalf."

Parks was frustrated by Bennett's disappearing act. He was fine without him around; he didn't entirely trust the kid, and felt that his priorities were slanted more toward the university's goods over the department's, but when the kid was needed every time he stepped

279

foot on the university grounds it was good to know where he was.

"No answer on his cell phone," Tippin called out from his desk, phone still ringing in his ear as he held onto the receiver, waiting to be told what to do next.

"Could you please get some patrolmen to take a swing by his place and check it out? Last thing I need is to find out he's bled to death on his kitchen floor."

"Isn't he the university's problem?" Fairmont asked. Parks glared at him and a look of regret spread across his face for having asked the question. "You got it, boss."

"What are we all gathered around here for?" Hardwick asked, entering the room. "I thought this case was finished?"

"With all due respect, ma'am, we still need some more damning evidence," Parks replied.

"Such as? I thought you said that Mrs. Knott knew her husband was cheating on her."

"She did."

"And that she lied about dying of cancer."

"She did that too."

"And that she paid off her doctor to keep quiet about it."

"And that too."

"And you and Levinson found her face up in a pile of her own vomit thanks to an OD. Sounds like guilty conscience to me. Wife kills husband in a fit of jealous rage and then offs herself with guilt. Sounds like another crime scene associated with this case that we're investigating. And didn't you also say you had the lipstick at the crime scene that didn't belong to Kelli?"

"We did."

"Check her out. What do you want to bet it matches the same brand that Elizabeth Knott uses. She's your third person."

"Something tells me it would. And that's what I don't buy. It's all fitting together too easily. Like it was all placed that way for us to find it."

"Picture yourself in a book or movie?" Hardwick snapped. "This isn't about a bunch of red herrings to throw us off. Usually the straightest line between two points is the only line. And it works. There's a reason these people get caught. Because the truth always comes out. What happened happened. You can't manipulate the facts."

"Exactly," Parks agreed. "That's why I'm not buying it. I think she's being set up. Just like Nick Martin's suicide. Two 'suicides' related to the same case? I'm not buying it. We know there was a male present at the crime scene. We have semen all over the crime scene. I know we said we thought there were two people who did the murders. In which case, who's this other person? We still need to catch them. Now, we believe it was Nick Martin, but we're still waiting for the test results to come back. So until they do..."

"I love how you've managed to take a simple double homicide and turn it into a freaking conspiracy theory. Okay, what now?"

"I'm not sure. I think we were thrown off. On purpose. I think our killer is male. The lipstick was brought there by the same person who killed them. After all, lipstick is lipstick. Just because I'm holding it doesn't mean it's mine. And vice versa. I think the semen and lipstick have been throwing us off. And it was done that way on purpose. To do just that. Throw us off. Our killer is smart. He knows what he's doing."

"Well, that's a fancy theory you got running around your head there but—"

"Sir," Tippin interrupted as he spun around in his desk chair his phone still attached at the side of his head. "Sir?"

"What is it Milo?" Parks asked.

"I got a Maryanne Chambers on the line."

"Who the hell's that?"

"She's Fredrick Knott's literary agent. You said to find her? Before. Not now. I mean—I left a message. She's calling us back. Well, me. I mean you."

"Yes. Yes," Parks said with a face that was asking for Hardwick to wait a minute. "Get me the line." Parks picked up a nearby phone. "Miss Chambers? This is Detective Dave Parks."

"Time is money, Detective. Think we can make this quick?" the woman replied with a sharp voice. She sounded as if she was walking somewhere—fast—though Parks doubted it was on a treadmill. More like the halls of her workplace.

"As quickly as I can. Tell me what I need to know and I'm done."

"Shoot."

"You're Fredrick Knott's literary agent?"

"I represented him through his last three books. What of it?"

"Rumor has it he's been shopping around a new book?"

"You ever heard of client confidentiality, Detective?"

"You're a book agent, not a lawyer or doctor, Miss Chambers. And with all due respect the man's dead and I have an ongoing murder investigation."

"True. Yes. Knott was shopping around a new book. Been a bidding war on it for the last month. Almost sold it until, well, Knott's death changed the players a bit. But it will work out."

"So the book's still being worked on even though Knott's dead?"

"You act as if Knott was the only writer I represent," Maryanne laughed. "I got dozens of them. And even more ghostwriters. I'll find one to finish it based on his notes. And now with his murder, we're guaranteed a half million-copy first printing. At least."

"Who's it about?"

"What's that?"

"The book? Who was Knott writing the book about? One of his patients, correct?"

"Even if I knew that information, I'm not sure I would tell you, Detective."

"Miss Chambers." Parks paused, breathed deeply and gathered his cool. He needed to be calm and in charge of the situation. "We believe that whoever it was Knott wrote about may have had a great reason to keep the book from ever seeing the light of day and that his murder may have been the result of trying to keep it from coming out. That makes them our prime suspect. If you don't assist me in whatever way I ask I will have no choice but to charge you with obstruction. You understand?"

There was silence from the other end for a moment while the agent mulled this thought over.

"Well, it looks like your killer may have succeeded," the agent sighed, sounding defeated and not happy about it.

"How's that?"

"Look. The truth is I've never seen a full copy of the book yet. Just the first three chapters. I don't even know who it was about officially. I'm not sure how he generated so much heat for it, but he did. He managed to stir up all the pre-publicity himself. Without my help. We were supposed to meet about it yesterday morning. But with him dying Friday night—"

"And you still plan on finishing the book?"

"One way or the other. I've got the first three chapters and Knott was famous for taking notes. Overtaking notes if you ask me. Just have to find the damn thing first. I tried to get a copy from the wife but she denied the book ever existed. I think she's full of it. She can make a mint off it and I think she's shopping it around. Lying bitch."

The line went silent as Maryanne paced from one room to the next, doors opening and closing around her.

"Is there any way you can send me those first three chapters? Fax? Email?"

"I already spoke to the kid before you. Should be getting an email shortly."

"Thank you for your time."

Parks hung up the phone and began to think. Fairmont shrugged at Moore as they hung up the lines they had been listening in on.

"We get that email yet?" Parks asked.

"Printing it as we speak," Tippin replied, as the printer next to him spat out several pages.

The first three chapters of Knott's manuscript printed out and Parks immediately began devouring the pages, passing each one on to Rachel who passed them on to Fairmont and so forth as each page was read. Tippin scanned through the pages on his iPad. Half an hour later, Parks finished and sat quietly, taking in what he had read, while everyone else caught up.

"Well, that was useless," Fairmont said. "He never named a single person. It was all about the school. And nothing that bad. Though you could tell something was being set up. But who cares?"

"What do you make of that?" Hardwick asked, ignoring Fairmont's comment.

"We've been going about this all wrong," Parks answered.

"How do you figure?"

"One of the theories behind the murders is money."

"Not just money, but a shitload of money," Fairmont replied.

"Money is often a motive for murder," Hardwick shrugged. "It's a good one. That's why it keeps being used as an excuse."

"Well, what if it is money? Just not someone's money?"

"What good is money if it doesn't belong to a person? And who else would it belong to?"

Parks began picking up the copies of Knott's patients' files. "What's the one thing all of Knott's patients have in common?"

"They're all patients of Knott's."

"But from where?"

"The school," Rachel Moore answered. "The university."

"Exactly," Parks said. "What if what there is multiple people he's got something on and all of *this* has nothing to do with *them*, but rather with what they all have in common? The university. What if it doesn't necessarily make them look bad, but makes the university look bad? What if he's coming clean, so to speak? Exposing what he and Norton had been doing? Would someone be willing to pay to stop that from coming out? Kill him? That's worth a hell of a lot more than several individual people."

"That's worth a hell of a lot more than just millions," Hardwick corrected.

"What did you tell us from the beginning? The school wants this buried. And quickly. Imagine it. Something bad enough to affect not only the enrollment of the school but also any grants or donations the school receives. The people who attend it. The people in high places who send their kids to this school. Like the governor. That's one hell of a motive."

"So then who does that lead us back to?"

"Who's the one person who has the most to lose from the school going financially under?"

Everyone stared at Parks.

"Bill Norton."

"But why?" Hardwick wanted to know. "Why write it? What's the point?"

Parks thought for a moment, staring up at the murder board, taking all of the information he had been given as he tried to form a workable hypothesis.

"Picture this: Knott's got his little dirty habits on the side. Black-mailing students into sex. Drugs. Whatnot. Whatever he feels like making them do. But they're costing him. Expensive video equipment. Keeping the right people paid off to keep quiet about it. Whatever. Maybe he's got other habits we don't know of. The drugs. Either way, he's going broke. But his wife's dying. So he'll inherit. Just keep his nose clean and all will be fine. But, she takes a turn for the better—or worse, if you're him. She's not dying any more. And since he hasn't been keeping his end of the bargain she's now going to leave him. Broke. Time for plan B. Write a scandalous tell-all. Just start writing, not about anything in particular, just a set up, and use it to blackmail again. And maybe at first he did use it to blackmail his wife, but Elizabeth doesn't care. Just so long as she gets away from her husband he can write whatever he wants. Besides, he probably doesn't know as much as he really thinks. So there goes that idea. But while he was writing—playing around really—he came up with a better idea. Something even more scandalous. Write about the students. Blackmail them when he can. But again, they're students. That's only going to get him so far. They're students. They're not only broke but are in debt. So then he thinks about the school. The same school that's been turning its back on his behavior for the past few years. The same school—and I'm talking about Norton here— that became involved with his sick games. Norton has more to protect here. More to lose. A wife. The school. His prestige. An empire, basically. He can't afford to turn his back on the blackmail. He must pay. But with what? He doesn't have as much money and he can't tell his wife what he needs the money for without implicating himself in the wrongdoings he's been carrying out with Knott. So what's the simplest solution that will solve everything?"

"Murder," Fairmont practically whispered.

"Murder," Parks agrees.

"But the book?" Hardwick asks.

"What about it? It's only three chapters so far and it's worthless. And anyone else who reads it will think the same thing. It could be about anyone and yet no one. Only Norton, whose primary interest is in the school, would believe that Knott would actually write a tell-all about them and the university. It fits. Knott betrayed Norton concerning the games they played. He's Judas."

"But let's say we buy this theory," Hardwick said playing devil's advocate. "There's no proof linking Norton to the crimes. Both concerning the students beforehand with Knott or Knott's murder. There's no proof. And as for the book, it's just Knott's word against an institution. He would need proof for it to stand up. Otherwise it's nothing more than slander and lawsuits galore."

"The video tapes?" Parks replied.

"What video tapes?"

"Bobby and Cynthia. We have their statements on Knott's behavior. They said there were videotapes of what went on. Where did Knott keep those? Definitely not at home where his wife could discover them. At his office? At work? No one had access there except for him. Did we find videotapes in his office?"

"No," Moore said defeated. "We've looked. His office. At home.

Bank deposit boxes. Everywhere. There's nothing anywhere."

"Which brings us back to square one," Hardwick said getting upset with being so close yet not able to do anything about it. "We've no proof. We can't do anything about it. It would be slander on our behalf and he'd have this entire department sued and closed before the end of the week."

"Unless we find them," Parks smiled.

"And you know where they are?"

"One thing at a time. This proves that Bill Norton is our killer. He's the only one besides Knott who knew or would have known about the videotapes. So if they're missing, he had to be the one to take them. Knowing that, we can work on him."

"But it's not likely that he'll ever turn them over," Fairmont said. "More than likely they've been burned to pieces by now."

"Agreed," Parks said. "But I've a feeling there's one videotape still out there. A back up plan so to speak. And insurance policy. Just in case. One without him in it. Just Knott. Norton would never know when he might need one to be able to blame everything on Knott."

"Again," Hardwick said, "it's not likely that he'll just turn it over."

"No," Parks agreed. "But I think we know someone who just might. He's got to have it, if not, at least a copy of it. It's the only way he's known all along what's going on. Why he's been one step ahead of us all this time."

"Who?"

"Christopher Stone," Parks answered.

"But why would he have a copy?"

"I think that's why he's been helping us this whole time. I think Nicole Dumas, and maybe even Christopher himself, are on one of those videotapes."

TWENTY-FIVE

"**H**e's not here," Fairmont said through the radio to Parks. Parks had a feeling that Bill Norton wouldn't be at his office at the university. Luckily, they had presented their case and were rewarded with several warrants. Now they just had to find him. That was also the reason why he had sent Fairmont and Tippin to the school and went with Rachel to the Norton residence. Just in case.

"Let's go check it out," Parks said as he and Rachel got out of his car and walked up to the Norton mansion.

Parks pounded on the front door and waited for an answer. As there was nothing but silence he knocked again and impatiently rang the doorbell. He was about to knock again when the butler answered.

"Can I help you?" he asked.

"I'm Detective Parks and this is Detective Moore. We're looking for Bill Norton," Parks answered.

"I'm sorry but he's not—"

"What's with all the ruckus?" Christopher entered the doorway from behind the doorman, also just as surprised to see the police

289

standing there. "Detective Parks. What's up?"

"Where's your father, Christopher?"

"Stepfather. And he's not here right now. I think he's at the school."

"He's not there either."

"He should be. I'm sorry, but I don't know where he is. I'm not his keeper."

"Is your mother home?"

"No. She's not here either. Not sure where she is. Out at some ladies lunch or something. Maybe they're out together somewhere. How should I know? What's going on?"

"We're arresting your father for the murders of Fredrick Knott and Kelli Davis."

"Took you long enough. You get proof?"

"We'll find it." Parks handed over the warrant as the door swung wide open and police men and women began filling the Norton mansion to search every room. "I want you to come with us. We have some more questions for you."

"If you're arresting my father for the murders then what do you need me for?"

"Are you coming or not?" Christopher didn't move to Parks's order. "Christopher, I will place you under arrest if I have to, now move."

"Arrest me? For what?" Christopher laughed.

"Where's the videotape?" Parks smiled back at the student. "Your videotape?" Christopher froze, the color draining from his face.

"How do you...you can't—"

"I'm tired of your games. Christopher Stone, you are under arrest for aiding and abetting in the murders of Fredrick Knott and Kelli Davis. And for obstruction of justice," Parks looked to Moore as if to say he was dead serious. Moore nodded that she would back up whatever decision he made and Parks took out his handcuffs and approached the young man.

"Obstruction of justice? Are you shitting me?" Christopher was so shocked by the accusation that he didn't notice Parks restraining him. "What the hell? Get off of me!"

"Fine. Consider yourself a material witness. Whatever you want to call it. Either way, you're coming with us. Christopher Stone, you have the right to remain silent," Parks began. "If you give up that right, anything you say can and will be used against you in a court of law."

"Fuck you!" Christopher spat. "You can't do this to me."

"You have the right to an attorney. If you cannot afford one, an attorney will be obtained for you before police questioning. Any questions?"

"You're making a hell of a big mistake," Christopher replied.

"Guess we'll just have to find out now, won't we?"

*   *   *

Parks entered the station with Christopher in front of him in cuffs as Matt Bennett came walking out from the break room with Fairmont at his heels.

"Where the hell have you been?" Parks all but shouted at Bennett.

"What are you doing with him?" Bennett asked. Despite trying to act cool and simply inquisitive, the tone in his voice gave away his concerns and worries, though what about exactly, Parks did not know.

"He's being questioned. Possibly booked," Parks informed his partner as he stared at Bennett's broken nose and black and blue eyes. "Jake. Put him in interrogation room one."

Parks passed Christopher off to the other detective and then grabbed Bennett by the arm and dragged him away from everyone else in the station staring at the two.

"Where the hell have you been?" Parks hissed in a loud whisper. "You look like shit."

"I fell in the shower yesterday morning," Bennett answered. "I had to go to the doctors and get sewn up. My leg's all ripped to shreds from the water faucet. I've been knocked out on pills ever since. I called and left a message."

"Well, I never got that message."

"Well, that's not my problem. Why don't you chew out your messaging system? I was kinda tied up."

Parks stared into Bennett's bloodshot eyes. "Are you high right now?"

"The doctor prescribed some medication for me. Sorry. I wasn't planning on coming in just yet. I was supposed to be off for seventy-two hours. But some patrolmen pounded on my door and said you demanded I show up. Well...I'm here now."

"Fine," Parks replied. This was not what he needed. Two detectives on the same case both high as kites. He tried to remember the last time he took some of his own pills and gave up on trying to concentrate that hard. Since the scene with Katherine in her foyer he hadn't taken a single pill or touched a drop of booze. He still needed sleep though. He was going on less than eight hours for the last sixty-two. "Go home. Keep resting. We're almost done with this anyway."

"You're charging Christopher for the Knott murder?"

"No. I'm just shaking him. We believe it's his stepfather."

"Bill Norton?"

"Now you see why Christopher knows so much? And why you were given the instructions to do what you did?" Bennett had a blank look on him. "Oh, come on. We all know you've been instructed to report every little detail we uncover back to Norton. Now we know why. Question is whether you're going to continue helping him cover up his tracks or get with the show."

"But Bill Norton had an alibi for the night of the murders. He's the president of the damn school for crying out loud. I thought we had enough people witness him around at all times?"

"I was rereading the witnesses statements from that night...and most of them are bullshit. Half of them don't know what the other half saw. But there was one thing."

"What's that?"

"Bill Norton gave a speech that night."

"Putting him in public sight."

"Yes. But before he did, one of the other professors gave an introduction for him which lasted over twenty minutes. During that time, Bill Norton was in a back room preparing for his own speech. He was alone back there. There's twenty-four minutes, right around the time of the murders, that absolutely no one can one-hundred percent attest for Bill Norton's whereabouts. He might have been in the back room preparing for a speech he already knew how to give."

"But you don't think so?"

"There's a back door to the room that leads out to a side hallway."

"That he could have easily disappeared out of and no one would have known about it.? Maybe. And let's say he did choose that time to do the murders? That's pretty iffy. I mean how could he possibly know how much time he would have until he was needed upon the stage and how much time the murders would have taken. There's no way to know for sure. You can't tell me he took that risk. He was *that* desperate to kill them. Besides, are you sure his wife wasn't back there with him?"

"According to witnesses she was already up on stage with Christopher, waiting for her husband to come out and give his speech. He was back in that room all by himself. And when he came out, according to a few eye witnesses, he appeared slightly off."

"So where is Bill Norton?"

"Can't find him. Not at the school and not at home. Christopher was at home. That's why we brought him in. To see what he knows."

"I'm staying around for this."

"No."

"Yes. You know damn well Christopher's a snake. He's hard to grab. You're going to need help getting any information out of him. And I can help. Unofficially or whatever. As an observer. Let me help you."

Parks thought about this.

"Besides," Bennett continued. "This is a joint case. You need me or someone to represent the school in this matter."

"Fine. Go grab some coffee. Try and sober up. I'll go over what we've found today and then we'll tackle Christopher. Let's let him sweat for now."

*   *   *

Two hours later Dave Parks and Matt Bennett entered Interrogation Room #1 to question Christopher Stone on what he knew about the Knott/Davis murders. Less than ten minutes later, all hell would break loose, and both detectives' lives would be forever turned upside down.

TWENTY-SIX

Parks entered the interrogation room. "Hello, Christopher."
Bennett entered behind Parks and stood off to the side, almost hidden in the shadows. Though he may have been invited, this was still an official LAPD investigation. Both detectives had bruised and cut faces, bags developing (or staying) under their eyes, adding to their worn down demeanors; the weight of the world appearing to be on both men's shoulders. Christopher stared intently at Bennett, making him somewhat uncomfortable. Parks wasn't sure why, or what had gone on between the two, but something was up. Bennett was on edge. And Christopher appeared to know what it was. Parks was about to excuse Bennett when Christopher spoke up.

"This is your last chance," Christopher said. "Let me go. You know I didn't murder Knott. You have no right to keep me here. I will tell you nothing you need or want to hear. So just let me go."

Parks remained quiet and stared at Christopher, noticing he was on edge and slightly defensive. He fidgeted, his legs bouncing, his eyes flying around the room. Parks had never seen him like this. Something was different this time. Why wasn't he his cool, calm self?

"What's the matter?" Parks asked, looking from Christopher to Bennett. "What am I missing?"

"Other than you have me locked up against my will for no legal reason?"

"You're a material witness. We think you might be in danger." Parks answered and Christopher laughed shrewdly. "What are you scared of?"

"Scared of?" Christopher smirked. "What the hell do I have to be scared of? I didn't do anything. And even if I did, you don't have anything on me."

"We have all sorts of—"

"Bullshit," Christopher snapped. "You got dick and you know it. Besides, even if you had a confession out of me it wouldn't do you any good in a court of law and you know it." Christopher turned his attention to Bennett and winked at him. "Now would it? Judge would take one look at this case and laugh in your faces and throw it all out."

"What the hell are you talking about?" Parks demanded to know without turning to look at his partner. "He's not LAPD."

"I mean you two aren't exactly the safest, surest bets to bring in a collar, are you?" Christopher was enjoying himself too much. "Do you trust him? Fully?" Christopher was talking about Bennett and Parks knew it. Something was going on. Had already happened. Had he been played? "You know if my father really did do what you suspect him of doing then how can you trust Matt? My father assigned him. What do you think he's been doing all this time? Playing fair. Agreeing with you. He's been spying. He's been tasked with manipulating this whole case."

"That's a fucking lie!" Bennett shouted as he rushed toward the desk. Parks jumped up and stopped him from getting close to Christopher. He already knew this. This wasn't news. Did anyone really think he wouldn't have already suspected this?

"I mean you're both high as kites," Christopher leaned forward and whispered, barely audible so as not to be heard by the numerous recording devices surrounding the room. "I'm sure that if either of you took a blood test right now you'd both be suspended."

"What are you talking about?" Parks planned on playing dumb as long as he could get away with it.

"It's called an insurance policy. Bennett was my father's. You were my mother's. They didn't realize they were playing against one another. And you're stronger. So you were harder to turn. But that's okay. Because that allowed me to play you two off each other and get one up on both of my parents. With what they've done—to me personally—they don't deserve insurance policies. They don't deserve their get out of jail free cards. But I do. You two are mine. Feeling the itch yet, Matthew? Has it all come back to you yet? I'm sure it's probable that his judgment is somewhat impaired. I mean what with stalking potential suspects during off-duty hours and then the drinking and the drugs—I wonder how that would look?"

"You fuck," Matt hissed.

Parks refused to comment, knowing that most likely Christopher spoke the truth. He didn't have all the details, but his imagination was beginning to fly. This was not good. They were about to lose the case. Their only hope was that the LAPD could distance themselves from the university. That would require Bennett to take the fall. It would mess up his future, and Parks felt bad for the kid, but whose fault was it really? He knew well enough what he was getting himself into.

"Oh, don't worry about it," Christopher said turning to Parks with a smile. "He's not so holy and mightier-than-thou. I mean after all, he did assault me. I'm sure that doesn't look too good on record either."

"What the hell are you talking about?" Parks spat. "I never assaulted you."

"True. Then again I haven't left this room yet. I give it five more minutes."

"Is it true?" Parks asked Bennett, ignoring Christopher's wild accusations. "Did you...what happened with him?"

"N-nothing," Bennett stammered. "I...I don't recall—I swear to you I don't know. I can't remember."

He was jittery. He loosened his tie and wiped his forehead, the perspiration soaking through his suit.

"You don't recall whether or not you did drugs with a potential suspect?" Parks asked.

"I have pictures," Christopher smiled. "And video. But the question is, of what? You still don't remember?"

Bennett licked his lips and breathed deeply in through his nose.

"Speaking of..." Christopher smiled. "Detective Parks, did you happen to go and visit Jennifer after I brought her up? I'm sure you did. I know you're a good detective like that. Like to make sure all your t's are crossed and i's dotted. Right? Had to find out what she spilled about, huh?"

"We're done here," Parks said turning and looking to the double-sided glass. "This interview is officially over."

"You see? He doesn't want you or anyone else to know," Christopher continued turning his attention to Bennett. "About her I mean. About his wife. And their baby."

"You shut the hell up!"

"So you see, he really can't judge."

"You don't know what you're talking about," Bennett said defensively of his partner.

"Oh? Don't I now?" Christopher said slyly looking to Parks. "They were young and in love. Then the attack happened. It was meant for you, I believe. But you weren't around. So they got her, didn't they? Barely lived through it. And when it was over, and all was said and done, she was pregnant. Isn't that right, Detective Parks? Only you weren't the father, now were you? How did that make you feel?"

"Shut up!" Bennett shouted at Christopher while Parks stood there, stunned, soaking in the words that were coming from Christopher's mouth. How could he possibly know what he was saying?

"Did you do something about it? Did you go after them like she wanted you to? Begged you to? Or were you too much of a coward to do anything about it?"

"Why are you defending your stepfather?" Parks talked over Christopher in hopes to regain control of the conversation.

"You think I'd defend that piece of shit?" Christopher barked. "Why would I? Who the hell is he to me? If you think he's guilty and you have the evidence to back it up then arrest his ass. See if I care. My life will go on with him in jail or not." Christopher laughed. "Everyone else can rot. My mother. Elizabeth—"

"Elizabeth Knott is dead," Parks interrupted.

"Bullshit."

"And even though it looks like an overdose, I don't buy it. And something tells me, you wouldn't either. She was force fed those pills. She's got bruises on her wrists and arms to prove it. Someone sat on top of her and held her down and shoved those pills down her damn throat. Who was it? You? You were sleeping with her on the side. Don't act as though I don't know. Your mother suspected someone, but I wonder if she ever thought it was her own son sleeping with her best friend."

Christopher glared at Parks and saw the truth on his face.

"What were you getting out of it? Elizabeth's small fortune? What happened? You knew her husband was blackmailing her for her money. Did that piss you off? Made you want to kill him? Did you actually have true feelings for her or were you just after her money too?"

"You can't prove dick. Now let me the hell out of here."

"Seems if my theory about your father's motive is bullshit then that leaves you as my lead suspect," Parks said. "Just sit tight. You're not going anywhere."

"Excuse me?"

"We're not done with you yet. You still know things about the case and I want to know what."

"Oh, yeah? Well you still know things I want to know. You never answered my question?"

"I've got nothing more to say to you."

"Did you visit Jennifer?"

"Get him out of here," Parks said to no one in particular. "I'm finished with him."

"Or did she not want to see you?"

Christopher turned his attention from Parks to Bennett.

"You know why she wouldn't be able to stand the sight of him, right? Did he tell you? I mean you guys are partners. It's only fair. He knows about your little pill popping twitch so why shouldn't you know about the baby he lost?"

Parks immediately turned back into the room and rushed at Christopher, grabbing him and shoving him up against the wall. "I'm warning you! Shut. The hell. Up."

"Or what?" Christopher whispered. "Tell me? Could she even stand the sight of you? Not that I blame her. Not that she has any reason to act better than you. I mean it's not like you could have done what you did without her permission. Could you have? I wonder. Whose idea was it? Did you help? Or did you try to stop her? Being the good Boy Scout that you are. Or did she just go behind your back and do it all on her own? Did she betray you?"

Parks slammed Christopher up against the wall, his head hitting the brick wall and sending an echo throughout the room. "Shut the hell up!"

"Dave...let him go," Bennett ordered, trying to pull him back.

"No. I thought not," Christopher smiled. "She knew. She probably asked you to do it. To help her. Pleaded. Begged you to help. What's wrong? Did neither of you want the baby? Was it just too much of an inconvenience? I bet. So then you had to go and take care of it."

"Shut up!" Parks ordered through clenched teeth.

"Only problem was it was too late, wasn't it?" Christopher continued. "No doctor would help you. So you guys had to get inventive. You had to take care of the problem yourself."

Parks went to hit Christopher when Bennett stopped him. "No! You can't. Then all of this will have been for nothing. Stop it."

Parks glared at his partner who started to lead him away.

"I'm already off it for sure though," Bennett said to his partner.

Before Parks could react Bennett turned around and slammed a fist into Christopher's stomach, quickly followed by a punch to his face. Christopher slammed back into the wall, cutting the back of his head as a spray of blood flew from his mouth and nose.

"I'm already off it," Bennett repeated as he led his partner away from Christopher who had begun laughing uncontrollably at the situation. "Leave it alone. It's not worth it. Leave the past in the past."

Christopher managed to get to his feet and worked his way over to the detectives, laughing the whole time.

"I have just one last question for you, Detective..." Christopher groaned in-between a few chuckles. "I just want to know one thing..."

Parks stopped walking and stared back at Christopher, knowing he shouldn't listen to a single word he said, but not caring, just wanting that one excuse to hurt him for everything he had put them through.

"You must have been considering keeping it. Even though she wasn't. I mean, after all, didn't you give your son a name?"

The fury had reached its limit and Parks exploded. By the time Fairmont and two other officers had entered the room and helped Bennett get Parks off Christopher it was already too late. The damage had been done.

And as Katherine Norton arrived with the family lawyer to help escort her son back home to safety with the promises of a lawsuit lingering in the air, both David Parks and Matthew Bennett had been removed from the Knott/Davis murder investigation and put on indefinite suspension.

PART 3
CHECKMATE

TWENTY-SEVEN

Parks and Bennett sat at the end of a dark, hole-in-the-wall bar, not far from the station, for almost an hour, sipping their beers and scotches, neither one contemplating the intelligence of such a move considering the medication both were currently on, though both did ponder their current predicament and the paths they had chosen that had led to that point. Parks had been suspended, pending further investigation by IAD; and while the assault on Christopher would probably not get him fired from his position, the lawsuit from the Nortons most likely would not do him any favors. There was also the other investigation into his activities with his former wife which, due to the presence of the Assistant District Attorney at the interrogation, would be carefully examined. Bennett had been fired and would be facing legal action once it could be determined what to fine him with. He wasn't as high on the food chain, so if he was lucky enough, he'd be forgotten and end up as mall security in Glendale. Or somewhere further away.

After twenty minutes Bennett finally took out his prescription bottle and popped a pill.

"Sure that's wise?" Parks asked.

305

"It's about the only thing I'm sure of," Bennett replied. "Besides, I'm in major pain. Little too late now. Might as well not feel the pain. Want one?"

Bennett offered the pill and when Parks didn't take it he popped it down his own mouth.

"He called it," Bennett muttered.

"Who? What?" Parks wondered as he stared at his half emptied glass.

"Christopher. He said he could have either one of us thrown off the case at any time. He wasn't joking."

"He played us from the beginning." Parks finished his shot and poured another from the bottle he'd had the bartender leave with them.

"But he never lied to us."

"We got too caught up in his games. We stopped paying attention to what we were doing. Let ourselves get overwhelmed. It's our own damn fault."

"If we would have just left him alone like he said..."

"Forget him. He was a person of interest and we were doing our jobs. So what about what he knew? We pushed him. I'll give you that. But he was scared in that interrogation room. Something was off—with him. I haven't seen him like that before. He only fought back like that because he was scared of something. Maybe of us finding out something we don't know yet."

"Like what?"

"Don't know," Parks shrugged. "It doesn't make sense. Everything we've said so far makes sense. About Norton being the killer. But maybe it's not. And maybe Christopher knows who the killer is and they don't know he's onto them yet."

"But if he knows and he's innocent, then we could have protected him. Why not just tell us and be done with it?"

"I don't know. But something changed when we brought him in." Parks finished his drink and sat there, taking in the smells and lights of the bar. "Why did you do that? Stick up for me? Attack Christopher on my behalf? You didn't have to do that, you know?"

"Fuck them," Bennett spat as he downed his beer. "They've been playing us both off each other since the beginning. Not that we haven't known it. They knew you wouldn't trust me and that's the only reason they put me on this case. I know what you think of me. And what they wanted of me. But I'll be damned if I'm anyone's pawn." Bennett played with his empty beer bottle. "I'm not for sale. You can believe me or not. It doesn't matter. I'm the only one who has to live with my decisions. It's my conscience. But I won't be bought. And right is right. And you didn't deserve what happened."

"Detectives?"

Both men turned around to find Nicole Dumas standing behind them. The woman was ravaged and beaten up. She had a black eye and a bruised face, the cuts of which appeared to have already been haphazardly cleaned up a short while before. The bruises were still forming. Two of the fingers on her right hand were swollen and bruised, having been broken. When Parks went to reach for her she jumped back, both out of distrust for any man around her and due to the bruises and pain her body currently felt.

"P-please don't," Nicole cried, tears flowing down her cheeks.

"Nicole," Bennett was out of his chair and at her side, wanting to hold her but knowing that he shouldn't. "What happened to you? Who did this to you?"

"Miss Dumas..." Parks tried reaching out to her in the most calming, soothing voice he could muster up under the circumstances. "How did you find us?"

"I was outside the police station. Waiting. Getting the courage to come in when I saw you two leave. I followed you here."

"Who did this to you, Nicole?" Bennett repeated not caring about formalities. He was out of a job anyway. What more could they do to him? "Who?"

Nicole looked him in the eye. "Christopher."

"What?" Bennett paused, almost stepping back from her.

"Christopher did this."

"Why?"

"When?" Parks added quickly, her accusation pinging something in his psyche as being wrong.

"He was furious. He found out that I stopped by your house," Nicole explained. "Today. After the funeral. To see if you needed anything? I swear I've never seen him that jealous before. I don't understand it. But he was furious."

"When was this?" Parks repeated.

"Just a few hours ago. Earlier."

"Nicole," Bennett whispered with a slight shake of his head, admitting that he knew she was lying.

"He was so angry. He began to throw things—" Nicole was somewhat confused by the detectives' reactions.

"Christopher Stone was in police custody for most of this evening," Parks interrupted. "Being questioned. And before that he was at home where we arrested him. Alone."

Nicole stood there like a child caught in a lie, not sure of what to say due to the fact that she had not considered this scenario.

"I...uh..."

"Dave. Matt," Fairmont called out as he entered the bar from behind Nicole. "Whoa. You, um . . .?"

Nicole turned from Fairmont, shame on her face.

"What's up, Jake?" Parks asked, getting the detective's attention back on track.

"I've been looking all over for you guys."

"Sure it's wise you found us?" Parks asked not taking his attention off Nicole.

"We just got something," Fairmont replied. "And I thought you would want to know about it."

"We're not on the case anymore," Parks reminded him.

"I know. I also know you still know more about it than anyone else. I thought you should know about this either way."

"What's up?'

"We got a call from Long Beach P.D. ten minutes ago," Fairmont explained. "Seems they found the body of a twenty-three-year-old male in one of the harbors."

"And?" Parks was curious to find out where this was headed.

"They're not sure how he died just yet, though he does have a nasty gash on the back of his head," Fairmont continued. "It looks as if he's been dead for at least a week. He was floating in the water."

"What does this have to do with our case?" Parks asked. "Get to the point."

"The kid's prints were in the system. His name is Ryan Lockhart." Fairmont finished, practically beaming.

"Oh my God." Nicole threw a hand to her mouth and began shaking in fear.

"Nicole?" Bennett reached out for Nicole who began backing away from the detectives.

"Nick Martin's roommate," Parks muttered "The one we couldn't find?"

"Oh, no. Oh my God. No," Nicole cried. "That wasn't supposed to happen. He—she lied. She said Ryan was okay. She lied. They lied to all of us."

"She?" Parks asked, turning to Nicole. "She who? They?"

But Nicole refused to answer, simply crying and shaking her head back and forth.

"There's more," Fairmont stated. "There was a gun found on him. Long Beach ran ballistics on it and it matches a double homicide that occurred up in Seattle a few weeks ago. They've contacted Seattle P.D. and they're faxing us a copy of the report."

"What the hell?" Parks was completely lost. "What the hell's going on here? A double homicide? Who? What? *What?*"

"Nicole," Bennett said as he reached for her.

"No." Nicole jerked back and wiped away a tear. "Stay the hell away from me. You don't get it. None of you do. We're fucked. We're all fucked. They lied to all of us. Both of them. Oh my God. I...I-I-I don't know what—Oh my God!"

Nicole turned from the threesome and bolted out of the bar.

"Nicole!" Bennett pushed past Fairmont and ran outside after her.

"Stay the hell away from me!" Nicole shouted halfway across the street when a car came barreling by, striking Nicole, sending her up over the hood.

Nicole's face slammed right into the windshield, shattering it into a million pieces as it ripped the flesh from her face. Her neck snapped in two instantly as her body was flung up over the hood of the car and onto the pavement behind it.

"Oh my—" Bennett stopped and turned away from the sight, a mixture of adrenaline, booze and the pills pumping through his bloodstream. He stood there shaking and then suddenly leaned over and threw up in the street.

As he did so Parks stared at the dead woman lying in the middle of the street and wondered how it had come to this.

And what was next?

*   *   *

"What the hell are we doing here, Dave?" Bennett kept in step behind Parks as they approached the Norton residence.

"Nicole lied to us," Parks said, reaching the door.

"And?"

"And there was a reason why. She was scared. Just like Christopher. Something's going on around here and I want to know what."

The lights outside of the house were all on, but inside was dark and the front door was slightly ajar.

Bennett grabbed Parks's arm to stop him from entering. "Our badges were taken away, remember? We're not official. We don't even have guns. And I'm sure by now they have a restraining order out on us."

"So what? I still took an oath to protect and serve. They may have taken my badge away but I'm still who I am. Something's wrong here and I'm going to find out what. There was a reason Nicole was told to blame Christopher. I want to know why. And who set her up to do it? If anyone knows who, it's Christopher. That kid was scared shitless out of his mind. Something was us. I think he's in danger somehow. Now either you're going to help me or not. We're just two civilians here to find out what's going on." Parks pushed the door open all the way and stepped out into the foyer. "Mr. Norton? Mrs. Norton? Christopher? Anyone home?"

"Maybe they didn't come back after they left the police station," Bennett suggested.

"No," Parks replied. "Mrs. Norton's BMW is in the garage. Saw it when we walked by."

"Stop," Bennett stopped him, keeping him quiet.

"What is it?"

"I can hear...I think it's coming from back there. By the kitchen."

Bennett walked past Parks down the dark hall and flipped on the lights when he reached the kitchen. Both men paused at the sight that was waiting for them on the kitchen floor. Christopher was lying there, in a pool of his own blood, staring up at the men, pale and lifeless. Next to him, on the floor, written in his own blood was the word: 'Sorry'.

"Christopher?"

Christopher's chest heaved upward as his stomach rolled and he turned his head slightly at the mention of his name.

"Oh my God, Christopher!" Bennett rushed to Christopher's side and looked down at the mess that had been made. Both of his wrists had been slashed.

"I'm calling an ambulance." Parks took out his cell phone.

Parks relayed the information needed to receive the quickest assistance while Bennett grabbed some towels off the sink and began to wrap up Christopher's arms, holding them up above the rest of his body.

"What the hell were you thinking?" Bennett shouted in a whisper as he wiped his forehead, getting Christopher's blood all over his hands and therefore across his face. "How the hell could you do this to yourself? What happened? What changed, Christopher? What's so bad that you thought this was the only way out? Who's after you?"

"Ambulance is on its way," Parks confirmed. "Here, let me help. Dammit, Christopher. What's going on?"

Parks helped Bennett finish securing Christopher's wounds as best he could.

"Dammit, he's lost a lot of blood." Parks knelt over to assist Bennett, not realizing that he was kneeling down in the blood, drenching his pants. "I'm not sure he's gonna make it."

"He's going to make it," Bennett shouted. "He'll make it. You hear me, Christopher? You're going to make it. I don't know what happened, but this isn't the end for you."

Christopher started to whisper something, not able to pull up enough strength to speak, before finally passing out.

TWENTY-EIGHT

Jake Fairmont was handling the Nicole Dumas accident scene, relaying what had happened to Hardwick on the phone, when Parks interrupted that call with information about Christopher Stone. Twenty minutes later Hardwick arrived at Cedars Sinai hospital in Hollywood at the same time as Katherine Norton. Parks stood in the lobby, oblivious to his blood-stained clothes as he talked to a doctor, while Bennett held back in a corner, watching everything unfold around him.

"You two aren't allowed here," Hardwick said, practically in Parks's face.

"We found him," Parks said. "We made sure he got here. What were we supposed to do? Run from the scene?"

"Detectives," Katherine said with tears in her eyes. Across her face were signs of concern and thankfulness for having found her son, despite her reservations about them from earlier that day. "I can't begin to tell you how grateful I am that you found my son. I just hope—what's his prognosis?"

"He'll live," the doctor standing next to Parks replied. "He's lost a lot of blood, so we can't sedate him right now but he's been sewn up

315

and receiving a transfusion as we speak. His arms are extremely tender and his body's in a state of shock, but he should be all right. As with all suicide attempts, we've put a watch on him, and restrained him to the bed so that he can't harm himself again. I'm also going to have to refer him to a few psychologists and programs to attend to for the next ninety days. Standard procedure."

"Suicide attempt?" Katherine gasped with tears flowing from her eyes. "But why? I don't understand."

Hardwick turned to Parks for answers. He might not have been on the case anymore but he had found the young man.

"We don't know," Parks admitted. He didn't feel like admitting what they had seen at the scene. "We haven't been able to talk to him just yet. He's been unconscious since we found him."

"What were you doing there in the first place?" Hardwick demanded to know.

"Nicole Dumas, Christopher's girlfriend, found me and Bennett. She had been attacked." Katherine looked appalled as she put a hand to her cheek. "She claimed Christopher did it to her, but the timeline didn't jive. He had been in with us at the same time. So we felt that maybe whoever attacked her might be going after Christopher next."

"So maybe he didn't hurt himself?" Katherine asked suddenly.

"We've no way to know until he wakes up and tells us his version of things," Parks said solemnly. "He was unconscious when we got there. We don't know anything more than that."

"Can I see him?" Katherine asked.

"He's up on the fifth floor," the doctor next to Parks said.

"Officer?" Hardwick motioned to one of the patrolmen standing guard by the elevators. He couldn't have been older than thirty. He was baby-faced, trying hard to grow the facial hair to help appear older. "Can you escort Mrs. Norton up to her son's room?"

"Oh, that's not necessary," Katherine protested as she retrieved a tissue from her purse and began to dab at her eyes. "I'm sure I can find it myself."

"Nonsense," Hardwick said, placing a hand on the distraught woman's arm. "In case you need anything he'll be able to contact me immediately."

"I'll go with Mrs. Norton," the doctor behind Parks said. "I can go over everything with her on the way up. We might need a few private moments at this time."

"Of course," Hardwick agreed.

"Thank you," Katherine nodded agreeably.

"But—" Parks started before he was cut off.

"You two stay right where you are," Hardwick ordered. "I'm not finished with you yet."

"Thank you," Katherine said as kindly as she could under the circumstances. "Thank you for everything."

"Not a problem," Hardwick replied. "Go and see your son."

"Thank you." Katherine tried to smile. She stepped onto the elevator and let the doctor press the button for the fifth floor.

Katherine disappeared and Hardwick turned to Parks.

"Do you think she's going to just be grateful you found her son and drop the lawsuits?" Hardwick all but hissed at the two men. "You two sure have messed this up royally."

"What about Bill Norton?" Parks asked.

"Not that it's your concern any more, but we've located him," Hardwick said. "He was at the university all day, or so he says, then downtown having dinner with the governor about one of his kids attending the school in the fall. We told him about Christopher, so he's on his way here now. We didn't tell him he was a suspect. We'll let him meet up with Katherine and then take both of them to Parker Center for questions about Christopher. That's when we'll question him about everything else."

"So he's still your primary suspect?"

"You two. Go home. Quit drinking, I can smell it on your breaths, and go to sleep. You'll be contacted. Now go."

Parks stared at Hardwick, both of them knowing she was right and that she was looking out for his best interest as well as that of the department. She wouldn't steer him wrong if she could help it. Parks finally nodded.

He turned to motion for Bennett to follow when an assistant nurse stepped off a second elevator.

"Chief Hardwick?" the nurse asked.

"Yes?"

"Have you seen Dr. Klein? I have the results from Christopher Stone's blood tests."

"He's up with the patient now," Hardwick said. She noticed a slight hesitation in the nurse. "Is there anything we should be aware of?"

"Well, normally I wouldn't say anything, but since there's so many police around, I feel like this might be a police matter."

"What is?"

"It's the wounds on Christopher's arms," the nurse explained. "We think there's a possibility he didn't do them to himself."

"What are you talking about?"

"When he was brought in Christopher couldn't move," the nurse continued. "I'm not talking blood loss not-able-to-move. I mean drugged not-able-to-move. So the doctor had him tested."

"He was poisoned?"

"We don't know just yet. But we did find a puncture wound in the back of his neck," the nurse said.

"So he was paralized?" Parks asked. "Suxamethonium chloride?"

Parks was well aware of the effects of Suxamethonium chloride, having been poisoned with the chemical himself some seven months prior by the Palisades Poisoner. A poison that had been obtained from the same university.

"Possibly. I don't know."

"And injection means someone got close to him. Real close," Parks surmised. "It had to be someone Christopher knows. Or trusts. Or not expects to do this to him."

"So he was drugged and then cut?" Hardwick asked skeptically. "But if someone was trying to kill him and make it look like a suicide why did they cut him like that? Why not like Nicholas Martin? The bleeding is more severe that way. He'd be dead for sure by the time we found him."

"But what if that"—Parks stopped talking as he stared at the elevator doors—"What if it's not Bill Norton? What if we were wrong?"

"What are you talking about?" Hardwick asked.

"He left the station with his mother." Parks slowly pieced everything together.

"You can't be serious." Hardwick was astounded by the accusation.

"Where was Katherine Norton?" Parks asked. "She left the station with him. It wasn't more than an hour later we found him. Where did she go? Why wasn't she with him? She wasn't anywhere near that house from what we could see, yet her car was still there. She did this."

"You can't be serious!" Hardwick shot out as Bennett rushed to the elevator and punched the button for it to come back to their floor.

"Dead serious," Parks replied. "It all makes sense. It's not just Bill Norton, it's her too. Somehow they're both a part of it. Maybe they don't realize it, or they're not working together, or maybe they are. But somehow they're both involved. She did it. That's what Christopher knew. That's what he's been trying to tell us from the beginning. He knew. Everything he's told us from the beginning—starting with Knott's affair with her. Its involved both of them. But if she did do it then she's got to be going to finish the job. We have to get up there."

"But you can't be—"

"Where the hell's my stepson?" Bill Norton shouted as he stormed through the lobby doors to the hospital.

"He's up a few floors with your wife," Hardwick replied. "We were just heading up there to speak to him and your wife."

"Why? What's going on? Has something else happened?" Bill Norton was distraught and frantic, his eyes bugged and a heavy sheen of sweat on his forehead. After frantically looking around he caught sight of Parks and Bennett. "What the hell are those two doing here? We've begun proceedings for a restraining order against them. I want them out of this hospital, immediately."

"They were just leaving," Hardwick answered. "Nothing's going on. I'll take you up there myself." She turned back to Parks and Bennett. "You two, go home. Now. I don't need any more trouble from you two let alone crazy, half-assed theories. I'll handle the situation upstairs. That's an order. Go."

*   *   *

Christopher had been nodding in and out of consciousness ever since he arrived at the hospital and was still foggy. His wrists were painfully sore as he had not been given any antibiotics. He wasn't quite so dizzy anymore, though his mouth felt as if he had swallowed an entire bag of cotton. He looked around for some water when he noticed the restraints on his arms, binding him to the sides of the bed. He jerked at the restraints and immediately regretted it as he felt a bolt of pain shoot up through both arms.

"Aww, there he is," came the sound of Katherine from the entrance of the room.

Christopher froze, with his back to the door. He knew he was trapped and he slowly turned to find his mother standing there with the doctor next to her. Christopher went to yell a warning to the doctor, only to find his throat was too dry and painful to elicit any sort of communication.

All pleasantness drained from Katherine's face as she came to realize what her son was up to and she quickly walked around the bed toward him.

"I don't like to see him upset like this," Katherine said, reaching down for her son who struggled to get away from her. "He seems upset. What's wrong with him?"

"I'm not sure." The doctor came around to the same side of the bed as Katherine and worked his way in between her and her son. "What's wrong, young man? Calm down. You're all right. You're going to be just fine."

Without another word Katherine grabbed the doctor by his hair with her left hand and pulled his head back while she placed the scalpel she had swiped off a nearby tray and quickly and violently jabbed it into his jugular and slashed it across his entire throat, sending a spray of blood out across Christopher's face.

The doctor grabbed his throat, blood leaking out through his fingers while he fell to his knees, his free hand grasping onto the side of Christopher's bed as he stained the once mint-green sheets a dark, crimson color. A few seconds later he fell over onto his side, his life pouring out onto the floor.

"Unfortunate, really," Katherine said. She noticed a spot of blood on one of her shoes and tried to wipe it off on the doctor's coat. "But I didn't have much of a choice. It had to be done. You're the only one who knows. Everything. You can ruin it all for me and your acts lately have proven just that. I'm sorry it's come to this. After everything. But I saw the videotapes. I know what he did to you. You're not safe. You'll never be safe again. I have to do this to protect you. It really is the lesser of two evils. It's time to finish this whole game once and for all."

TWENTY-NINE

"Oh my God. Dave! You don't know how glad I am to see you," Rachel Moore said as she approached the two detectives standing out in front of the hospital.

"Rachel? What's up?" Parks asked.

"We just got a fax from Seattle PD," she said.

"My God—oh, right. Seattle. The two murders that the gun found on Nick's roommate are tied to. So what? Who died? The deceased's roommate's dog walker?"

"A Mr. Glenn Marsh," Moore answered.

"Never heard the name." Parks said. "Who is he?"

"He's this computer tech millionaire who lives in Seattle," she answered.

"How many millions are we talking about?"

"Close to eighty million."

"Shit. How'd he die?"

"He and his wife were gunned down in front of a restaurant in the downtown area," Moore continued. "Two weeks ago. No witnesses. They don't know who did it. Until we gave them a call about the matching gun with Nicholas Martin's roommate."

323

"Both dead?"

"Yes."

"He's that rich and they didn't have bodyguards? Guess they have some rich kids now, don't they?"

"Didn't have any kids. He had no family whatsoever to speak of and the only living relative she has left is a brother."

"So she has a brother who just became a multi-millionaire? Who's that lucky guy?"

"William Norton."

"Oh my God! Oh my—that's it!" Parks exclaimed. "That's the connection."

"What is?" Moore asked.

"Her! Katherine! We crossed our black widow theory off because Bill Norton wasn't worth any amount of money. But we were wrong. It was all a set up. From the beginning. She knew what he was worth even though it wasn't his directly. She figured out a way to buck the system and get around it without being a suspect. She was buying time. Christopher knew about it. He's always known. And now she's wrapping it all up. We have to get to the fifth— where's Bennett?"

Moore looked around, just as confused as Parks. Bennett was nowhere to be seen.

*　　　　　*　　　　　*

"How much longer is this elevator going to take?" Bill Norton asked, fidgeting from one foot to the next.

"Sorry, Mr. Norton," Hardwick said shaking her head and pressing the button for the fifth floor again. "We're almost there."

Bill Norton looked up at the neon red numbers and saw the floor change from a 3 to 4. He then quickly took the Glock 23 handgun from his left jacket pocket and aimed it at Hardwick, firing two shots in the woman's direction without looking where they went as he stared at the front of the elevator and waited for the doors to open.

The chime went off and Bill Norton prepared himself for any oncoming adversaries who might have been alarmed by the sound of the gunshots from the elevator, but was pleasantly surprised to find the hallway abandoned. As late as it was, he wasn't all that surprised. He pulled the emergency stop button on the elevator, freezing it on their floor.

He found the deserted nurses' station and walked over and began to flip through files and charts until he found the one containing his stepson. He dropped the chart and started down the hallway until he found room 513 and peered in through the open door.

Lying on the bed, covered in blood and sweat was his stepson, chewing through one of his wrists, trying to free himself from the bed that held him prisoner.

"You little shit," Bill Norton hissed. "I bet you helped plan all of this, didn't you? Huh? Thought you could get away with this? You and that cunt mother of yours. Planning. All along. My inheritance? Well fuck you! You can't! Not now. Not ever!"

Bill Norton walked around to the side of Christopher's bed and found the doctor on the ground with his hand still at his throat, in a puddle of his own blood.

"You sick bastard," Bill Norton shouted.

And with those words Bill Norton grabbed Christopher's arm and began pulling apart the stitches that held his stepson's life together.

*   *   *

"Fifth floor! Fifth floor!" Parks shouted as he and Moore ran up each flight in the side stairwell, deciding to not wait for the non-moving elevator. As they made it up each flight of stairs, Parks found himself coming short of breath as he broke out in a sweat as head swirled. They reached the landing of the fifth floor and burst out of the stairwell and onto the main floor when Parks saw Hardwick laying half in and out of the elevator in the opposite direction. "Jane!"

He ran for the elevator and grabbed his boss to determine her status.

"Jane? What happened?" Parks asked

Rachel looked around and saw a nurse coming out of a room down the hallway. "You! I need a doctor out here now! This woman's been shot. Hurry!"

The nurse came running toward the pile on the floor of the elevator and yelled at one of her coworkers as she reached the injured person.

"Call Doctor Klein, now!" the head nurse ordered to another nurse coming out of a nearby room.

"Jane? Jane, I need you to tell me what happened? Who did this to you?"

"Sir, I need you to back off," the nurse ordered. "I need room. Now back off."

"Jane?"

"Norton," Hardwick breathed deeply.

And before she could add another word the screaming began to come from down the hall. Instinctively, Parks reached into Hardwick's coat and retrieved his boss's gun and then started down the hallway as fast as he could possibly go.

*   *   *

"You sick little—"

Before Bill Norton could get another word out his wife appeared from the shadows of the restroom and swiftly stuck the surgeon's scalpel deep into the side of his neck, hitting his carotid artery and sending a spray of blood out of his body.

Bill Norton spun around and swung a fist at his wife's face, sending her flying back into the surgeon's tray. Katherine held her ground and started after her husband once again, when he aimed his gun and fired at her, sending her back against the wall.

With his wife taken care of, Bill turned back to Christopher when a loud, animalistic scream came from behind him. Before he could react, Katherine collided with her husband, running into Christopher's bed, sending the whole thing toppling over and onto its side.

Christopher let out a scream when his head slammed against the hard hospital floor, dazing him. His parents continued to fight on top of him as his body weight pulled against his handcuffs, sending a bolt of pain through both of his wrists and up his arms.

Katherine scratched at Bill's face with her fingernails, breaking one off on his mouth when he bit at her finger. Bill grabbed his wife's throat and began to choke her. Katherine frantically searched around the ground for something to fight him off with when she felt the scalpel she had attacked him with. She picked the knife up and drove it into the back of her husband's neck, hitting a mess of nerves and tendons, but not causing him to loosen up on his grip at all. Katherine's face began to turn blue, her eyes bugging out, when a pair of hands grabbed the back of Bill's jacket and spun him around, pitting him face to face with Matthew Bennett.

Summoning up all of his fury and rage, Bill released his wife and grabbed the detective and charged out of the room with the man, forcing their way through a wall of glass, sliding out onto the hospital hallway.

Bill struggled with his opponent, slamming Bennett's head against the floor a few times. The back of Bennett's skull cracked upon contact, sending a loud gunshot-like sound echoing throughout the hallways as blood splattered across the floor from a wound on the back of his head. Bill managed to sit up and went to slam Bennett's head against the floor again when a shot rang out, a bullet ripping through his chest.

Parks fired two more times, the first hitting Norton in the chest and the second taking the top of his head clean off as the bullet shattered his skull. Bill sat there, on top of Bennett, as he stared out into nowhere. When his life finally left his body, he slumped over onto the detective.

Parks ran to check on Bennett. The younger detective was dazed as the damage to his head hadn't helped his already delicate physical condition. Blood continued to flow steadily out of the back of his head as his eyes closed and he blacked out. Parks turned to Katherine Norton who sat against the wall, her body slowly going into shock from everything that had happened to her. He yelled for help from every direction he could get it.

Several nurses ran down the hall and began tending to both Bennett and Katherine. A few more arrived and began to care for Christopher, who was still handcuffed to his bed. As Parks watched on, the doctors proclaimed Bill Norton dead at 11:27 that evening.

Parks walked away from the operating rooms and silently and happily thanked God that justice had been served and that no amount of money could have turned out any other result.

THIRTY

"**D**etective Parks," Chief Reed welcomed Parks with a firm handshake. In his late-fifties, with close cut silver hair and a gruff, if not somewhat soothing, voice that was balanced by his usually fair demeanor, Thomas Reed was considered by most to be the perfect person to run the LAPD. He was handsome and, despite the stressful job, had aged well, always giving off the appearance of being in good health, yet had the stern ruthlessness to make the impossible decisions when needed. Though they had met on occasion, for the frequent fundraiser or yearly reviews, Parks never had all that much interaction with the man as most of his day-to-day dealings were with his direct superior and one of Reed's three right-hand people, Assistant Chief Hardwick.

"Sir," Parks nodded, taking a seat opposite Reed.

It had been ten days since the fiasco at Cedars-Sinai hospital. Hardwick was still on leave, recovering from her gunshot wounds, one of which simply grazed her left arm, the other hitting her in the stomach and missing any vital organs.

"We'll get to the legal ramifications of this past case in a minute. Before that, I know you've been waiting patiently this past month to see what the final results of our redistributing within the department would be. I know this hasn't been easy. But it was inevitable. All of the other teams have been disbanded. Yours is all that's left. It was only a matter of time. And this case hasn't helped. Despite objections by AC Hardwick, it has been decided by myself and the board to dissolve your team at this point and time."

Parks closed his eyes and breathed deeply as he took this in. He knew this was coming. He shouldn't have been surprised. But part of him, deep in the back, had still been hoping against hope.

"The changes have already been put into effect. You, having been gone for the past week, are not yet aware of them, but they are. You will be required to take the rest of your two week mandatory leave of unpaid absence before returning, but you are returning. Don't ask me how, or who's looking out for you, but no charges are being brought against you, despite the ADA being present for your last interview against Christopher Stone. I wasn't present for that, but no one has anything to say about it and all evidence of it ever taking place seems to have been...misplaced. Now, I know you haven't been here for the last week, so I'm not even going to insult you by asking about it. Just consider yourself lucky. Take the time off. Relax. You look like crap. Then come back and start anew. You're lucky. You've had a colorful career filled with positive results and your future can be just as bright. The Palisades Poisoner case did wonders for protecting you within this department but it doesn't make you invincible. Luckily for you, the Nortons are all dead or in jail or withdrawing their suits."

Reed looked down at his desk, collected his thoughts, and soon got back on track.

"Upon your return next week you'll be reassigned to Robbery-Homicide with Detective Moore as your partner. She's informed us there are no issues between the two of you or with the two of you being partners. Do you have any objections?"

Parks cleared his throat. "No, sir."

"You'll also no longer be reporting to AC Hardwick. You'll now be part of my division as I'm helping oversee Robbery-Homicide and AC Hardwick is moving over to Major Crimes. You'll report directly to me."

"Yes, sir."

"Good. Apparently there was some sort of a situation between Detective Moore and Detective Fairmont that you failed to take care of. I'm not sure what this all entailed, but as they no longer work together, I don't see how this is a problem, let alone one to keep record of. Detective Fairmont has been reassigned back to the CSI division, though he may even go back to patrol. We need men on the streets right now. We'll see how that plays out. He may be reassigned back to the Detectives' Division at a later date depending on where we need bodies. For now, he's there."

Parks remained silent but showed across his face that he understood.

"And Milo Tippin is the newest member of your team. He's young and not yet ready to be a detective. Being a detective used to take time. Years. Experience. Not simply passing a test. Somehow he got around the four years of experience as a patrol officer. Probably because he's still technically part of SID. He'll be going back to the Cyber Crimes Online Division with Computer Forensics. And that takes care of the members of your team. On a side note, let me say that I am sorry to see your team go this way. There had been talks within the department of keeping your team whole, but considering everything that's gone on with the Knott/Norton case we just can't justify keeping you together."

"Excuse me, sir," Parks interrupted, knowing he was walking on thin ice as it was. "But what exactly is it my team and I are being charged with? Negligent wise, I mean. I mean, we did apprehend Fredrick Knott's and Kelli Davis's killer, didn't we? And the scandal at the university was hardly our doing. We got a crooked university president and professor away from the student body. Isn't this all seen as good things? For the department, I mean?" Reed stayed quiet. "I understand this is your department, sir. And I mean no disrespect. All I ask for in return is the same. If you have or had no intention of keeping my team together, then that's your call. But to blame the decision on my team, saying they didn't fully carry out their duties according to the law, when in fact they had..." Parks wasn't sure what else there was to say. What was done was done.

"Your team has been instrumental in helping keep the citizens of Los Angeles safer. There's no arguing that. You and your team have done a lot of good. But times change. The economy's changing. We have to change with it. No one's being reprimanded or fired. Nor will there be any commendations. This was a nasty case that was never going to have a good outcome. From the second it began."

"It's just best for the department if we sweep it under the rug," Parks commented, without any emotion one way or the other. "And that includes the team that worked on it. If we don't exist, then this case never did either, right?" Reed remained quiet, neither offended by Parks's comment or acknowledging them. Parks could think of nothing more to say. "I understand, sir."

THIRTY-ONE

"**A**re you going away?" Parks asked as he approached Christopher from his car across the street.

Christopher had just finished stowing away the last of his luggage into the airport limo parked in front of his house.

"Just a little vacation. I'll have to be back for mother's trial. They want me to testify," Christopher replied, staring at the empty mansion.

"For the prosecution or the defense?"

"Both, actually," Christopher chuckled. "Guess that's up to me, though, isn't it?"

Katherine had been booked and the DA was working on a case against her for at least four deaths, though Parks doubted that they would stick. Katherine had money, and with it came the best defense it could buy. Adam Wolfe was having a field day with all the publicity coming from the case.

The scandal of the "High Society Black Widow" had been all the talk of the town for the last few weeks. Katherine Norton had been on the front page of every major newspaper and magazine. Radio DJs and talk show hosts all gossiped, eagerly awaiting the trial to

333

come. There were talks of book deals and TV movies. Today was the first day Parks hadn't noticed a camera crew stalking outside the Norton residence.

"Besides, I don't think I need a house this large all to myself. It has too many memories."

"Are you feeling better?"

"I'll live," Christopher said looking at his wrists before looking up at Parks and all of his bruises. "And you?"

"After everything's been more or less cleared up—and since you didn't press any charges—I'll live too. Though I'm sure once the trial digs things up...well who knows? Screw it. Whatever."

"You're welcome. The force needs good men like you."

"Go figure the university didn't take Matt back. But at least no charges are being issued against him. Not sure what he'll do next. Future doesn't look too bright for him right now."

"Oh, I think he'll survive," Christopher said. "I offered him Ryan Lockhart's standing invitation for rehab. He took it. He'll be in there for ninety days. It's more like a paid vacation, so I'm not really surprised. But I felt it was only fair considering I helped get him into his current predicament. He'll do schooling or something after. Maybe get into private security. But who knows. What about your legal troubles?" Christopher asked, the sun glaring into his eyes. It was one of those rare, beautiful LA afternoons where the smog appeared to have disappeared, leaving the sky wholesome and healthy.

"You know, funny enough, it seems the entire interrogation Matt and I did with you has vanished. All proof it ever happened, all recordings, all paperwork. Vanished. And the ADA's not pressing charges."

"Oh, I'm sure he's got bigger fish to fry. You know there's a new election coming up in a year. He's going to run for the DA's office.

He needs funding. And I'm sure he wouldn't want to do anything to jeopardize his biggest contributor." Christopher smiled as if there was nothing else to say. For once, the rich bought something that Parks knew he shouldn't—couldn't—have any real objection over.

"Wonder how that will look to your mother's case? The prosecutor's biggest donor is the son of the woman he's prosecuting for murder?"

Christopher shrugged. It wasn't his worry. He didn't care what people thought about him or his mother. Somehow he thought his mother would come out of this just fine. She usually did. More like a cat with nine lives than a deadly spider. And he'd only have to worry about her then. Until that day when she was freed he was on his own.

"Why?"

"Why what?"

"Why all this? Why are you helping us?"

"Believe it or not, Detective, I was never against you. When I saw the situation the two of you were in, thanks to my mother and stepfather, I could think of no reason not to help you." Parks simply stared back. "Let's say I believe in Karma and I'm making sure I don't get screwed over too much anymore."

"But then why put us through all of this in the first place?"

Christopher thought about the question but decided to ignore it.

"I had no proof. No evidence. I knew about the videotapes but not where they were or how they could be used against me. I had to play both sides. Sorry about that. My mother found out about your past affairs with Jennifer through a PI she had hired. It wasn't meant for me to find out. But I did. By accident. But you do have to admit you pushed me into a corner."

"Why did she do it? Months ago? I mean how could she have known I would be the detective on Knott's murder?"

"How do you know you're the only person she dug stuff up on? Maybe it wasn't an accident that you were on duty that night. Or maybe it wasn't an accident the murders happened when they did. Who knows? You'd have to ask my mother about that."

"You really don't know what you're going to do?" Parks asked. "About your mother?"

"Bill meant nothing to me," Christopher replied coldly. "She, on the other hand, is my mother. Yes. She loves me. And I her. But not in the way that a mother should love her son. To her I'm simply an object. A means to an end she desires. You know my birth father died trying to provide for her?"

"I've heard bits and pieces," Parks admitted.

"He gambled," Christopher said. "Every day. In and out of working two jobs while she sat at home or went out with her girlfriends to spend his money. He worked to pay for her lifestyle. When that didn't pay enough he gambled. And he did it poorly. He lost a lot. When he was killed, she did nothing about it. Simply took me and ran. And we continued to run until she met her second husband. Millionaire extraordinaire. There were plenty of men out there with money. And she was an attractive woman. But you see, there was something else she was looking for. That was one thing my mother was good at. Digging up dirt. These men she found she found for another reason besides money."

"What was it?"

"My mother didn't like attachments."

"Attachments?"

"She wanted the money. But not the men. So she had to find men she didn't see worth keeping around for that long. Or men she could get rid of without losing the money."

"How?"

"First stepfather, James Keller, he loved me. But not like a son. The neighborhood parents who wined and dined with him thought nothing of the fact that he allowed them to bring their children over while they socialized with him. He even had a room in the house made up for them. All the toys a child could ever want. What they didn't know about was the costumes. The changing. And the videotaping. I tried to escape from him, but I couldn't. How could I? After the parties were over and the other children went home—well, where was I to go? I *was* home. With a monster. And my mother wouldn't do anything about him. He was worth money. A lot of it. And she wasn't going to let me ruin it. If I didn't want him around anymore then I needed to do something about it. Her hands were tied. She made that much clear to me. I may have only been eight but I knew what had to be done."

"My God..."

"The thing is there was proof of his actions. Others had come forward and reported him. But as you know, as I learned early in life, money can buy a lot of things. Including freedom. I realized it didn't matter what I said or proved. He would always be around. He had to be dealt with. Permanently. And who would say a thing against it? A child defending himself from a pedophile."

"How did you? The boat..."

"My stepfather didn't actually own a boat. It belonged to a friend of his. He too had a son that was all too familiar with my stepfather. And he found out and wasn't all too happy about his own son. All alone. Out at the sea. Hell, I was eight at the time. What did I know? But the father's rage wasn't enough to consume my stepfather and both men ended up killing each other and blowing up the boat in the process. Fortunately, for me, at the time when the man planned to do the job he had me in a life vest, swimming off the side of the boat so as not to be around to witness anything."

"They found you out at sea."

"Yep. She thought I had planned it all. An eight-year-old! That's what my mother thought of me. Six months later we inherited. Or rather my mother inherited. Until she started going through it. Quite quickly might I add. Almost four years. But then she found Howard Price, another millionaire with the same addiction as my first stepfather. And though I was a few years older, I was still young enough for him to desire me. And well, you know how that story goes by now."

"My God, how could she...you..."

"She cares more about the money she can inherit from these men than she does about her own flesh and blood's safety. She's blinded. Living in her own world. Always has. By her own rules. She means nothing to me now. I learned all I needed to from her. She isn't useful anymore. I'm old enough to leave. But you saw her. She didn't want me to leave. Not now. Not ever. She won't let me. She needs me. I'm her comfort blanket. Her stability. She's uneven and uncomfortable around the world without me at her side. She needs me there. To help her. To protect her. Well, that's not my job. I'm her son. It's her job to protect me. Me!"

Parks stared in shock at Christopher.

"How did it all start? This time."

"Mother picked him out. Bill Norton. Not because he had money but because he had access to money. She set up his sister and her husband in Seattle. You can bet on that. But this was years ago. We moved her, settled in, lived our lives. She had plenty of money back then, so it wasn't like she needed it right away. She was planning. For the future. Mind you, I didn't know any of this. It's not like she told me her plans. I know the way she thinks. What she likes and is usually after. But I'm not always sure. When she married Bill I knew there had to be more to it. My mother's not capable of love."

Christopher paused and took this thought in.

"She made friends with Elizabeth. A legitimate friendship. I'm sure she had something to do with setting Elizabeth and Knott up, but I'm not entirely sure. Or why. Maybe they were both pawns all along. But she sent me to Knott when she became worried about me. I told her no but she forced me. So, as a way to get back at her I told him everything. Not what she was planning, because that I wasn't aware of, but everything that had happened in the past. This was years ago when it started. Part of why Knott broke up with her. He knew her MO and didn't care to be next. But after she married Bill he started to figure out what she was planning. Even if he wasn't sure how or why. Considering Bill had no money. That's what threw everyone off. Even me. We all knew she had more than him. She should have been satisfied. She could have been taken care of for life. But not my mother. She always wanted more.

"In that aspect Knott and my mother were perfect for each other. He was greedy too. And broke. And when he found out that Elizabeth was no longer ill and was leaving him he came up with a back-up plan that involved blackmailing my mother. About her history and her plans for Bill and his millions. How she would inherit it through him. Through his sister. See, Knott had the drug thing going on the side. With the heroin. I knew about that from Nick and Kelli when I hung around their place with Ryan."

"The heroin?"

"Yep. It was no secret on campus that Knott was a dealer. He had access. From other students. So Ryan got it from him."

"So Ryan Lockhart is the one who killed Bill's sister and her husband up in Seattle?"

Christopher nodded in a half shrug.

"How did that happen?"

"You building a case for the prosecution?"

"Off the record," Parks said honestly. "Just between you and me. Call it the need to know."

"You know what happened to the curious cat, right?" Christopher smiled. "Ryan got involved through my mother. Through me. See what being a friend with me brings? Go figure I can never keep any. She knew about his habits. And a user always needs more. And money. And when he got busted for the porn thing, she came in and saved him. She'd keep him in the school and supply him with an endless amount of cash for his drugs if he did this one little favor for her. And somewhere when he met up with her to collect payment she double crossed him. As is expected with my mother. She never paid up. Not with Ryan and not with Knott."

"I'm beginning to see that."

"She could have afforded to pay whatever it was any of them asked for. But she's greedy. Just like the rest of them. So she killed Ryan and manipulated Bill to take care of Knott."

"How'd that all work out?"

"Best I can tell? She double double-crossed them both. Knott knew she was trying to get Bill's inheritance and in exchange for his silence he wanted a part of it. He probably even supplied her with the information about the students and videotaping and rapes. Oh, yeah. There were rapes. So she used it how she could. Then she probably told Bill some story about Knott raping her or blackmailing her or whatever. Didn't matter. It was all lies. But it was enough. See, Bill had wanted Knott gone from the first time he heard about him and mother together. Bill Norton was a wildly jealous man. If you would have investigated into his personal history, you would have found that out for yourself. He's got two ex-wives, both of whom had filed restraining orders against him. My mother knew that. She was counting on that."

"So Bill's the one who..."

"Killed them? Yes. Knott and Kelli Davis were killed for reasons their killer wasn't aware of. Kelli was just in the way. Knott was killed out of jealousy and for revenge for what Bill had thought he'd done to my mother. Bill was simply a pawn. But it was all just a game. My mother planned on the murders to get rid of Knott and then Bill would go to prison for the murders and she'd still get his inheritance. He began to piece it all together, though. My mother knew that. You see, she did what she did to me"—Christopher motioned to his arms—"not to hurt me, but to protect me. She said as much. But I didn't realize that at the time. She knew Bill had found out the truth about her. And what he would do to her. Hurt her. Through me."

"So she hurt you? Why?"

"Her plan was to call for an ambulance as soon as she was done but you two came in and disrupted her. She panicked and fled. She knew that because of what she did I would be taken to the hospital. Into a sort of protective custody, you could say. And she hoped that at least there I would be guarded. Safe from Bill. She hoped you'd keep my condition secret from him. But someone called him. That's why what happened...happened. And so now you know."

Detective Parks stood there, feeling dirty and used, not sure how else he was supposed to feel. So many people had been used and mis-led. Himself included. Here was a boy who had been used and abused, mistreated from youth, who had simply learned how to sur-vive, adapting to his environment. But still he felt wrong about it all.

"Where are you going?" Parks asked.

"All of my mother's assets are frozen until after the trial. And then it will be anywhere from six months to a year before both mother's and Bill's inheritances become mine. Provided she doesn't get to keep it herself. But we'll see what happens. Until then I still have enough money of my own. Not sure where I'm going. Just need to get away for a few weeks. At least get out of this city. For a while. But don't worry, Detective. I'll be back. You think this was a sick game...wait until the trial begins. Talk about skeletons in the closet."

Christopher smiled at Parks and then slipped into the back of the limo which pulled out and drove down the street heading for Sunset Boulevard, disappearing to God only knew where.

AFTERWORD

If my first novel *The Poisonous Ten* is seen as a sprawling epic LA-type novel, then the opposite could be said of *Wicked Games,* which has more of an intimate, almost claustrophobic feel to it. *P10* took place over weeks and bounced around from location to location. Whereas the majority of the scenes in *Wicked Games* take place at the downtown LAPD station or at the fictional Pacific Southwest University. Sure there are a few scenes here and there where Parks visits local dives and whatnot, but overall the novel feels simpler and scaled down in tone.

Wicked Games has a weird, if not interesting, history to it as I had actually written it before *The Poisonous Ten.* But it goes back even further than that.

When I first moved to Los Angeles, I had given up on writing novels for a while, switching over to screenplays instead. Of the many that I had attempted, one was a murder mystery, influenced by *Basic Instinct* and other 90's thrillers. The script was called *Diversion* and remained unfinished at about 50 pages. I couldn't figure out how to wrap it all up. Eventually I put it aside...unfinished.

A few years later, when I had picked back up the novel format and had already finished two novels and almost a third (which at over 600 pages still remains unfinished), I was searching for a new idea to tackle. One day, when scanning over old screenplays, I came across *Diversion* and realized that I wanted to finish it. I wanted to know who the killer was and why everything that had been written so far had happen. And while I couldn't wrap my brain around how to continue it in the screenplay format maybe I would have better luck expanding on the world in novel format. And so I did.

I adapted the first fifty pages and then continued on, without so much as a blink as how to continue. Characters changed. Plot points changed. Heck, even the title changed. And three months later the book was finished. And then began to wonder what was next for Det. Parks and his gang. That's when I began research for *P10*. Throughout writing *P10*, I came to realize that it was no longer a sequel, following the events of *Wicked Games*, but rather a standalone novel all on its own. Eventually I put *Wicked Games* in the bottom of a drawer and forgot about it, referring to its 300 pages more as the character outlines I needed to help fully realize my players.

Wicked Games to me is fun. A good guilty pleasure. And sometimes that's all the more we need. I felt I could go back, do some rewriting and possibly salvage the novel. It's stronger than it was before but there are still times when even I'm not sure what I was saying with it. Though, honestly, I don't feel I'm saying anything. It simply is. It's a fun, slick thriller. A whodunit, that's about who did it and not about the lessons or reflections on life that some novels have. I've had some people tell me they like it more than *P10*. Others the opposite. I can live with either. I don't regret this novel—nor do I apologize for it. It is what it is.

Like I said, it's a guilty pleasure.

And sometimes that's exactly what we need.

TC

ABOUT THE AUTHOR

Tyler Compton graduated from CSU, Sacramento in 2002 with a BA in Theatre Arts and a minor in Film Studies. He currently resides in Los Angeles where he's witnessed various forms of crime, including someone breaking into his apartment while he was in it.

His first book, *The Poisonous Ten*, was released in June 2013 and was named an Award-Winning Finalist in the Fiction: Mystery/Suspense category of the 2013 USA Best Book Awards, sponsored by USA Book News.

The third book in the Detective Parks series will be released in June 2016. Tyler is currently at work on his next novel.

Follow @tscompton on Twitter or visit TylerComptonBooks.com for the latest news and details about future releases.

www.ingramcontent.com/pod-product-compliance
Lightning Source LLC
Chambersburg PA
CBHW020327180626
46812CB00001B/83